"OH, CARRIE, IT'S GONE! COME ON, HELP ME LOOK."

Margo thrust the sheet of paper into Carrie's hands and seized the laundry hamper. Before Carrie could stop her, she had ripped the white covering loose from the lid, and with her shiny red fingernails flashing, was pulling the pad beneath it into shreds.

"One lousy page," she wailed, "when we know he must have had more than a hundred! What do you think happened, Carrie?"

But Carrie was giving her attention to Millie, who was standing in the doorway with Ben. Her face was a chalky white and her voice trembled as she said, "May I see that please, Carrie?"

In silence, Carrie handed Millie the page of manuscript and watched as she quickly scanned it. When she looked up, her dark eyes were filled with tears.

She said, "I've seen this before. It's one of my pages. It was Paul who stole them from me!"

———————— ★ ————————

Finders
KEEPERS

ELIZABETH TRAVIS

W☉RLDWIDE®

TORONTO • NEW YORK • LONDON
AMSTERDAM • PARIS • SYDNEY • HAMBURG
STOCKHOLM • ATHENS • TOKYO • MILAN
MADRID • WARSAW • BUDAPEST • AUCKLAND

FINDERS KEEPERS

A Worldwide Mystery/March 1993

First published by St. Martin's Press, Incorporated.

ISBN 0-373-26116-0

To Kay, who, with unflagging energy and total disregard for personal safety, helped research the setting for this book

ONE

THE WARM Mediterranean sun shone down on the silent house, piercing through the branches of the olive trees to dapple the roof tiles with a lazily shifting pattern. The movement of the air was gentle, seeming to stir the leaves almost timidly, as if still in awe of the famous author, Charles Melton, who for so many years had demanded quiet in the morning. The black poodle, Finesse, napped on a sunny patch of lawn, as he did every morning, whimpering gratefully when he dreamed his master called him. A fat marmalade cat watched him from the nearby stone balustrade, her eyes narrowing to almond slivers when his outstretched legs twitched.

The house was made of stone coated with pale, coral-colored stucco which deepened to terra-cotta in the damp areas close to the shrubs. The broad facade was punctuated with two rows of tall, slightly arched windows, their green wooden shutters held open with S-shaped iron brackets. Since they faced east, the front windows were always curtained in the morning to protect the rugs and furniture from sun damage. This gave the house a blank look that was relieved by the front door, an ancient, cracked slab of wood carved with the oval faces of sorrowful saints, possibly grieving over their own broken-off noses. An intricately wrought iron bell topped with a tiny bird hung from the stone door jamb, its chain dangling listlessly in the quiet air.

While Melton was alive the household had stayed quiet in the mornings to accommodate his work routine, and the habit of silence still prevailed nearly a month after his death. The silence was so profound, in fact, that when Noel Wright opened the door of his small upstairs office, he paused to listen intently, almost afraid he had lost his hearing. Then he heard a faint tinkle he recognized as the chime of Charles Melton's hunting watch from the bedroom across the hall. Soon it would stop, he hoped, unless the zealous housekeeper, Lila, kept the thing wound.

He stepped carefully into the corridor, wondering where Lila was at this moment. Marketing in the village, he should think, and probably being delayed by questions about the house and about Melton's estate. Had the will been read? Who would inherit? What about the furniture, and the books and paintings? Had they been appraised?

Noel Wright hesitated outside his door, glancing up and down the corridor while he fought a repugnance toward his task that nearly immobilized him. He glared at the open door to Melton's room. If the fiendish old coot had possessed an ounce of decency he, Noel, a cultivated, middle-aged man of breeding and professional achievement, would not now find himself playing the role of common sneak thief.

A tawny Bokhara rug stretched two-thirds of the length of the hallway, then was joined by a shorter strip that was probably even more valuable. Noel felt smug when he looked at it, remembering that it was he who had persuaded Charles to add the rug to the already overloaded carton of purchases they were shipping home from Morocco. On either side of the carpets the uneven floorboards gleamed nearly black from years of polishing. They squeaked unpredictably underfoot, but Noel felt quite certain there was no one in the house to hear.

He drew a deep breath and wiped his damp palms on his trousers. Then he stepped onto the center of the Bokhara, where the floor was firmest, and walked swiftly down the hall to the room next to Melton's. Its polished walnut door stood slightly ajar, a fact Noel hadn't been able to observe from his own doorway, so he rapped firmly once, then again, and listened for a full minute before pushing the door open and stepping into the room.

There, as in Melton's room, the only activity came from a clock: the soft click of the digital alarm beside the bed as the numbers fell into place. They read 10:30, the bright green squares glowing through the room's dimness. Noel glanced impatiently at the closed draperies, wishing he dared to pull them. Between the bed and the window the bathroom door stood open. Noel strode over and peered inside at the white-tiled walls and floor and the old-fashioned porcelain fixtures; then he entered the room to look behind the shower curtain.

The tub was empty, of course, and Noel stood for a moment appreciating the texture of the fine-loomed white voile overcurtain that had been lavishly draped over the waterproof liner. The hem had been done by hand, he noted approvingly, with an insert of red piqué piping that many people wouldn't have bothered with.

The towels were nice too: the carnation print from Porthault that he would have ordered for himself if the color of the cotton binding had matched it better. The slightly faded red had been picked up in a way he liked: two strips of antique ribbon bordering the white damask wall covering, which he also admired.

He sniffed at the scent that pervaded the air, trying to place it, then picked up a crystal bottle of bath salts from the floor beside the tub. *L'Homme,* the label read, and Noel gave a snort. L'Homme; how touching.

Before he replaced the bottle he wiped it off with his handkerchief, feeling a little foolish but telling himself he would feel even more ridiculous if somehow his presence here were revealed by his fingerprints.

He returned to the bedroom and stood waiting for his eyes to adjust to the dimness. If the walls had not been covered with a deep red chintz the room would be brighter even with the curtains drawn; as it was, he had to grope his way to the closet on the opposite side of the room. He stepped inside and partially closed the door—he had to be able to hear—before turning on the small flashlight he had brought along. Then he saw a double row of jackets and trousers on evenly spaced, polished wood hangers and, below them, a shelf of neatly ranked shoes, each on its wooden tree. Paul had very small feet, he observed enviously; his own had always been an embarrassment, even though they were narrow at least.

One end of the closet had been given to a stack of drawers, painted the same ivory as the woodwork. Noel drew them open one by one, admiring the neatness with which the underwear and socks and handkerchiefs were stacked. He felt reluctant to search among the clothing—it seemed so terribly intimate—but he forced himself, carefully lifting a few pieces at a time, so he could feel any hidden papers, then looking under the scented flannel drawer linings before putting everything back in place.

When he had finished with the drawers he searched through the boxes stacked on the top shelf of the closet and was amused to find in one of them, wrapped in blue tissue, an elaborate lace dresser scarf from the shop on the Rue Duphot where they had gone together to order some pillowcases. Paul had pretended to be shocked by the price, he remembered; he had a thing about ostentation, yet he obviously treated himself to the best.

Noel switched off his flashlight and stepped out of the closet. With his handkerchief over the brass knob, he closed the door, then walked to the square mahogany desk that stood in front of the windows, sat down in the chair behind it, and began going through the drawers as methodically as he had searched the closet.

A faint sound caused him to stop and tilt his head toward the window to listen intently. The hand in which he held a sheaf of notepaper was suddenly perspiring, and he quickly replaced the paper in the drawer and slid it shut. He got to his feet, slowly, carefully, and stepped close to the beige linen curtain; the sound had seemed to come from the driveway below. He looked again at the clock, which now read 11:10. Lila could be returning, but it seemed unlikely. Or Paul. Paul might have forgotten something.

Noel Wright could feel his dry breath scraping his throat as he strained to hear. He stood stiffly beside the window, longing to twitch the curtain for a look. Instead he began moving cautiously toward the door. The sound had come from outside the house, he felt certain.

He had reached the foot of the narrow, carved wooden bed when he heard the sound again, much nearer, and this time he knew it for the squeak of a floorboard in the hall. A nearby one, from the loudness of it.

Noel swiveled instantly and headed back to the curtained window. He slipped behind the hanging folds of linen at the far end, where the window gave way to several feel of wall; no light would silhouette his shadow there, and because the draperies had been installed some inches out from the wall, to accommodate glass curtains, he wouldn't make a bulge.

A minute went by, enough time for Noel to regret his choice and wish he had gone into the closet, which probably had a lock. Then he heard a door slowly opening and saw the room grow lighter, then immediately darken again as the door was quietly closed.

He could not see the figure that had entered, but he was aware of a density, an unmistakable solidity that moved soundlessly across the room, coming nearer, then stopping; he tried to picture where.

Noel heard, very near, the felty sound of furniture moving on carpet, then a creak, as someone sat down in the chair behind the desk. He heard a drawer being pulled open, followed by the soft rustling of paper. It was comical, this replay of his own actions; listening, predicting the next move, he came close to hysteria. He could feel the panicky laughter bubbling against his ribs.

There was a whispered exclamation: "Damn!"

Then the chair was pushed back, and in a moment a strip of light appeared in the center of the windowed wall. The draperies were being opened and Noel, wtihout thought, seized some of the folds that covered him and held them tightly.

The parting of the curtains stopped immediately, so abruptly that the long panels swung sharply outward, then back against the wall with a thud.

Noel heard the desk drawer pushed shut, then footsteps running on the carpet. A flicker of light from the hall, then the closing of the door.

He slumped against the wall, still clutching the linen drapery across his body. He did not know who had entered the room, and that person did not know who had gotten there before him, only that someone had. The morning had been an exercise in futility for them both, and listening to his pulse thudding in his temples, Noel thought it had probably raised his blood pressure and shortened his life-span as well.

He stepped out of his hiding place cursing the name of Charles Melton.

TWO

LYING ON A CHAISE beside the pool of the Hôtel des Fleurs, Carrie Porter could hear snatches of conversations in several languages, none of them English, which meant the chatter did not intrude on her thoughts. Such as they were. Carrie was finding it easier than she had expected to keep her mind off home, children, and work.

She amused herself by sorting out the nationalities of the people around the pool. There were several French, of course, the nearest the two women who had fallen silent as she walked past them. She had taken it as a compliment that Frenchwomen—two chic Frenchwomen with thin, tanned bodies and alert, sharp-nosed faces—should stop talking to watch her pass. Now, stretched on her stomach with her eyes closed, she listened to their light, cultivated voices and regretted that she could not share in the lazy exchange of comments and soft, tantalizing laughter.

A flow of emphatic Italian came from beyond the two women: a man and woman talking without pause—possibly hoping to drown out the Oriental tongue that stabbed so jarringly from the couple beside them.

The incomprehensible babble around her was in perfect accord with the unreality of Carrie's world at that moment. The heat of the sun on the backs of her legs, the soft air scented with thyme, jasmine, lavender, and pine, the gentle thud of surf from the beach beyond the pool, made up a cloud of well-being on which she seemed to float like a swimmer on a raft.

It was all the more wonderful for being unexpected. No one had told her the Riviera would be like this. Her friends had called it beautiful, but no one had described the roads that slanted up into the sunlit hills, arching over white stone bridges, descending to run close beside the fanciful, turreted hotels and gleaming shops, then down to the edge of beaches surprisingly covered with fat pebbles.

The words *Nice; Côte d'Azur* on the air terminal had seemed the open sesame to a magical world. Carrie murmured them to herself while Ben steered their small car along the road that followed the coast from Nice to Cap Ferrat. Nearing Villefranche, they passed a jewel-like château that was the most elegant building Carrie had ever seen. She had a moment's glimpse of a gold-crested iron grille set between baroque stone pillars and, behind it, a white facade with high, lace-filled windows; then the road curved around to the sea once more.

At the edge of the village they looked down at a cluster of ancient buildings and docks far below, while on their other side the rugged mountain tilted against the golden afternoon sky. Peering up, Carrie could see the Grand Corniche, the highest of three roads that curled across the slope between tile-roofed stone farmhouses and terraced plots of vegetables and flowers.

It was at that point that she first became aware of the scent that wafted down from the hills like a benison on the slopes and beaches below, and every day since then she had identified more of the ingredients. There were flowers, certainly—roses, marguerites, mimosa, jasmine, and a hundred others—but it was the tang of pine and the ripeness of peaches, plums, and grapes that made the Riviera air so intoxicating. No perfume could duplicate that fragrance; it was alive, the breath of the living earth.

The sun was burning into her legs, and Carrie turned herself over, moving slowly and carefully so as not to rumple the towel that had been wrapped around her mattress by an astoundingly slim and tawny beach boy. Sitting up, she saw the same boy adjusting an umbrella for a blond girl who wore nothing but a minuscule bikini bottom. Casting solemn, measuring glances from the sun to the girl's bare breasts, the lad tilted the umbrella to shade them, but when she admonished, *"Non, non, plus de soleil!"* he shrugged and smiled as neutrally as a eunuch.

He was accustomed to nudity, of course; everyone on the Riviera was, with the exception of Ben Porter, who could not keep from staring, even when Carrie jabbed him with her elbow. Thinking of that, she glanced down at her own well-proportioned body, the one Ben had plenty of chances to appraise and which she knew he still admired, even if after nine years of marriage he didn't frequently say so. Her skin was still pale—they had arrived only two days earlier—but when Ben saw her tanned like these women around her, and wearing the new white bikini she was saving for the tan . . .

Carrie smiled. He would go right on looking at the others, she knew that; it was a fact of life, and a healthy sign, she'd always heard.

The blond girl was sitting up, waving her arm to a swarthy man who stood near the entrance to the deck area, scowling in the bright sun. His curly black hair was as glossy as if he had just dipped it into a vat of oil, and after leaving a space for his broad face and muscular shoulders, the curls continued in a thick, less glossy mat that covered his body to the waist. Wrapped tightly around it and reaching to his ankles was a skirtlike cotton pareau, printed in pumpkin and mauve. On his feet he wore sandals with thick rubber soles, and when he saw the blond girl he began clumping over to her chaise and the empty one beside it she was saving for him.

The poolside chatter had ceased, but the sunbathers were not actually staring at the new arrival, only listening with animal alertness while they wriggled and turned on their mattresses, glancing from under hat brims, umbrellas, and sunglasses to see the blond girl get to her feet as the man approached, then bend to kiss him on both cheeks. She was a good two inches taller than he, even with his thick sandals, and Carrie observed that as the two kissed they held themselves apart. It was the etiquette of nudity, she guessed; it would not do for onlookers to watch the smooth, bare body press itself against the bristling mat.

"Delaunay?" Carrie heard from the Frenchwomen two spaces away. *"C'est Delaunay, n'est ce pas?"* Then, *"Non, non, non, ce n'est pas!"* in emphatic disagreement.

Carrie sank back on her mattress, wondering whether the swarthy man really was Georges Delaunay, the film director. If so, the blond girl might be Marcelle Briard, the nineteen-year-old beauty for whom he had left his wife, and who had subsequently borne him triplet daughters.

Triplets? Carrie's eyes flew open, and she pushed herself up for another look at the pair, who were still on their feet, arranging their towels and lotions and magazines as fussily as if they expected to spend a week in that same spot. The blond girl's figure, as she bent and reached, was exquisite; never could that waist have accommodated triplets, so she must be the successor to the prolific nymphet—if her companion was indeed Delaunay.

A tall man wearing madras trunks and a wide-brimmed straw hat appeared on the deck, and Carrie felt a lift of her heart as she recognized Ben. One of the hotel's blue-striped towels was draped over his shoulder, and he carried an armful of books and newspapers. He stood peering at the sunbathers over horn-rimmed dark glasses that had slipped down on his nose; then he started walking toward her, and she watched him take one unbelieving glance at the nearly naked blond girl as he passed and quickly wrench his eyes away. When he reached her his greeting was, "Whew, did you see that blonde by the steps?"

"I was afraid you'd missed her. You didn't stub your toe or drop anything." Leaning back on her elbows, Carrie smiled up at her husband, and he set his armload of reading materials on the nearby plastic table and bent to kiss her.

"I'm learning to be cool."

Ben straightened, peering around for an attendant to bring another chaise, while Carrie studied him lazily through half-closed eyes. He might have been taken for a college boy, with his long, bony legs and somewhat awkward stance, except for the composure that made him appear at home wherever he went. He stood looking around with an expression of amused tolerance, as if he were some nobleman waiting to be recognized. It was that manner of his that had first attracted her when he started at Foote and Marshall, the publishing company where they had both worked as editors. To her such poise promised a kind of security; it was not until later that she realized Ben's self-possession had also posed a challenge.

"You look like a sleepy cat," he said, sitting down on the end of her chaise while the beach boy ran to find another.

"I should. I feel like purring." Carrie moved her legs to make room for him. "Why didn't you tell me the Riviera would be like this?"

"The last time I was here it wasn't. The ladies still wore clothes ... I think. Of course I was only nine; I might not have noticed."

"You'd have noticed. But I wasn't talking about the nudity, Ben. It's all so beautiful and serene, and it smells so good."

"The eats aren't bad, either. Let's get a menu and order lunch."

"I'm still thinking about breakfast. That croissant...and the honey. I've never tasted honey like that. And the butter, all that butter...melting in the sun." She opened her eyes and grinned up at Ben. "Let's go back to our balcony and have breakfast again."

He squeezed her ankle. "It pays to take you places because you enjoy them so much. You could teach a course called Travel Appreciation."

The boy was back, having brought a chaise, menus, towels, an umbrella in case it was needed, and the suggestion of drinks, which was immediately accepted.

When he had trotted off to get their wine spritzers Ben stretched out on his mattress and said, "I tried to call Millicent Girard, but she wasn't home. I *think* I left a message asking her to call me here. I'm not sure it got through."

"Maybe you should try her again after a while in case it didn't. I'm dying to meet her, aren't you?"

"It ought to be pleasant if she's as good-looking as Hank said she was."

"You know, Ben, a French wife is exactly what Hank needs."

"Wife? He's met her exactly once, you may remember."

"I don't care; he's hooked, I can tell. 'Millicent Girard.' I love her name. She would understand his business—Frenchwomen always do—and she could travel with him and help him entertain." Carrie paused, smiling reflectively. "And Eunice would flip, absolutely."

Keeping his eyes closed, Ben rolled his head back and forth marveling. "You have a whole new life worked out for Hank, haven't you? But Mademoiselle Girard may have other plans. A lot of doors will be open to her after her years with Charles Melton."

The beach boy had returned with their drinks, which he set carefully on the table between them. Ben pushed himself up to sign the bill, saying, "Come back in five minutes and we'll order lunch," then swung his legs over the side of the chaise and reached for the menu.

Carrie took a long sip of her drink and said, "I'll have a mushroom omelet and a salad."

Ben looked up from the menu, frowning. "Where's that boy? I meant to ask about the *moules*."

"Oh, yes. If they're those little pink ones I'll have some too. Ben, do you have Hank's letter with you?"

"No, but I remember it pretty well."

"Did he say Charles Melton had left Millicent a manuscript in his will, or that he gave it to her before he died?"

"She'll have to clear that up for us. The important point is that she has only part of a manuscript, three chapters. They're no good to her or anyone else without the rest of it."

"I should think even a fragment of an unpublished work by Melton would be of great value, now that he's dead."

"If that's all that exists, sure, it would be worth something to scholars, at least. But Hank said Millicent is certain that other of Melton's close associates were given sections of the manuscript as well. Obviously, whoever gets hold of the entire thing will make a fortune."

Ben looked up from his menu with a welcoming smile for the waiter, who had returned for the luncheon order.

"Très bien," Ben said, glancing at his watch. *"Cinq minutes, exactement."*

The boy made a slight bow, holding his pencil and pad in readiness while Ben composed his next sentence.

"Les moules," he said slowly, *"Sont-elles grandes ou petites?"*

"Ben," Carrie interrupted, but he ignored her to concentrate on the waiter's reply, which was unexpectedly lengthy and seemed to contain no words relating to size.

"Fine," Ben said decisively when the boy had finished. "We'll both have them. And a salad—right, Carrie?—a green salad, *salade verte,* that is. And a nice white Bordeaux."

After he had made a selection from the wine list and the waiter had departed, Carrie said, "I'm surprised that you ordered the mussels after what he told you."

"Oh? You caught some of that?"

"They probably won't hurt us, even if they do come from Beirut. I'm not going to worry about it."

"Carrie! Why didn't you speak up?" The *International Herald Tribune* slid onto the deck as Ben hastily got to his feet. "Where is that boy? I've got to cancel our order."

"Darling, relax. I'm just trying to make the point that you ought to practice your French on something less important to you than food."

"Hell, you had me believing..." Ben collected the disarranged newspaper and sat down again. "You're right, I suppose, but I keep hoping for a breakthrough."

"So do I. I have the idea that if I hear enough French spoken around me I'll start to understand it—by osmosis. Maybe if we come to the Riviera every year, or even twice a year..."

"What a dreamer. The only reason we're here now is because the trip will pay for itself, you know that. Even if we don't track down the manuscript—and then, by some miracle, get the rights to publish it—we can write off part of the expenses as literary consultation. Howard checked that out before we left."

"And *Deathwatch* will take care of the rest." Carrie sighed happily and lay back in her chaise. "What a lovely shock to have Sam Blake come up with a best seller. Do you think he's good for another one?"

"I wouldn't be surprised. His books have been improving steadily."

"With the help of your editing, Ben. You've taught Sam a lot; I hope he realizes that."

"Well, thanks. At the moment I think he's more excited about the way we've been marketing *Deathwatch,* and that's mostly your contribution." Ben reached across the table between them to take Carrie's hand. "We're a hell of a team, you know that?"

She smiled at him, the big, wholehearted grin that set perfect white teeth gleaming against red lips, her blue eyes crinkling nearly shut behind her sunglasses. Carrie didn't hold back; she could light up a room with that smile.

Ben would never forget the first time he'd seen it—the day he reported for work at Foote and Marshall and was introduced to his new colleagues. Centered in the group of editors who had gathered to meet him, Carrie, with her shining blond hair and laughing face, had stood out like a jewel in a box of cotton. When he shook her hand she smiled into his eyes with so much friendly curiosity that he felt an almost irresistible urge to draw her off to some corner where they could be alone.

After that first day only one or two of the women on the staff made any effort to capture Ben's attention, and within six months they were planning Carrie's bridal shower.

So Ben and Carrie had been "a hell of a team" from the first, though the partnership had developed along lines neither of them could have predicted. Two years after the wedding it had produced their son, Terry, and it was when he was still tiny that Ben began to balk at the demands and restrictions of his work.

"I never have any time with him," he would complain; and it was true that the work of acquiring new authors,

then seeing their books produced and promoted, took all of
his office time. The necessary reading and editing had to be
done in the evenings and on weekends. He not only had
little time for his son, but the painting that had been an
important interest was totally neglected.

Carrie, on the other hand, was surprised to find that she
missed office life. She was given some editing jobs that she
could do at home, but it was the business end of publishing that had intrigued her, she now realized: the dealing
with authors and agents, and the packaging and marketing
of the books. Much as she enjoyed her baby, his waking
periods were brief at first, leaving her far more leisure time
than she needed.

In search of ways to make their lives more satisfactory,
the Porters began a period of what could be called squirm-
ing around. They spent weekends looking at houses in the
suburbs, then ventured to northern Connecticut and Ver-
mont, thinking they might give up the city altogether. They
considered dairy farming, or inn-keeping; Ben thought he
might go to law school; Carrie talked to friends in real estate and interior decorating.

But it was book publishing that engaged their minds and
talents, and when a friend suggested that they start their
own business, the idea was immediately appealing, if scary.
Publishing did not *have* to take place in New York, after all,
and did not demand a large staff or elaborate offices.

The friend, Ted Marsh, had his own dreams of a better
life-style. He also had a trust fund with which he offered to
help support the Porters' venture if they would give him
some part-time work that would pay his living expenses and
leave him free to paint.

So, not quite able to believe they were doing it, Ben and
Carrie bought a converted farmhouse in Riverdale, a pretty
village in the hills of central Connecticut. The town's com-
mercial area was concentrated in a few blocks of Victorian
houses along the river bank, and in one of these they rented
office space for the Porter Publishing Company.

Five years later, holding hands beside the pool of the
Hôtel des Fleurs, feeling slightly dazed by the combination

of hot sun and cold wine, Ben and Carrie could not find much to complain about. Porter Publishing was slowly establishing a reputation for quality as well as originality—not always a compatible pairing. And Sam Blake's best seller had given the Porters a heady taste of success. They were beginning to speak of paying off their debts and adding to the staff.

But Ben and Carrie were discovering that the greatest benefit of independence was just that—the freedom to work when and where they wanted to instead of adapting themselves to a rigid office routine.

Ben, dropping Carrie's hand now to prepare for the lunch he saw being wheeled toward them, spent most of his days at home painting in one end of their big family kitchen. At the other end of it he cooked—creatively, daringly, often but not always successfully. And when manuscripts needed editing he took time out for that.

Carrie, who was taking a quick plunge now while the waiter fussed over their table, worked in the office every day—usually dropping Terry and Brooke, his five-year-old sister, at school on her way. Carrie was the one who negotiated with authors, agents, and printers; it was she who prepared contracts and supervised sales—always following plans she and Ben had worked out together. If it sometimes wore her out she'd stay home for a day and Ben would take over.

This unusual working style had evolved during the first year, when Brooke was born and Ben, giving Carrie a hand, found he really enjoyed cooking and marketing. He also loved painting in the spacious, kitchen-family room, especially in the winter, when often a smoldering log fire matched the warmth of a fragrant stew simmering on the stove.

Carrie, seeing the reluctance with which Ben left this haven, began to volunteer to take his place in the office. "I'll just run over and meet the lawyer," she might say. "You can sign the contract later." And soon she was "running over" to the office every day. Or she would visit the printer,

hire a free-lance copy editor, travel to New York to lunch
with an agent.

"Carrie and I are interchangeable," Ben would explain
to curious friends, and they just about were. Either could
run the office or the house, and because they switched roles
when they wanted a change, neither of them got rusty.

Vacations, however, they kept traditional. "I suppose
one of us should stay in the office and run things," Carrie
had suggested tentatively, and had been delighted with
Ben's shocked reaction.

"Take separate vacations? Forget it. We're not that pro-
gressive."

"But you could call this one a business trip," Carrie had
replied, "and since I handle the mundane details . . ."

"Including a mundane trip to the Riviera? By yourself?
Staying in the Hôtel des Fleurs with all those scheming international types?" Ben was almost choking. "You're not
serious, I hope?"

"Well, maybe you should go. Hank Stovall is your
friend. You're the one he wrote to."

"And this Millicent Girard he's raving about probably
isn't really so great looking." Ben paused, but Carrie's face
remained unnaturally serene. "And you don't like French
cooking as much as I do." He stopped again. "And who
wants to see where Charles Melton lived? I can't think of
anything more boring." Still Carrie lay back in her chair,
gazing dreamily out the window.

"Carrie?" he asked. "What are you up to anyway?"

She reached beneath a cushion and pulled out a fat envelope, which she handed to Ben. "Two tickets on Air
France," she said. "I tried to get practical when I saw how
much they cost, but I couldn't bear to go without you. *Or*
vice versa."

So they had persuaded Ted Marsh to keep the office
running and hired reliable Mrs. Duffy to babysit and taken
off on their first major trip since their honeymoon. Pre-
dictably, parting from their children had been a wrench for
Carrie, and she comforted herself by picturing their daily
activities.

"What time is it now, Ben?" she asked as she brushed out her dripping hair. "At home, I mean?"

Ben peered at the clock mounted on the wall of the bath house. "It's one thirty here; must be seven thirty there. A.M., that is. They're just waking up."

Carrie tied a flowered cotton skirt over her suit and sat in one of the chairs the waiter had placed at the table. "How nice," she said, smiling as she surveyed the starched white tablecloth, the crystal vase of anemones, the dewy wine bottle in its silver cooler, and the covered tureens of *moules marinière*. "I see you told them how I like things done."

Ben handed her a folded piece of paper. "This came with the lunch," he said. "Unless she hears to the contrary, Millicent Girard will meet us at the hotel at four."

Carrie quickly scanned the message, then set it aside and picked up her wineglass. "*À votre santé, mon mari.*" Then she frowned. "That isn't right, is it? Should it be '*à ton santé,*' or something?"

"A ton of *santé* won't be enough if these mussels are really from Lebanon."

Ignoring Carrie's groan of disgust at the pun, Ben apprehensively lifted the cover from his tureen of *moules;* then, as he sniffed at the plume of wine-scented steam rising from the dish, his lips curved in a beatific smile. "Be nice to Mademoiselle Girard," he said as he reverently transferred a spoonful of tiny coral mussels in their glistening black shells to his soup plate. "Be so nice that she'll invite us back year after year while we slowly—get that, Carrie?—*slowly* help her find the rest of Charles Melton's unpublished novel."

THREE

To the Porters' surprise, and somewhat to their relief, Millicent Girard turned out to be an American, a young and charming one with wistful dark brown eyes. She responded in kind to their laboriously composed French greeting, then said, "Let's speak English, shall we?" Studying their faces, she added, "Unless you prefer French, of course."

"No, no, that's fine, wonderful, much easier," Ben and Carrie chorused, as if, given a moment's hesitation, she might irretrievably change her mind.

"We thought you were French, of course," said Carrie. "Your name..."

"My father was from Quebec." Millicent Girard looked from Ben to Carrie with a faint smile trembling on her lips, her huge dark eyes glowing. "So I grew up speaking French—thank goodness. I'm not much good at learning languages, really."

"Carrie and I are finding we're not particularly gifted in that line either," Ben replied.

He glanced around the lobby of the hotel, a tall octagon composed of ceiling-high mullioned windows. Pots of blooming flowers set at the base of each bordered the room with color while symbolizing the spirit of the Hôtel des Fleurs. In the center of the space a massive oval reception desk stood on an Aubusson rug whose rich colors had faded to a tender mélange of rose and ivory and pale blue-greens. Six Louis XV fauteuils covered in threadbare ochre tapestry formed a semicircle in front of the desk. French doors opened at the front of the room to a circular gravel drive and on the inner side to an awninged terrace where Ben could see white-coated waiters passing trays of cakes and sandwiches.

"Shall we have tea?" he asked, and Millicent Girard responded with the same rather shy smile.

"That would be lovely," she said, and Ben took her arm, then Carrie's as well, and began leading them out to the terrace.

Millicent was several inches shorter than Carrie; her head reached only to Ben's shoulder. She had shining dark hair cut to curve across her forehead, framing her rather squarely modeled face and long-lashed brown eyes, then turning up to reveal the wide gold loops she wore in her ears. The tailored lines of her ivory silk dress emphasized the delicate curves of her body. Her waist, circled with a honey-colored crocodile belt, looked to Ben to be about the size of his five-year-old daughter's.

In contrast, Carrie, with her blond hair swinging, her face alight with pleasure and curiosity as she looked around at the tea drinkers on the terrace, might have been an adventurous Viking queen. Ben stifled a smile at the image; Carrie, having always wanted to be petite, would hardly enjoy being compared to a Viking.

The maître d'hôtel seated them at a low round table at the edge of the terrace and, after they had ordered tea, left them to enjoy the prospect of the broad green lawn that sloped toward the sea, bordered on either side with cypresses and umbrella pines. A light breeze blew up to them from the water, and Carrie inhaled the scent she recognized, the mingling of flowers and herbs with tangy pine.

"Do you still enjoy that wonderful aroma?" she asked Millicent. "Or do you stop being aware of it when you've lived here for a while?"

Millicent smiled. "I never have," she said. "But perhaps the French do, having known it since they were born. I've never thought to ask."

She studied Carrie's face, intrigued by the notion. "Now that I think of it, Melton referred to the special scent of Riviera air whenever he wrote about the area, so I guess he never took it for granted either."

Carrie said, "You must know Melton's works almost as well as he did after—how many years was it, exactly?"

"Only five." Gazing toward the distant sea, Millicent slowly shook her head. "I can hardly believe it was such a short time." She paused and when she spoke again her voice was thick. "I can't believe it's over."

Carefully avoiding Ben's eyes, Carrie patted Millicent's hand. "You must have been devoted to him—and he to you."

"We had become very close, yes. Working together as we did, we sometimes anticipated each other's thoughts. It always amused him when that happened; he said we were like an old married couple." She smiled briefly at the memory.

"Then it's not surprising that he left his unpublished manuscript to you." Carrie bent over the table eagerly. "I wonder if he wanted you to finish it? Because you were the only one he could trust..."

"The only one he could trust!" Millicent laughed harshly, then immediately apologized. "Forgive me, Carrie," she said. "You will see how how ironic that is when I tell you that Charles Melton left me only one section of his manuscript—three chapters, to be exact—and he also left parts of it to at least four other people, maybe more; we can't be certain. It is extremely doubtful that the whole book will ever be assembled."

"Why is that? I should think you would put them all together and..." Carrie was stopped by the bitterness that suddenly appeared on Millicent Girard's pretty face. "I'm sorry," she faltered, "I must have said..."

"What you said was perfectly logical, but it will never happen because of the way Melton left things in his will." Millicent looked from Carrie to Ben. "You understand copyright law, of course, so you know that at an author's death his work falls into the public domain unless he has assigned the copyright to some specific person."

Ben nodded. "Then in this case..."

"Charles Melton ordered that the copyright to his unpublished novel should be awarded to whichever of his heirs gains possession of the entire manuscript within the year following his death. Can you see what a terrible thing he's done? Can you imagine the rivalry he's stirred up?" Millicent threw up her hands. "It's positively wicked of him to have done this to us!"

Both Carrie and Ben began to speak at once, but stopped when the waiter arrived with the tea service, which he set, after a questioning glance, at Carrie's place. While she poured out the tea, he took a platter of tiny sandwiches from his assistant and offered it to Millicent.

Ben said carefully, "Now let me get this straight. Charles Melton has divided an unpublished manuscript among several of his close associates—five that we know of. The copyright to the work will go to the one who somehow gets all the parts for himself. Is that right?"

Millicent nodded. "Within one year," she reminded as she placed a thin watercress sandwich on her plate beside one each of smoked salmon and cucumber.

"No wonder Hank was so intrigued." Ben wore a quizzical grin as he weighed the possibilities. "The old guy really put you on the spot, didn't he? How is everybody taking it? Are you still on speaking terms?"

"Oh, of course we're all pretending we don't care a fig about material gain. No, no, we're just a group of disciples, grateful to have received a keepsake from the hand of the great master." Her dark eyes were unreadable, opaque as ebony. "We are far too intellectual to engage in some childish competition, and Melton knew that—knew it before we did."

"Then I wonder what his motive was."

"That's what none of us can figure out. Or if Noel or any of the others have any ideas, they're not sharing them with me." Millicent's lips twisted bitterly. "I had no idea Melton was capable of such cruelty."

"Well, is it really so cruel?" Carrie asked. "I mean, how do you know the manuscript is worth all this fuss? He was an old man, after all. Maybe he was written out."

Millicent smiled. "In my one hundred fifty or so pages the writing is absolutely mesmerizing, and Paul Clifford tells me the same is true of his. If the rest is as good, it's a masterpiece."

"Oh, Millicent—Millie—you just have to get it together. Bribe, steal, whatever you have to do!" Carrie's eyes were shining with excitement. "Think of it: Charles Melton's final and most brilliant novel!"

"Charles Melton's most valuable literary property, that's what it is—or could be." Ben shook his head. "No wonder nobody wants to give up any part of it."

He took a pencil out of the pocket of his blazer and reached for a menu to write on. "Would you tell us something about the other heirs?" he said.

Millicent sipped her tea, then she began, "First there is Noel Wright. Noel was Melton's agent and for years his closest friend. I've thought he might be behind this scheme, but I can't see any benefit in it for him. Quite the contrary, in fact."

Ben shook his head, frowning. "I can't either, at this point."

"We also have Paul Clifford, Melton's secretary. He and Noel live in the house, by the way, and so do I. Paul hates Noel; I'm not sure why." Millicent paused to take a sip of tea. "The other local heir is Margo Honeywell. I imagine you know who she is?"

"Oh, sure. Though I didn't know she was close to Charles Melton."

"He found her very entertaining. In fact, I would say Margo was a necessary ingredient in his life; she brought the world to him. She has a villa here in Cap Ferrat, and she could produce anyone he wanted to see: the oil barons, the intellectuals, the painters and dancers and actors, all the headline makers. Naturally, they were all dying to meet him, and Margo could control it, serving them up when he was in the mood and keeping them away when he wasn't."

"How does a woman get so powerful?" Carrie marveled.

Millicent shook her head, smiling. "Wouldn't we all like to know? Margo simply has a way of making people do what she wants; you'll feel it when you meet her. And she's in awe of nobody. If she wants to go somewhere she'll call up Prince Rainier and ask to borrow a plane. What's more, she usually gets it.''

''I don't think we'd better meet her. What if she decides she wants Ben?''

''Margo isn't predatory about men; she's too smart for that. Also a bit over the hill. You might look out for Jeanette Melton, though, *cousin* Jeanette, Melton's other heir. She'll collect any man who might be useful to her career, if she can.'' Glancing from Carrie to Ben, Millicent added, ''I'd say in this case she can't, but she's one to look out for in other ways. I never let down my guard around dear cousin Jeanette.''

''What is this demanding career of hers?'' Ben asked.

''She's an editor of *World Beat,* and she wants to live up to the name in both senses: cover the hot spots and beat out the competition. She'll be editor-in-chief some day, I've no doubt of that—unless she makes some fatal mistake, which isn't likely.''

''Obviously, she doesn't live here.''

''No, Jeanette is based in New York, but she often gets to Europe and always comes here when she does. At least while Melton was alive. She was well aware of the fact that she was his closest living relative.'' Millicent stopped and a look of malicious pleasure appeared on her face. ''I wish I'd been around when she heard that her legacy was three chapters of a probably unpublishable novel.''

''Is that really all he left her?'' Ben said. ''Then who inherited his fortune? He certainly must have made one.''

''Everything goes to scholarships he set up in various colleges in the States. Except the house, which he and Noel Wright owned jointly. I imagine Noel will buy the other half from the estate.'' Millicent held out her cup for more tea, and Carrie took it from her.

''I wonder if Melton finished the book he left you. Maybe not, and that's the reason . . .'' Ben looked up from the notes he'd been scribbling. ''If each of the five of you has three chapters, that's a total of fifteen. What about length? Do they add up to enough pages for a complete novel?''

"Paul and Margo have roughly the same number of pages I do: between one hundred forty and one hundred seventy. Noel won't even tell me that much, and I haven't had a chance to ask Jeanette, but if they had about the same amount, yes, that could certainly be a Charles Melton novel." Millicent sat back helplessly. "But we're deadlocked. We're all so afraid one of the others may get the whole thing that we'll probably go to our graves still clutching our miserable few pages."

Carrie added solemnly, "And possibly doing the world out of a literary treasure."

"That as well." Millicent forced a wan smile. "You can see why I need help."

Ben was slowly shaking his head. "I wonder if Hank knew what he was getting us into. He sent you his best regards, by the way..."

Carrie interjected, "His love, I think he said, Ben," and was gratified to see Millicent Girard's smooth skin turn faintly pink.

"I believe he'll be over some time this month," she said. "But you see, I didn't tell Hank the whole story. We had just met, I hardly knew him, and I had no idea he would want to get involved—in the matter of the manuscript, that is."

Carrie said, "I have the impression he wants to get *very* involved."

Ben said sternly, "Carrie!" and her blue eyes widened innocently. He turned once more to Millicent.

"I'm curious about your work. You weren't Melton's secretary, I gather; that was this Paul Clifford..."

"He called me his literary assistant. I hunted down references for him and did whatever research he needed—there's a surprising amount of legwork involved in writing fiction. I also acted as a sounding board." She paused to take a sip of her tea, then said slowly, "I'll always treasure the memory of long, quiet afternoons, when he had had his lunch and his rest and we would sit alone while he read me what he had written in the morning."

"How did you happen to get such an enviable job, Millie?" Ben asked.

He was astonished to see her fumble for a reply.

"How did I get the job?" she repeated. "Oh, I had some connections. My father was in publishing, you see." She swept her fingers through the glossy wave of hair that fell across her forehead. "Well, not exactly in publishing." She laughed shortly. "He was a consultant to several publishers, so he knew many people in the inner circles of that world: agents, literary lawyers, and publicists. And he knew I would practically kill for a chance to meet Charles Melton, let alone work for him."

"So would thousands of literature majors." Ben smiled admiringly. "You must have been especially well qualified."

"I was lucky," Millicent replied, "and I spoke French, which was one of the requirements." She was smiling as she added, "Melton refused to take the time to learn the language, but he was determined to live here, so everyone around him had to be fluent."

She paused to make a selection from a tray of pastries brought by the waiter. When he had placed a flowerlike apricot tart on her plate and had moved along to Carrie, Millicent said, "You can imagine how I felt about having a chance to work for such a giant of literature. I kept a diary; in my mind I stood off and watched and listened to every exchange between us; I felt I was living history."

"And you were." Carrie breathed. She was loving this, Ben could see. The story of the aging genius and his beautiful young disciple had totally captured her imagination.

"I'll bet you fell in love with him," she added. "And he with you. After all, he was lucky too."

Ben glanced sharply at his wife, wondering what she was up to; all the world knew Charles Melton's sexual preference.

Apparently Millicent also wished to skirt that issue, for she said, "To be true to his gift a man like Charles Melton has to isolate himself, not only from the mundane details of daily life, but from ordinary emotions as well. He couldn't allow himself to care for anyone intensely, to fall in love the way the rest of us do…although there may have been one important exception; I'll never know for sure."

"Are you suggesting that he wasn't always homosexual?"

Ben asked the question bluntly, but instead of reacting with shock, Millicent suddenly turned businesslike.

Studying her watch, she said, "I think we should save the question of Melton's sexuality for another time. Right now would be a good moment to catch Noel and Paul at the house, and possibly Margo too. What do you say? Would you like to come with me?"

Carrie said instantly, "We certainly would."

Ben was more cautious. "I'm not sure we can help you; I'm not even sure we ought to try." Seeing the fire that sprang up in Carrie's eyes, he hurried on, "But I'd very much like to meet these people you've been telling us about, if you can think of some way to explain us."

Millicent was pushing back her chair. "I'll just tell them you're friends of Hank's, that's all they need to know." But she stopped then and sat frowning thoughtfully while the waiter brought the check for Ben to sign.

"I'm wrong about that," she said, when he had gone. "I think we'd better invent another career for you. It wouldn't do for any of those vultures to discover that you're in publishing."

"Well, I am also a painter," Ben said. "I can bring my sketch pad." He got to his feet and helped the two women out of their chairs.

"And I'm also a mommy," said Carrie, smoothing her skirt. "I can bring pictures of the children."

Taking an arm of each while they left the terrace, Millicent said, softly but urgently, "I hope you're serious, because if any one of them finds out the truth, it won't merely be awkward. Forgive me for sounding melodramatic, but it could also be highly dangerous."

FOUR

PAUL CLIFFORD opened his curtains wider to admit more of the fading afternoon light, then reached across the deep embrasure to partially close the window. The stone sill was warm from the sun, and he rested against it, looking out at the square of lawn beyond the gravel drive and the jumble of shrubs and flowers at the base of the stone wall that bordered the property. What he could have done with that garden if only Charles had let him; but, typically, Charles would never take the time to listen to Paul's suggestions. It hurt, even in retrospect, especially when he recalled how extravagantly Charles had praised Margo's newly planted courtyard.

Theirs could be just as stunning, he thought, turning away to adjust his needlepoint frame to the changed light; but now it was too late. Noel, even if he decided to keep the house, had the bourgeois taste one might expect of an agent. Thank God he, Paul, would not be there to see his desecrations.

But just where would he be? Paul felt his throat tighten as a wave of sadness threatened to overwhelm him. He could not afford to give in to it just then, so he seized his needle and bent to the embroidery frame for distraction. He was doing the coat of a fawn, changing thread frequently for the subtle tones that from only inches away gave the impression of real fur. Not many had the patience for such fine work, but it was worth it when he thought of the piece lasting long beyond him, possibly hanging in a museum where some people would notice his initials placed modestly in the lower righthand corner.

Two more rows, then he would have to dress for dinner at the Delaneys'. He glanced at the digital clock, as always offended by the glaring green numbers. He hated that clock; it was completely wrong in the room, but Charles had given it to him. Sometimes he wondered if he did such things for spite, like keeping the garden a mess and a hundred other examples he could think of.

Paul got up and moved the needlepoint away from the window in case of rain. Loosening the cord sash of his silk dressing gown, he went to the closet, frowning as he observed that it was unraveling at one end. He could catch that up in the morning, and next time he went to Paris he would order a new sash from Charvet.

He hung the robe on a brass hanger, then took the foulard from around his neck, and placed it in a drawer. He had chosen his costume that morning, so now he didn't have to think about it, just reach down the red-striped white shirt and the deep-red linen trousers and then, the fun part, select a foulard that would harmonize and at the same time add a bit of spice. He would wear the hopsacking blazer, or, on second thought, might the Delaneys think it a bit too casual?

Delaneys! From New Jersey! Was it possible he was going to dinner with such people? He could not imagine how they had ever found their way to Cap Ferrat, but Margo had assured him that Michael Delaney was an important magazine publisher and had all the money in the world. Even so, he wouldn't have considered accepting the invitation if Margo hadn't practically ordered him to go. She knew how badly he needed a job, and the Delaneys had connections that could be useful, but God, how he dreaded the evening ahead!

He stepped out of the closet carrying the shirt and, pushing the door to, caught sight of himself in the full-length mirror. He ran his eye over his reflection, searching for something to like, but the best he could do was note that in spite of the way he'd been indulging himself since Charles's death, his waistline had not perceptibly changed. He squared his narrow shoulders and pulled in his stomach, but the contours of his body remained what they had always been: rounded, sloping, soft-looking, as if the bones had been removed.

His face looked soft as well, rather like a cookie with the round eyes and mouth stuck in by a child's finger. His nose was short and blunt, his chin not exactly weak, but decidedly small and rounded.

And white! If he had realized how pale he was he certainly would have gone to the beach that afternoon. With his graying, sandy hair and light hazel eyes he needed color in his skin. He rethought his choice of neckwear; he would look terminal in the curry and red.

Still, he had suffered a bereavement. Turning away from the mirror, Paul thought cynically that the pallor could be an effective touch as long as he was seeking a new post— job hunting, the Delaneys would call it, no doubt. They could see at a glance that he was a man of strong loyalties, one who truly cared about the welfare of his employer.

Yes, and how had he been rewarded? With an annuity befitting twenty years of devotion? No; the thick manila envelope for which he had signed the postal receipt with a shaking hand and thumping heart had contained nothing more than 117 pages of manuscript, chapters 16 through 18 of an unpublished and probably unfinished novel.

And then there had been the added shock, while he tried to believe he had been singled out for a sacred literary honor, of discovering that Charles had not entrusted his final lines to him alone but had diluted whatever value they might have by dividing the rest of the work among four others.

His throat tightened again, this time with anger. He'd not make such a mistake again, he told himself firmly as he strode to the closet to get his trousers. Whoever thought Paul Clifford would be easy to get—be they Delaneys or Rockefellers—had a surprise in store. This time he would spell it out, as might be expected of the trusted private secretary to Charles Melton. He would demand benefits, paid vacations, and, above all, a solid retirement plan.

Maybe, instead of hiring out to another self-centered genius, he would write a book himself—a lurid exposé of Charles Melton. If he did it quickly, while people still cared, he might make big money, and nobody could ever prove what was true and what wasn't.

The idea was so startling that he froze in the midst of pulling on his socks and stared openmouthed into space. Had he the courage, not to mention the skill it would take? What if Noel thought of it too?

The crunch of tires on gravel broke through his whirling thoughts, and Paul jumped guiltily. He rose from his seat on the end of the chaise, cocking his ears for the sound of voices. Car doors slammed; a man's voice asked some questions about the house. Could Noel have offered it to the real estate agents already?

Paul reached the window in time to catch a glimpse of a blond woman approaching the front door, followed by Millicent. Well, well.

Paul was tingling with curiosity as he slipped into his loafers. He put on his blazer, switched on the bedside lamp to make his homecoming less bleak, and very quietly opened the door and peered down the hall. Noel's door was closed, which might mean he was out, or dressing, or asleep; Paul didn't care which as long as they didn't have to meet. He stepped into the corridor and cautiously tiptoed to the staircase.

MILLICENT GIRARD led the Porters across the polished, rose-tinged quarry tiles that paved the entrance hall and down two steps into the drawing room. There they all stopped abruptly. A man stood just inside one of the French doors that led to the inner courtyard, apparently talking to himself.

"If you can't get these tasks accomplished during the day, you should employ a helper," he was saying in a voice tight with annoyance. He was a tall, thin man, wearing white trousers and a dark blue blazer, and he stood with his head cocked at an uncomfortable angle while he addressed whoever occupied what the others could now see was a ladder leaning against the outer wall of the house.

"It is nearly six o'clock, Lila," he went on. "I often have guests at this hour, as you well know, and they would not

find it entertaining to watch you plastering or whatever you
think you're doing."

Millicent's face was alight with suppressed laughter, but
she said calmly, "Good evening, Noel. Come and meet
some visitors."

The tall man turned his attention to the newcomers with
the air of one being asked to endure yet another trial, his
black eyebrows arching, his thin mouth tightening. Still, he
came over to them at once, holding himself stiffly erect,
arms straight at his sides, while his cold blue eyes raked
them in swift appraisal.

"Carrie and Ben Porter, Noel Wright."

As Millicent introduced them he lifted Carrie's hand to
his lips, then straightened and briskly shook hands with
Ben.

"How do you do?" he said, then stepped back and
waited for Millicent to explain their presence.

"The Porters are great friends of Hank's," she began;
then when Noel's expression did not change, she added,
"Hank Stovall. You met him, Noel, when he was here last
month."

"I think I remember. Yes, of course." Noel Wright
sighed. Looking from Carrie to Ben, he said, "There were
so many people coming and going, you understand, and I
was so...we all were, weren't we, Millicent?...so undone, so distraught."

"It was just a few days after Melton's death," Millicent
murmured, and Carrie and Ben nodded sympathetically.

"What a sad loss, for you and for the whole world."
Carrie feared she had overdone it, but Noel Wright looked
so pleased that she added, "It must have been wonderful to
have such a great writer for a friend. You were also his
agent, weren't you?"

"Well, of course we never spoke in such terms, not since
the beginning, which was more than twenty years ago." He
smiled mistily. "No, Charles and I talked of many wonderful things...I venture to claim that we shared a special
sensitivity...but we rarely mentioned business matters."

A metallic banging resounded from the inner courtyard, causing Noel to wince. He slowly closed his eyes, as if to be spared the sight of whatever offense was being committed, and kept them closed while a woman's voice called, "It's nothing breakable! Dropped the trowel, that's all!"

The base of the ladder, visible through the long windows, vibrated noisily as a pair of feet wearing paint-stained sneakers stumped down the treads. The feet belonged to legs clad in blue workman's pants which were soon seen to be belted around the waist of a woman.

Impatient to be down, she jumped to the ground from the third rung, swinging a bucket of plaster in one hand. She set the bucket on the ground, then seized the ladder and tipped it on its side, apparently preparing to put it away.

"Here, let me help you with that!" Ben darted through the open door, reaching for the ladder while the woman watched his approach in astonishment. She was about Carrie's height but solidly built, with a tanned, lively face and curly brown hair lightly streaked with gray.

"It's all right, Ben," Millicent called after him. "Lila does this all the time." Following him to the courtyard, she said, "This is Ben Porter, Lila." She turned to include Carrie. "And Carrie Porter. Lila Baines, you two. Lila keeps this house glued together."

"Welcome to La Rêverie!" The woman had propped the ladder against her legs in order to clasp Ben's hand in both of hers. Her snapping brown eyes peered intently into his face, then she swiveled around to Carrie and seized her hand with the same warmth. As she studied Carrie's face her eyes brightened with pleasure. "What a beauty you are, Carrie Porter! That coloring...!"

She stepped back, allowing the ladder to crash to the ground, and, glancing from Carrie to Millicent, said, "The two of them are quite a sight, wouldn't you agree, Ben? The contrast... But let's not spoil them. Where did you come from? How long are you staying with us?"

Millicent replied, "The Porters are staying at the hotel, Lila; for about a week, I think." She looked questioningly at Ben and he nodded. "They're friends of Hank Stovall's."

"That darling man! I hope he comes back when we're in better shape to entertain him." Lila looked past them, to where Noel Wright could be seen in the drawing room, then lowered her voice. "We were all at sixes and sevens when Hank was here; I guess you know why." She cast her eyes upward, indicating either heaven or Charles Melton's study.

"Hank was sorry to intrude at such a time," said Carrie. "But when he met Millicent . . ."

"I know." Lila Baines was beaming again. "I know what happens when a man meets Millicent."

"Lila . . ."

"Well, enough of that. You go in and have a drink while I stow my gear. No, no, I can manage." Grinning at Ben as she batted his hands away from the ladder, she picked it up, then the bucket, and trudged toward the rear of the courtyard.

Noel Wright had appeared in the doorway, apparently to make his departure. "I regret that a dinner engagement compels me to leave you," he began, then stopped as Paul Clifford entered the courtyard from the direction of the driveway.

Taking charge of the introductions, Noel said, "Good evening, Paul, these are Millicent's guests, the Porters." He nodded stiffly in the direction of Ben and Carrie, and as Paul moved up to them, fixing a shy smile on his face, added, "It has been a pleasure, Mr. and Mrs. Porter. I hope we will meet again."

Millicent said, "Noel, I am hoping you will join the Porters and me for lunch tomorrow." She turned to Paul Clifford, who was shaking hands with Ben, and said, "And you too, of course, Paul. We're going to Le Petit Jardin."

Slowly shaking his head, Noel said, "I am sorry, Millicent. I can't possibly do it." He glanced briefly, impassively, at Paul, and said, with another curt nod at the Porters, "Enjoy your stay." Then he was gone.

FIVE

"WELL, I MIGHT HAVE accepted if I had known you were coming along, but it's too late now." Noel Wright sounded petulant, but he did muster a faint smile as he watched Margo Honeywell pour coffee into two of her delicate Limoges cups.

Margo did everything with such style; he knew it was one reason he admired her. Even at this early hour her face was perfectly made up, her prominent cheekbones touched with rouge, her lips painted with her custom-blended rosy red, and her surprising amber eyes outlined to emphasize their rather exotic tilt. Her silver-streaked black hair was smoothly brushed back from her face and turned up on the ends in the simple, dramatic style she had worn for twenty years. The streaks gleamed in the sunlight, too artfully placed to be natural, though of course Margo was old enough.

Noel placed his cup on the stone table, then sat down in a wrought-iron chair across from Margo's. It was 10:00 A.M., their favorite time in the garden, when the sun had been up long enough to warm the flagstone patio but hadn't yet baked it too hot for comfort.

"I hope you appreciate these cups, Margo," he said. "You really shouldn't be using them."

"And if I didn't use my museum-quality china and crystal and furniture what on earth would I drink from and sit on? You know I'm too broke to go to Printemps and buy cheap ones." Margo laughed her famous raucous laugh, which sounded more appropriate to a waterfront bar than a Cap Ferrat villa.

Noel looked pained. "I wish you wouldn't talk that way when we're alone, Margo," he said. "I'm not some dealer who's going to overcharge you. Not that you're fooling them either when you talk poor, merely insulting their intelligence.''

Again the bawdy laugh rang out, with Margo's generous mouth opened wide, her eyes disappearing behind thickly blackened lashes. A tear escaped, and she quickly blinked her eyes wide open and sat up to dab with her hanky before the makeup could run.

''I detest this new stuff Annette made me try,'' she said, while Noel looked on sympathetically. ''Arden may cost more, but I know it's waterproof.'' She took a sip of her coffee, then peered at Noel over the rim of the cup. ''Come on, pick up the phone and tell Millie you've changed your mind. Otherwise you'll do yourself out of an excellent lunch and possibly an amusing afternoon.''

But he was shaking his head like an obstinate little boy, which was just what he looked like, Margo thought, sitting there with his dark blue espadrilles pressed together and a lace-edged napkin spread across his bony knees.

''I won't let you talk me into it,'' he said firmly. ''And you know why.''

''Noel, you've got to get over this foolishness about Paul. It's like an elephant and a flea. You can reduce him to jelly with one look.''

''He hates me, Margo.''

''Probably with good reason. But what do you care? You made a fortune...''

''Far from it.''

''...as Melton's agent; you must have, unlike poor Paul, with that pittance he paid him. And then to be left a few measly pages...'' Margo set her cup on the table with such haste that it rattled, and Noel looked at her reproachfully. ''I can't figure out what the old fool was trying to do!'' She tossed up her hands, setting up a musical jingle in the dozen or so gold bangles she wore on her wrists.

''That's a nice way to refer to the leading novelist of our day.'' Noel and Margo smiled at each other in perfect understanding. He held out his cup for more coffee, and she reached for the silver pot, pushing her flowered silk caftan up on her arm.

"What do you really think, Noel?" she asked as she poured. "Was he just torturing us, or are those damn chapters worth something if they're put together?"

"Margo, you're a big girl, and you know as well as I do that any unpublished work of Melton's is practically priceless. Any complete work, that is. Every author has fragments of this and that kicking around, beginnings that didn't work out, scenes that were dropped." He sighed, but his voice was heavy with complacency as he continued, "That's going to be one of my tasks, I'm sure, compiling an anthology of Charles Melton's false starts—comparing them with the finished product. The publishers have already approached me."

"That's very nice. But first, how about helping me get my hands on the rest of this manuscript he spread around in such a maddening way? Obviously, you don't need it."

"I beg your pardon! Are you suggesting that I should sacrifice part of my inheritance to enrich you?" Noel threw his head back and laughed more spontaneously than Margo could ever remember him doing. "Look around you, for heaven's sake! Your villa, your paintings, your...you, yourself, Margo, the personification of elegance... My God, why would you think I'd deprive myself to get you more?"

"Because you owe me, Noel Wright, and you bloody well know it." There was steel in her voice, and Noel stiffened.

"I suppose you're referring to that cocktail party a thousand years ago, when Charles and I met. My dear, we would have met sooner or later; we were in the same world. I hardly think..."

"That is not what I meant, Noel. Who set you up in Cap Ferrat, where you could keep your volatile genius under control? Who supplied the entertainment he needed when he got restless? You know he was just as fascinated with celebrities as any salesman from Peoria. That kind of simplicity was part of his genius, which I doubt you ever realized."

Margo had risen and come over to his chair, where she stood looking down on him so sternly that he felt his heart give a little flutter of alarm. He got to his feet, rather awkwardly since she was standing so close, and reached out to place a placating hand on her arm.

"Look, my darling," he began, but she shrugged off his hand and stepped away from him. He had never seen her in this imperious mood; he couldn't think how to cope.

"Here's the way I see it, Noel. You have arrived at an enviable state of financial security partly through your own cleverness, of course, but also because of what I did to keep Charles Melton happily isolated here for all those years. You found the treasure, you might say, but I was the one who kept it under lock and key for you."

"But Margo, you enjoyed it. You loved being the only one who could guarantee an audience with his holiness. Everything you did for Charles or, as you see it, for me, paid off in prestige for you."

"I can't eat prestige. I can't pay the electric bill with social position. Why can't you get it through your head that I need money just like everybody else?"

She turned away and the hem of her light silk caftan swirled up as she strode back to the coffeepot. She refilled her cup, not because she really wanted any more, but as stage business to help her gain control. She was coming too close to panic, and if Noel caught a whiff of it she'd be finished. He needed her to be tough, which he perceived as being strong, invincible. When he was with her he felt stronger himself, and if he stopped getting that feeling from her he would look for it elsewhere. She wasn't ready for that; she needed to be indispensable to Noel Wright for a little while longer.

Holding the coffeepot high in one hand, she turned around and reached for Noel's cup. "Damn it," she said huskily, "I think my problem is that I really miss Charles. It isn't the money I want, it's the old bastard himself, sitting there in that terrible dressing gown, springing all the insults he made up during the day." She grinned, the sad grin of a street-wise urchin. "Nobody will ever insult me the way Charles Melton did; nobody else has the talent."

"He adored you, Margo." Noel felt so relieved he adored her himself at that moment. He took a grateful sip of his coffee, then said carefully, "I *don't* want to insult you—unlike Charles." He flashed her a look of mischief. "But have you thought of selling something? If you're serious about money, that is? Your Vuillard must have quadrupled by now."

"Certainly I've thought of it, and I get offers all the time, but I'm not quite ready. The market isn't ripe yet for my kind of stuff. I've bought according to a plan, you see, Noel. All this is capital investment." She circled one hand in the air, and Noel nodded. "It's also part of my persona, if you know what I mean, and I can't cash it in until I'm through using it. Till I'm ready to shut the doors and turn into a little old lady. And relax." Again she wore the broad, knowing grin. "It's beginning to sound tempting."

Noel laughed. "Never!" he cried. "Your fans won't let you!" He paused, wearing a teasing smile while he studied her face. He went on, "Seriously, love, you'll always let me come through those doors, won't you?"

"Seriously, that will depend on what we work out, Noel."

"You can't mean you actually expect me to give you my bit of Charles's manuscript? Not that it will ever have any value. Don't you see that, Margo? If these fragments he left us aren't put together they're worthless, and you know how the others will hang on to theirs."

"Yes, every one of them is like a squirrel clutching an acorn in his greedy paws." She smiled. "Obviously, the only way to get the nut away is to give him something better. Such as money, which you should be well able to supply..."

"Oh now, Margo, you mustn't think..." With the corners of his mouth turned down, Noel was shaking his head.

"Or information, which I have always made it a point to store up in case of possible need." She gazed dreamily toward the tall poplar hedge that bordered the garden. "Together we might accomplish something, Noel," she said very softly.

For a moment there was silence in the garden. Margo continued staring into the distance, idly pleating the folds of her caftan with one hand, while Noel concentrated his attention on the flower painted in the bottom of his empty coffee cup.

Finally he said, "Charles's will specifically states that one of us must get hold of the whole manuscript. There's to be no sharing, so why should I help you? Why not go after the whole prize myself?"

Margo replied calmly, "Because you can't do it by yourself."

"Oh?"

"Right. Even if you got the rest of it somehow, Paul Clifford hates you too much to give you his part. Even for money. He told me he'd rather die a pauper." She sat back and folded her arms. "But he'll give it to me, or sell it, rather, to keep me quiet. So will the others if I can sweeten the pot with your money."

"So I'm to be a silent partner, am I? Well, not before you sign an ironclad agreement, my dear, though I don't quite see how we can get away with that legally."

"I know a Swiss lawyer who will be glad to help us out." Margo's tone was sweetly reasonable as she added, "After all, my interests need protection too."

"You have thought this through, I see. Tell me, who do you have in mind for our first victim?"

Margo gave no sign of being pleased or surprised by his apparent capitulation as she replied, "My idea is to start with Jeanette. She's the toughest and she's also a total opportunist. She'll go in with me, hoping to steal the whole thing for herself in the end."

"But you won't let that happen?"

"No, I won't."

For the second time that morning Noel was startled into explosive laughter. Margo watched calmly while he pulled a handkerchief from his pocket and dried his eyes.

"I've never known anyone so shameless," he said, "but how dull life would be without you!" He glanced at his watch and got to his feet. "Something tells me you can bring it off, so I guess I'd better cooperate."

Margo smiled up at him for a moment, then stood, shaking out the folds of her caftan. "We'd better get together tomorrow and work out the details. Jeanette is coming over next week."

"At your suggestion, no doubt?"

"Not exactly. I merely told her Sonny Devere would be visiting the Marchands."

"Formidable!" Noel kissed her cheek, then stepped back, and she saw that the laughter had gone from his face. He stood very still, his pale blue eyes boring into hers as he said, "I will not find it amusing if you try to manipulate me, Margo. Please don't forget that."

He turned away then, and strode across the lawn to the gate.

BEN AND CARRIE PORTER drove to Le Petit Jardin with Millicent in her little blue Fiat. Since it had never been Margo Honeywell's style to squeeze herself into a small, crowded car if she had access to a large, luxurious one, she and Paul were being driven to lunch by the Marchands' handsome gardener in their Citroën. "I exercise it for them when they're in Paris," Margo had told Paul on the phone, "and incidentally give Jacques a breather from his sex life. The maids don't give him much time off, poor guy."

Listening to her throaty cackle, Paul had shuddered at her coarseness and instantly accepted the invitation. As always, she was late picking him up, however, giving the others a good twenty-minute wait.

The restaurant was situated on the outskirts of an ancient village in the hills above Cap Ferrat. It had been a farm for several hundred years before being turned into a restaurant, and the parking lot into which Ben pulled the Fiat was the former barnyard. While some of the old stone walls had been left to crumble in a picturesque way, the farmhouse itself had been rebuilt into three small dining rooms that opened onto a vine-shaded terrace where in good weather luncheon could be served. Millicent and the

Porters were led to a table overlooking the charming garden, and menus were brought for them to study while they waited for the others.

"*Terrine de lapereau à la Sariette*. How it rolls off the tongue!" Ben looked up from the large, tasseled folder with an expression of total contentment.

"I agree that's ever so much more euphonious than 'rabbit paste,'" said Carrie. "On the other hand, I'd much rather ask for puff pastry than '*feuilletée*.'"

"And you'd have a better chance of being understood." Ben's eyes twinkled as he shifted his attention from the menu to his wife, then back again. "Tell me, Millie, what are *queues d'ecrevisses*?"

"Crawfish tails, which I strongly recommend. They do them in an amazing sauce; the ingredients are one of their best-kept secrets."

"And *terrine de grives*? Oh, never mind; I think this must be our friends sweeping in."

Ben pushed back his chair and got to his feet, taking his time, since Margo Honeywell was engaged in a voluble discussion with the owner, who had conducted her in from her car. Paul Clifford trailed along, wearing his usual shy, pleased smile.

Margo, on the other hand, was chuckling lustily as she approached the table, apparently having told the proprietor a scandalous story, for he was blushing and rolling up his eyes as he laughed along with her.

"There you are, darling," she said as Millicent stood up to kiss her, "what a perfect day to be here!"

Millicent introduced them. "This is Ben Porter, Margo, and Carrie Porter. Come and sit next to me, Paul."

Margo was wearing a white linen jacket over a lemon-yellow silk dress with a pleated skirt. At her throat an ancient, greenish Roman coin hung on a thick gold chain; her gold earrings were Byzantine and carved in the shape of rams' heads.

When she and Paul were settled and had ordered drinks, Margo looked from Ben to Carrie and nodded approvingly. "How nice to see some attractive new faces," she said, "don't you agree, Paul? By now we are all sick to death of each other, but it's too beautiful to leave."

"Unlike many beautiful places, the Riviera is never dull, at least not to me." Paul sat very straight in his chair as he added bravely, "Margo may be tired of everyone, but I'll never cease to be entertained by the people one finds here."

"Well, you move in exalted circles, as we all know." Margo grinned broadly around the table, having turned her own notoriety into a joke they could share together. "And you, Ben and Carrie Porter, surely with such plain names you are celebrities in disguise. Tell me the truth."

"'In disguise.' I believe I'll start looking at myself that way," said Ben. "It sounds so much better than 'unknown.'"

"Ben is a painter," Millicent said distinctly, "and you really are promising, Ben, or so Hank tells me."

"Ah, Hank—another plain name that stirs excitement. In certain quarters, at least." Margo's grin focused on Millicent, then moved on to Paul.

"Did you meet Millie's handsome new friend, Paul? And did Noel? I can't remember what he told me."

"Of course, Margo, you were there some of the time he was in and out. It was such unfortunate timing; we were all so distracted by our loss." Paul's small features had puckered unhappily, and Millicent patted his hand.

"Charles Melton's death was a loss for the whole world," said Ben, and Paul nodded in silent agreement.

Carrie said, "Will you help me with the menu, Mr. Clifford? My French is so hopeless."

Indeed the waiter had arrived to take their orders, and everyone spent the next moments weighing the enticing options as anxiously as if there were a chance they might miss out on the one dish worth having. When at last he had gone they looked around at each other with relief, and all began talking at once.

Paul turned to Margo and said, "Did you have some special reason for asking whether Noel knows Millie's friend?" Before she could reply he hurried on, "Because I thought you noticed, as I certainly did, what a perfect fool he made of himself."

"Oh, Paul darling, I didn't mean anything by my silly question. You know how I babble on."

"I know how Noel Wright babbles on; that's exactly what he did every time he came near that nice young man. I couldn't stay in the room. I mean it, I was forced to leave." He peered at Margo indignantly until his lips began to tremble, and he whispered, "And at such a time, Margo. I'll never forgive him."

"Come on, Paul. Noel is human, and we all needed distraction just then. I'm sure that's why Millie brought the man around—to give us all a lift."

Paul sat back, aware that Margo was smiling at Millie, who was now listening to them attentively.

"You are so wise, Millie," he said, turning to grasp her hand. "You always understand people's needs better than they do themselves."

"I can't believe that, Paul, but thank you for saying it. Now here's your lovely soup; doesn't it smell delicious!"

They all watched eagerly as the first courses were brought and soon were lost in enjoyment of the beautifully cooked food. Ben tasted Carrie's *mousse de truite* and she his *foie gras,* each declaring his own choice the better, and the pleasant competition continued until Carrie's dessert, a *soufflé glacé au Grand Marnier,* briefly rendered them speechless.

Margo said, sprinkling sugar on her *fraises des bois,* "I think this was Melton's favorite place, don't you, Millie? I always think of him sitting at the table over there under the plane tree . . ."

"Excuse me, Margo, but Charles's favorite table was that corner one where he could watch the people. I don't see how you could forget, but then I was here with him more than anyone else." Paul sounded simultaneously reproachful and proud. "I had misgivings about coming today, to tell you the truth, but it is wonderful remembering him here."

"Paul, your loyalty astounds me. When I think of how it was rewarded...well, I'd best say no more." Shaking her head in wonderment, Margo took a spoonful of tiny strawberries.

Millie spoke up instantly. "Paul never thought of reward, did you, dear? Not at all. Paul is the most unselfish person I know."

"That's fortunate." Margo lifted a delicate chocolate leaf to her lips, ignoring Paul's expression of shock.

"Margo, you are being deliberately cruel!"

"Never mind, Millie. I know Margo's values are very different from mine. We've always managed to be friends in spite of that." Paul spoke with exaggerated dignity, but his face was pale, and he had taken only one bite of his chocolate mousse before pushing the plate away.

"Darling, that's exactly the point." Margo put down her spoon and bent toward him earnestly. "If we weren't so close I wouldn't be so angry about the way that man used you—yes he did, Paul, you've got to face it—and then left you nothing but a few pages of his so-called deathless prose, as if you were no more important to him than the rest of us. Three chapters of an unfinished novel..." Margo was shaking her head sadly, "...in return for years of devotion."

"Three chapters—well, hardly!" Paul was sitting up very straight; his watery eyes had taken on a defiant glitter. "You seem to have forgotten, Margo, that I was not only Charles's secretary but his closest friend and confidant. I should have thought it obvious that he would leave the bulk of his manuscript to me."

"But, my love, you certainly gave me the impression..."

"Am I not entitled to some privacy, Margo, in personal matters? Am I not allowed to keep just a few secrets—even from you?" He made himself taller in his chair as he added, "Eventually you will find out how mistaken you are. Meanwhile, I suggest we talk about something else."

Giving Margo a lordly nod of dismissal, Paul turned to Carrie and began asking about her children.

SIX

AFTER LUNCH Millie had found a cable waiting to tell her that Hank Stovall would arrive in Nice the following afternoon. Since she had made a luncheon engagement and felt it would be a tactical error, at this point, to break it for his convenience, she gratefully accepted Ben and Carrie's offer to meet him at the airport.

"We'll take him to Le Chat Noir for dinner," Millie proposed.

But Lila Baines had other ideas. "The Porters haven't had a chance to taste Marie's cooking," she said, "and she told me this morning she's in the mood for bouillabaisse."

Lila had been washing Melton's black Mercedes in the driveway when they came home. A stream of soapy water coursed through the cobblestone gutter while Lila, wearing Wellington boots and blue jeans, rinsed the car with the garden hose. The poodle, Finesse, watched from the lawn, keeping his legs tensed to bound away when Lila turned the spray on him, as she did at unpredictable intervals.

The Porters were happy to accept the dinner invitation. Lila's hospitality did not extend to offering the Mercedes for the airport trip, however. When the last drop of water had been sponged away, she carefully pulled the sparkling car into the garage, climbed out, and pocketed the keys.

"She won't let anyone touch the car," Millie said, when Lila had disappeared into the house. "And the funny thing is that Melton hated it, called it a prime example of bourgeois pomposity. He made it clear that he'd bought it only because it was the one issue on which Paul and Noel saw eye to eye—that a man in his position had to have a black Mercedes. Left to himself he'd have gone around in one of those little tin Renaults."

Ben said, "I'm beginning to like Charles Melton."

"Yes, you would have liked him, and he would have enjoyed you. Of course he would have adored Carrie." Millicent smiled, remembering. "When he met a woman who combined beauty, intelligence, and style, Melton came pretty close to worship."

"Then it's a good thing they never met," said Ben. "I've never thought worship would be good for Carrie."

"Although you, of course, would thrive on it." Carrie climbed into the rental car in which the Porters had driven over that morning. "Thank you for that wonderful lunch, Millie. We'll bring Hank around four o'clock, I should think, if the flight's on time."

From Carrie Porter's journal, dated May 10, 1989:

I've always thought of journal keeping as an activity for lonely ladies—usually British—with literary pretensions, but life around here is getting so fascinating and complex that I have to record what goes on—especially since Ben seems to be seriously caught up in this mystery of Charles Melton's manuscript. I'm afraid he has illusions of being a detective, probably because of the way he really did help figure out Greg Dillon's murder last year. He's been making a lot of notes, and a couple of times at lunch he looked very wise and knowing after somebody made a remark that seemed significant—to him. I might as well play along, especially since it is an intriguing puzzle, and the people involved are such characters.

Margo Honeywell, for one, is exactly the strong, colorful personality I would have expected her to be, and obviously very smart. I had the feeling there was purpose behind her every remark—especially when she began torturing poor little Paul Clifford about how shabbily Melton had treated him.

Millie's reaction to that was a little bit puzzling. She was very gentle and soothing with Paul, but in a way that allowed Margo to go right on turning the knife. It was almost as if they had set it up between them, in order to goad Paul into revealing exactly how much of the manuscript he'd been awarded. I have to wonder whether he really received more than everybody else's three chapters, or whether he was merely boasting.

I can't believe Millie is a schemer; don't want to, I guess, because she's so charming and attractive and would be so perfect for Hank. I can easily believe it of Margo, however, and, little as I've seen of him, of Noel Wright as well. Paul Clifford? Can't tell yet.

Yesterday afternoon Ben and I picked up Hank at the Nice airport, and I was glad to see that he'd gained a little of the weight he lost over the past two years when Eunice was putting him through such hell. He looked very boyish and attractive, I thought—trying to see him through Millie's eyes and deciding yes, that healthy, blue-eyed look had great appeal. He couldn't hide his disappointment that Millie wasn't with us, especially since he had only twenty-four hours to spend en route to a business meeting in Lyons. Still, since it was only three o'clock and we didn't think Millie would be home yet, we stopped in Villefranche to see the little fishermen's chapel that Cocteau decorated with wonderful fish designs that are playful and spiritual at the same time. I could have spent an hour there at least, but Hank was too itchy, so we left after only a quick look and dropped his bag at a tiny little hotel in the village—where, by the way, you can get a double room for 240 francs—then took him to La Rêverie. And there we found a major *crise* had taken place.

Millie was pacing around in the driveway when we pulled in, and instead of giving Hank the welcome he might have anticipated, she accosted us quite fiercely, demanding to know what in the world we'd been doing since the flight got in. She was really distraught, we saw that right away. She was pale, her hair was flying around, and her eyes, which are impressively large and dark anyway, looked black in her white face and were rimmed with pink, so she'd obviously been crying.

Hank put his arms around her, of course, and we all started moving toward the house, but she resisted; she didn't want to go in just yet, she said; first she had to tell us

what had happened. She almost seemed afraid to go into
the house, so we went with her around to the back, where
a path leads to a little grove of olive trees with a couple of
wooden benches in the middle of it, and there Millie told us
that someone had come into her room and stolen her por-
tion of Charles Melton's manuscript.

"Everyone thought I was going out for lunch, remember?" she said. "But Nadia got sick and called it off at the
last minute, which gave me a chance to wash my hair. My
bathroom was an afterthought, made out of what was
originally a maid's room on the other side of my closet. So
a person in the bedroom wouldn't necessarily hear the
shower going, or the hair dryer. Strangely enough, though,
whoever it was came in just as I started to open the door,
so *I* heard him—or her."

Millie started trembling so hard that Hank held her tight,
glaring around as if he'd like to kill whoever had upset her
so much. I encouraged her to keep talking—I always think
it helps to get things out—and, naturally, Ben was beside
himself with curiosity, so she went on to tell us that she had
instinctively frozen when she heard the sounds in her room,
then had very carefully and silently closed the bathroom
door again. She had tried to lock it and then come close to
panic when she recalled that the lock was broken and she'd
forgotten to ask Lila to fix it.

Ben asked exactly what sounds she heard, whether she
could tell what the intruder was doing, and she said she
could easily. "He wasn't being particularly quiet," she said,
"because he thought I'd gone out. Maybe he knew that all
the others were out as well. It was Lila's usual time for
marketing, and Marie was to go with her today to pick out
fish for the bouillabaisse. Anyway, I distinctly heard
drawers being opened and closed, first the ones in my
dresser—it's an antique and they squeak—then the ones in
my desk, which is just outside the closet."

I said, "Where had you hidden the manuscript?" and
Millie said she hadn't actually tried to conceal it.

"It never occurred to me. After all, we all knew who had
been given sections of it and who hadn't. I guess I thought

it was so unlikely that we'd ever get the whole thing together, I'd begun to think of my pages as nothing more than a keepsake. So I simply put them in a drawer of my desk, which I've never thought of locking.''

She looked miserable when she said that, and went on to apologize for being so stupid, etc., which both Hank and Ben hastened to assure her she wasn't. I kept quiet, rather thinking she was, if not stupid, certainly unimaginative. I pictured myself in her place slipping the envelope of pages beneath the carpet or taping it to the underside of the bed. Millie had been very trusting, but I reminded myself that all the people likely to steal the manuscript were her close friends, or anyway longtime associates, and she wasn't in the habit of hiding things from them.

Ben asked if she had noticed any change at all in her room when she finally gathered the courage to emerge from the bathroom; any scent, for instance, of cologne or tobacco, or any footprints on the carpet. Millie said the latter wouldn't show because her rug is one of those colorful Portuguese ones without any nap, and no, she didn't notice any aroma, either. I thought it was significant, in view of her casual treatment of the manuscript, that she immediately thought of that as the object of the intrusion and looked in the drawer to find it gone. (Did I make this point to Ben? Check for sure.)

Millie seemed to feel much better after she had told us all this; in fact, she apparently wanted nothing more than to forget all about it and start enjoying Hank's visit. The sun was sinking, and the light that pierced through the trees gave all of our faces a flattering rosy glow. When we stepped out of the little pine grove we were hit by a wonderful aroma coming from the kitchen, where Marie was cooking the bouillabaisse, and Ben started sniffing like a bird dog. He couldn't bear being left out, so he said he'd see us shortly and loped across the lawn to the back door.

The evening ahead was beginning to look very interesting, possibly unbearably so, it occurred to me, with four of us on the alert for signals that might indicate which of the

other four—Paul, Noel, Margo, and Lila—had visited
Millie's room.

I was about to suggest that we go out for dinner after all
when Ben struck his head out of the kitchen door and insisted that I come in and see the wonders that were taking
place. I knew then that there was no chance of prying him
away from La Rêverie that night, so I left Hank and Millie
and went to join him.

MARIE'S BOUILLABAISSE was a triumph, and the complex-
ities of serving and eating it proved distracting enough to
keep dinner from being as "unbearably interesting" as
Carrie had feared. Lila presided at an enormous tureen
from which she served the herb-scented broth in which the
fish had been cooked. Marie stood by to pass the bowls, her
black eyes anxiously following every dip of the ladle while
she murmured advice to Lila. The soup was followed by
helpings of lobster and local varieties of snapper, mullet,
bass, hogfish, and haddock, all of which had contributed
their special flavors to the bouillon.

Toasted croutons of French bread were passed to eat with
the fish, accompanied by a dish of the pungent garlic sauce
known as *rouille* and a bowl of freshly chopped parsley.
Ben had chosen a delightful white Bordeaux with which he
constantly replenished everyone's glasses, and soon all the
faces around the table were flushed, noses were shining,
and the conversation had become noisily competitive.

Margo had been invited to welcome Hank and share in
the feast, and, watching her, Carrie saw none of the ma-
neuvering she thought she had noticed at lunch the day before. Instead, Margo gave herself over to a lusty enjoyment
of the food and wine and company, and made the table so
lively that it was easy to see why she was a sought-after
dinner guest.

She lifted her glass, at one point, in a toast to Charles
Melton—"I hope he can see the wonderful time we're having at his table tonight"—but as she immediately em-
barked on an amusing reminiscence of another

bouillabaisse party, in which Melton had shared, the festive mood was undampened.

Noel Wright, on Carrie's left, seemed as caught up in the evening as the others. Instead of exhibiting the cool, superior manner he had worn when they met, he exerted himself to charm her. She would miss none of the attractions of the Riviera if he had his way; he wanted her to love it enough to come back, he said, and he offered to fill in any gaps by taking her around himself.

"I suppose we'll have to include your husband," he added, with a puckish glance across the table, "or he'll never allow us to become friends."

They arranged to lunch the next day in the ancient walled city of St.-Paul-de-Vence at the restaurant Colombe d'Or, where the walls were hung with Picassos, Legers, Braques, and Utrillos. This was unlikely to interfere with any plans made by Millie and Hank, who were having some difficulty entering into the general merriment, since they so clearly longed to be off by themselves.

The bouillabaisse was followed by a simple green salad, then an assortment of cheeses. When Marie reappeared in the doorway, wearing a look of triumph on her round, pink face and carrying a perfectly glazed *tarte Tatin,* Ben sprang up to open the champagne he had brought to go with dessert.

They toasted the cook, then Lila, then Charles Melton once more; they paused while Ben opened more champagne, then went on with it until Lila pushed back her chair and announced that it was time to give Marie a break, so coffee would be served on the terrace.

She produced a bottle of venerable cognac to go with the coffee, then while Noel poured it, slipped into the drawing room, put an Astor Piazzola tango on the stereo, and began rolling up the rug.

The resulting scene more nearly resembled New Year's Eve at an Elks Club than a gathering of literati in the south of France. Noel and Margo set the pace, lampooning with half-closed eyes and swooping strides the passionate intensity of a Spanish dance team. Ben pulled Millie from

Hank's side and followed their example, and Carrie, inspired by the combination of cognac and the throbbing Latin beat, seized Paul Clifford by his narrow shoulders and, with her eyes locked on his, began propelling him around the room.

"That was possibly the sexiest experience of the guy's entire life," Ben commented the next day, and indeed Paul's eyes shone with reckless pleasure as he stood on tiptoe to spin Carrie in circles.

More records were played—Charles Melton had been a collector of Latin-American music—and more cognac poured. The pairings shifted, the dancers' inventiveness increasing with each new partner, and they were all too lost in their own enjoyment to notice who left the room, or for how long, or who stayed and with whom. And of course they never dreamed it would matter.

SEVEN

THE MORNING following the bouillabaisse party Carrie slept until ten, forcing her eyes open only when she became aware that Ben was standing beside the bed staring down at her.

"Go away," she muttered, and rolled to the far side, pulling the sheet over her face.

"Just checking your vital signs," he replied. "You haven't moved since I got up; I was getting worried."

"I need to sleep some more," she breathed through the sheet.

"You need a swim, that's what you need." From the foot of the bed Ben tugged the bedclothes away and Carrie moaned. "A swim, then maybe a run on the beach and a sauna..."

"Ben, you are at your most revolting in the morning. Have I ever told you that?" She opened her eyes and sat up, then immediately fell back on her pillow, not yet able to face the sun that poured through the tall French doors opening onto the balcony.

"Is this the *première danseuse* of Cap Ferrat—the seductress even confirmed homosexuals can't resist? I was impressed, Carrie. I've never seen anything like it."

"Would you please stop talking and pour me a cup of coffee?"

Carrie got out of bed and headed for the bathroom, and Ben stepped out onto the tiny balcony where he had already eaten his breakfast. Their room was at the back of the hotel and overlooked the flower-bordered sweep of lawn that sloped to a small stone building from which one rode a funicular down to the terraced pool or onto the beach several hundred yards farther below. He could see the Mediterranean just beyond, a brilliant slice of travel-poster

blue against the rocky thumb of land that led to Pointe de
St. Hospice. Pouring coffee and hot milk into a cup, he
smiled at the improbability of being there amidst all that
beauty.

As he turned into the bedroom with Carrie's coffee, the
telephone rang and he strode to the bedside to pick it up.
When she came into the room a minute later he was still
listening, gazing at her somberly as he held out the cup to
her. Her knees began to buckle, and she turned so white
that Ben immediately interrupted his caller.

"It isn't the children," he said; then, as she shakily sat
down on the bed, "It's Paul Clifford. He's been shot."

"Oh no. That nice man . . ."

"He's dead, Carrie. He's been murdered."

LA RÊVERIE WAS HUSHED. All morning people had been in
and out of the rooms, entering the drawing room, for instance, or the study, often forgetting why they had come
there and stopping to think, then hurrying purposefully
away. They moved quietly, however, and spoke to each
other softly, almost timidly. It was as if the docile spirit of
the dead man ruled the household now as it never had in
life.

The police and ambulance attendants had caught the
mood and kept their voices low as they photographed Paul
Clifford's body lying on the floor of his bedroom, then
gently placed it on a stretcher and took it away.

Police Inspector Robert Foch spent the next two hours
asking questions of Noel, Lila, Marie, and Millie as Paul's
fellow occupants of the house. The inspector was a small
man in his late thirties with a solemn, courteous manner
that made him seem older. His thin black hair was neatly
combed to cover the top of a round head that seemed too
large for his compact body.

As soon as the ambulance had driven away he invited
Noel to come with him to Charles Melton's upstairs study,
where Sergeant Jean Clement waited to take notes of the
interrogation.

The sergeant asked politely if he might open the draperies to make the room lighter, and Noel replied, "Yes, by all
means." As the curtains swung wide he stepped behind the
desk and seated himself in Melton's chair. "Make yourselves comfortable," he said to the two policemen, and after a moment's hesitation they pulled two chairs up to the
desk and sat down.

When he had elicited Noel's personal history, Inspector
Foch said, "My aim this morning is to discover your fresh
impressions of what may have happened to M. Clifford.
Did you hear any unusual sounds during the night?" In the
low chair the inspector had to sit up very straight to face
Noel across the desk.

Noel shook his head. "No. Ordinarily I am a light
sleeper, but last night we drank cognac after dinner—perhaps a bit more than we should have." A slight, shamefaced smile appeared on his thin face, and the inspector
nodded understandingly. "I heard nothing until I was
awakened this morning by Marie's cries. It was a terrible
shock, terrible. I'll never in my life forget the sounds she
made."

"I can imagine," said Inspector Foch. "What did you
do? Did you leap up and run out to see . . . ?"

"Oh, of course. I simply bolted out of bed and into the
hall. I thought the woman was being attacked. I even . . ."
Again Noel wore an embarrassed grin. "I even grabbed a
lamp on my way out: it's an ormolu figure, and quite lumpy
and heavy. I wrenched the cord out of the wall and knocked
the shade off. Thank God I didn't hit anyone with it in my
confusion. We would have had two deaths in the house."

Sergeant Clement was a tall, muscular young man, and
at Noel's words he looked up and ran his eyes over him
skeptically, as if he doubted that such a man could kill
anyone, however hard he struck.

Noel felt his face grow warm. How he detested these
brawny types who measured every man by physical standards. The fellow belonged in a locker room; he could
never comprehend the subtleties that governed the life of La
Rêverie.

Inspector Foch received short answers to the rest of his questions. Noel had known Paul Clifford for almost twenty years; they were not close friends but maintained a comfortable working relationship; he could imagine no reason anyone would want to kill such a gentle man. Certainly no one among his acquaintances; surely Paul must have surprised a thief?

That possibility would be thoroughly examined, the inspector replied. His men would be as unobtrusive as possible, but he hoped Noel understood that they would have to be in and around the house for several days.

"You'd better explain that to our housekeeper, Lila Baines," said Noel as he rose from his seat behind the desk, "or she may give you some trouble."

"Thank you for warning me. I'll be talking to her next," said the inspector as they shook hands.

With a curt nod to Sergeant Clement, Noel took his leave. In the hall he found Lila waiting her turn, looking so apprehensive that he took pity on her and murmured, "It's not bad at all" as he passed her. Still, he felt edgy and resentful as he started downstairs.

He was relieved to see that Margo Honeywell had arrived while he was closeted with the police. She hurried to meet him at the foot of the stairs.

"I just can't believe it, Noel, can you?" He shook his head sadly and she went on, her voice trembling. "Who would shoot that defenseless little man? Some horrible pervert, do you suppose?" She shuddered. "Have they figured out how he got in? I mean, you were all here; didn't anyone hear anything?"

Noel put his arm around her shoulders and led her into the dining room, where coffee and biscuits had been put out on the sideboard. He offered her a chair, but she shook her head. "I can't sit still; I couldn't even put my face on. Look, I got halfway through and had to stop, my hands were shaking so."

She looked pleadingly into his face, and he noted that in spite of her shock she had managed to apply the eyeliner that dramatized the contrast between her amber eyes and silver-streaked black hair. She must have been quite a beauty once, he thought, then realized she had asked him a question.

"Was it robbery?" she was saying. "Is anything missing? Maybe no one has thought of looking." She glanced around, energized, as if she were quite prepared to take inventory of the house.

He poured her a cup of coffee and said, "We haven't noticed anything missing, but of course we're all so distracted..." He gave himself only half a cup so he wouldn't get jittery. "And so far the police haven't found any sign of forced entry; though to tell the truth, we left things pretty wide open last night."

"I should think so. I'm not quite sure how I got home."

"*I* drove you home, Margo, and what's more I helped you into the house *and* up the stairs to your room."

"I don't believe it. I've never in my life drunk so much that I had to be helped, as you put it."

"The miracle is that I got out of there unscathed. You practically wrestled me to the ground to get me to stay." Pouting demurely, he added, "You had designs on me, you naughty girl."

"For Christ's sake, Noel, are you out of your mind?" She glared at him, outraged, until she saw that his eyes were twinkling with mischief, whereupon she began to laugh helplessly.

"You're right, I must have had a snootful or it wouldn't seem so hilarious. Oh God, I can just see you hauling the old lady up the stairs..."

"And then fending off your advances."

"My advances indeed! How about you? Were you drunk enough... for once... the first time ever...? Oh God, it's too wonderful!"

They were leaning on each other, shaking with laughter, when Millie walked into the room and stopped short, staring in amazement.

Margo instantly left Noel and embraced Millie, pressing her cheek against hers. In a second her laughter had switched to sobs. "It's just so awful, Millie, isn't it? I can't believe it about darling Paul."

Noel had pulled out a handkerchief to blow his nose. "Margo and I are distraught, as you can see. All that cognac, and then a shock like this. Well, it's undone us, Millie."

"I'm just as shaken up as you are. I can't seem to take it in. It's the strangest feeling."

"Darling, what do the police think happened? Paul was shot, is that right?"

Millie nodded. "With a very small pistol, apparently, and only once. There was no sign of a struggle. He was in his pajamas..." Her voice faltered and she stopped to take a deep breath. "He always wore the most beautiful silk pajamas, didn't he, Noel? From Charvet, I suppose."

"Always." Noel was nodding approvingly. "For a man of moderate means, Paul had exquisite taste."

"He was absolutely meticulous. The last person on earth one could imagine meeting a violent death." Margo sighed. "Let's go outside, shall we? I feel oppressed in here."

As they started for the hallway Marie poked her head into the dining room to ask if they would like more coffee, and at the sight of her red-rimmed eyes Margo hurried to hug her.

"You're the one who's keeping us all going," she said, "and I know how terrible you must feel. He was devoted to you."

"Les gendarmes," Marie said. *"J'ai peur..."*

Margo turned to Noel in alarm, and he said, "They're questioning everyone in the house, of course." He said to the cook, "You must not be afraid, Marie. No one suspects you of harming M. Clifford. Oh, God, there she goes again!"

Marie had begun to sob, and seeing the exasperation on Noel's face, she spun around and darted back into the kitchen.

"Let her go," he said to Margo. "She's been carrying on like this all morning. I hope they question her soon and get it over with."

"She's next, as it happens." Lila Baines had appeared in the doorway. "I'll just go and tell her." She started for the kitchen, and Millie, Noel, and Margo walked slowly out of the room and down the short tiled corridor to the terrace, where, five minutes later, Ben and Carrie found them.

The poodle, Finesse, had met the Porters' car in the driveway, prancing expectantly on his long, stiff legs. He sniffed hopefully at Ben as he climbed out, then all the spring left his body and he sat down on the gravel to wait for the next arrival.

"Poor fella," Ben murmured, "you've had a hard time recently."

Carrie knelt down to hug the dog. She tousled his curly topknot while he gazed into her eyes with dignity and solemnly thumped his tail.

"He was Paul's dog after Melton died," she said as they started for the house. "I wonder if he'll adopt Noel now."

"Where was Finesse when the murder took place?" said Ben. "I hadn't thought about that."

He paused to scribble in the notebook he had brought, then followed Carrie through the door and out to where they heard the voices of the others on the terrace.

Millie and Noel were seated with a pad and pencil at a rectangular slate-topped table where lunch was often served. Margo had stretched herself out on a wrought-iron chaise nearby. She was wearing pants of jade-green silk with a flower-printed silk shirt wrapped at the waist with a long matching scarf. From her prone position the trailing ends of the scarf fell to the flagstone in a colorful heap of silk.

"We're making lists," she told the Porters after they had exchanged greetings and commiserations. "It seems to help."

Noel picked up his pencil. "People to notify, when to have the service, what to do about Paul's things. As I was saying, Millie, we must get in touch with his lawyer at once."

"We have no idea who might inherit from Paul," Millie explained to Ben and Carrie. "He had no immediate relatives. He may not have made a will."

"My money is on Jeanette," said Noel, tapping his eraser on the pad decisively. "And since she'll be arriving tonight..."

"Oh? I thought Jeanette lived in New York," said Ben.

"She does," Noel replied. "But she and Paul were very close, so Millie called her first thing this morning."

"She was coming over next week on business anyway." Margo's voice was faint. She had closed her eyes and she kept them closed as she added, "Is it almost time for a Bloody Mary?"

Ben said, "Is there anything on your list about who might have murdered Paul, or why? Are the police trying to find out?"

"They're working on it," Millie said, "but I'm afraid we weren't much help to them. Hank and I stayed up pretty late, and we didn't hear a thing."

"And the rest of us were too saturated with wine and cognac." Noel was shaking his head. "*Such* a rowdy evening. I don't know what came over us."

Ben got to his feet and paced to the end of the terrace and back. Ignoring a warning glance from Carrie, he said, "Has anyone had a look around Paul's room?" They all gazed at him blankly, and he went on, "I don't mean to intrude, of course, but the killer may have been after something. Paul's section of Charles Melton's novel, for example."

"One would hardly kill for that," said Noel, "considering how little use it would be without the pages belonging to the rest of us."

"You're probably right, but I think it might be a good idea to look for it, just the same. Unless, of course, you feel hesitant..."

"Not at all." Margo was attempting to push herself out of the chaise while gathering up the ends of her long scarf. "It is absolutely necessary...damn it, Noel, give me a hand. The police wouldn't have known what to look for, would they?"

"I wonder if Ben is thinking what I suddenly am." An icy light gleamed in Noel's pale eyes as he stepped over to help Margo haul herself up.

Millie was appalled. "I have to object," she said. "I can't stand the idea of pawing through Paul's belongings. We have no right to do that."

Carrie said, "I know exactly what you mean, Millie, but when you remember what happened to your pages, don't you think it would be in Paul's best interests to find his, if they're findable, and lock them up somewhere?"

"Let's see what Lila thinks." Millie turned toward the entrance to the house, but Margo stopped her.

"Think a minute, darling," she said. "Fond as we all are of Lila, she really has no stake in this, has she? Charles didn't leave any of his manuscript to her, so she can't possibly understand what it could mean to the rest of us."

"Especially to you, Millie." Noel took her hand and tucked it beneath his arm. "Paul was fondest of you, we all know that. If he could he'd probably give you his pages himself to make up for yours being stolen."

Still murmuring to her in his most coaxing voice, Noel drew Millie into the house with him, and the others followed them inside and up the stairs to Paul Clifford's empty room.

On the threshold they paused. The long hallway was brightened by the morning sun that poured through from the bedrooms on the east side of the house. Paul's room, however, stood in shadow, and the dimness gave a spectral quality to his neatly made bed, now so flat and empty, and the abandoned embroidery frame beside his chair. A loop of beige yarn dangled from the needle he had left stuck in the fawn's coat.

Even Noel hesitated, tightening his grasp on Millie's hand, until Margo gave him a little push. Once they were inside, she flicked a wall switch to turn on the bedside lamps, then stood looking curiously around the room.

"Very attractive," she said. She might have been approving a hotel room. She walked over to the dresser, where a silver-framed photograph of Charles Melton stood beside Paul's tortoiseshell brushes and an assortment of bibelots.

With a squeal of delight Margo cried, "I gave him this," and pounced on an intricately carved ivory netsuke, which she dangled before them from its black silk cord. "This is so dreadfully naughty," she said, chuckling softly, "that I know Paul wouldn't want anyone but me to have it."

Smiling brightly at the group who still hovered near the door, Margo dropped the little figure into the handbag which she had conveniently brought along.

Noel was frowning. "I don't think we should touch another thing," he said, "until Jeanette arrives. That's assuming she is Paul's heir; if not..."

Margo might not have heard him. She was at the desk, saying, "Noel, come over here and help me get this drawer out. Millie, you can make a list of everything, so it will be nice and legal. And Ben, why don't you and Carrie start on the closet?"

"I wouldn't bother with the closet," Noel said as he seized one end of the desk drawer. Margo looked at him sharply, and he added, "I think we should concentrate our efforts on the desk; it's the logical place, after all."

"So wise to do this before the lawyers get involved," Margo muttered as she helped Noel upend the drawer.

"Careful!" Millie reached out to keep the contents from cascading to the floor, and all three began sifting through Paul's papers, replacing them in the drawer as they finished.

In Paul's lighted closet Ben and Carrie searched among the drawers and boxes, marveling at the quality of his shirts, ties, and other accessories and the care he had taken of them.

Sniffing at a scented flannel drawer lining, Ben said, "We have a lot to learn about closets, I can see that."

"And what to put in them." Carrie fingered one of Paul's silky-textured shirts appreciatively, then examined the label. "Turnbull & Asser. Remember that, Ben."

In less than an hour Paul's desk, closet, and dresser had been thoroughly turned out, and his bookshelves and bedside tables gone over with equal care. Ben had crawled under the bed for a look in the springs; he had even investigated the lining of the tailored dust ruffle while Millie, who was now caught up in the challenge, helped Noel take the pictures off the walls and look behind them.

Carrie and Margo moved into the bathroom and searched through stacks of carnation-printed towels and boxes of red and white soap in Paul's linen closet.

Margo then turned to the large bottle of bath salts that stood beside the tub. She lifted off the top and stirred the crystals with her finger. "He could put a roll of paper in here," she said. Noticing the name on the bottle, she held it up for Carrie to see.

"*L'Homme.* That's very revealing." Carrie smiled sadly. "Poor man. He must have wanted to be normal, Margo, don't you think so?"

"Paul was perfectly content with his lot—at least by the time I knew him." Margo replaced the bath salts and turned back the fleecy white rug to look beneath it. "It saves them a great deal of trouble, you know, and money too: no wife to support, no tuition to pay, no teeth to straighten. Leaves them free to indulge their own expensive tastes."

Carrie was smiling. "I never thought of it that way. Really, Margo, knowing you is very broadening."

She opened the white wicker laundry hamper that stood against the wall and found it empty. Saying, "Marie must have done his laundry already," she closed the padded top, which was covered with the same white piqué that trimmed the curtains, then bent to slip her fingers into an opening where the fabric had come loose.

"Margo," she said, "how about this for a hiding spot?"

It was obvious that the covering had once been tightly held in place by the same piqué-covered tacks that continued around the edge of the lid. At the back, however, several inches of fabric were loose—the one bit of disrepair they had found in Paul's exquisitely appointed rooms.

Instantly Margo's eyes narrowed to slits, and like a greedy cat she pounced at the opening in the cover and tried to pull it wider. The hamper tilted under her efforts, and as

Carrie seized it she saw a piece of paper lying on the floor beneath it.

"Hold it!" she cried, and swooped upon a typewritten sheet which she immediately recognized as a page of a manuscript. She snatched it up and began reading aloud:

Page 261.... blood was trickling into his eyes, but Robert de Laine was unaware of it, nor was he conscious of the slightest pain. Instead, his entire being was suffused with the familiar exhilaration that told him he was winning. In the grip of his fingers Abu Sahid's neck felt as scrawny as a chicken's. De Laine gave it a firm shake and laughed out loud at the sight of Sahid's round head bobbing helplessly from side to side.

"Shall I twist it off for you?" De Laine shouted into his ear. "I could, you know, and then send it to Ysabel in a velvet box. Would she like that, Sahid? Would she treasure that ugly head of yours?"

But Sahid was past replying, to that question or to any other. Robert de Laine slowly relaxed his grip, and the body of his enemy slid to the ground and lay crumpled there, nothing now but a pile of bones covered with the brilliant embroidered silks that were to have been Sahid's coronation costume and now would serve as his shroud.

The men who had followed Abu Sahid stood gazing at de Laine with a mixture of fear and horror, but he turned his back on them and swiftly mounted the steps to the golden dais. There the jeweled dagger flickered in the torchlight, appearing to flame like the avenger's sword it would shortly prove itself to be.

"Oh, Carrie, isn't there more? Come on, help me look."

Margo thrust the sheet of paper into Carrie's hands and seized the laundry hamper. Before Carrie could stop her she had ripped the white covering loose from the lid and with her shiny red fingernails flashing, was pulling the pad beneath it into shreds.

"One lousy page," she wailed, "when we know he must have had more than a hundred! What do you think happened, Carrie?"

But Carrie was giving her attention to Millie, who was standing in the doorway with Ben. Her face was a chalky white and her voice trembled as she said, "May I see that, please, Carrie?"

In silence Carrie handed Millie the page of manuscript and watched as she quickly scanned it. When she looked up her dark eyes were filled with tears.

She said, "I've seen this before. It's one of my pages. It was Paul who stole them from me!"

EIGHT

"BUT MILLIE, there's no reason for you to hang around here any more, can't you see that? Those people have already made you miserable enough with their crazy scheming..."

"I'm not miserable, and anyway *those people* happen to be my friends—my dear friends."

"Fine, fine. You have a right to pick your own friends..."

"Thanks very much!"

"...But Millie, you've gotten so involved with them you can't think straight. You can't seem to see that your great literary adventure is over. The thing for you to do now is go home and capitalize on it."

"Making money, that's all you think about. You can't possibly imagine what it meant to me to work with Charles Melton, to be his friend and share his life."

Millie scrambled awkwardly to her feet, brushing bread crumbs from her jeans. Hank reached for her plastic glass of wine to keep it from tumbling down the grassy slope where they had eaten their picnic lunch.

"So you think I'm an ignoramus, do you, like all businessmen? Well, tell me, Millie, have you read all of Dos Passos, all of Faulkner, Hemingway, Fitzgerald, Edith Wharton, and Thomas Hardy? Not to mention Milton, Shakespeare, and all the guys we had in school, and not to mention—"

"I never accused you..."

"Not to mention most of *A Dance to the Music of Time*!!" The triumph in Hank's voice could have been due to ending his recital or to the fact that he'd risen to his feet, no hands, without spilling a drop from their two glasses of wine.

Still holding the glasses in his hands, he wrapped his arms around her, and they swayed together on the hillside while he begged, "Please don't make me fight with you. Please let us enjoy our last few hours together. Please don't think I'm a jerk because I want you on my side of the ocean!"

"Oh, darling, you know I don't think you're a jerk. Life would be simpler if I did!" She kissed him, and then when she saw the expression that came to his eyes, carefully took the wineglasses and set them on the ground. "We'll want that later," she murmured as he drew her to the blanket they had spread beneath a rather scruffy evergreen oak.

Sometime later they did indeed finish the wine, not minding the way the sun had warmed it or that a few tiny insects had to be flicked out of it. They sat with their feet braced on the slope and stared across the tree-filled valley toward the opposite hillside with its terraced vineyards and tile-roofed farmhouses. In the distance beyond, the blue sea gleamed against the deepening, duller blue of the afternoon sky.

"I'll tell you what," Millie said slowly. "As soon as this manuscript business is settled I'll go to New York and look around."

Hank pulled a leaf from her hair and tossed it away. He said, "It's quite possible the manuscript will never be sorted out. What then?"

She sighed. "I don't know. But I can't stay on at La Rêverie indefinitely; I know you're right about that. It's just . . . I've felt so sheltered there, so safe . . ."

"Until yesterday, when you had the bejesus scared out of you."

"Yes, until yesterday. And then to discover that it was Paul . . . I don't suppose there can be any doubt about that, can there?" Millie's dark eyes beseeched him to contradict her, but Hank shook his head.

"I don't know how else that page of manuscript landed in his room." He stroked her cheek with his finger as he went on. "That's the kind of thing that makes me crazy to get you out of here. You thought Paul Clifford was your friend; and look what he did to you. What about the rest of that bunch? I know you don't want to believe it, but one of them must have murdered Paul.''

"I really can't believe that, Hank. Not only because I know them so well—or think I do.'' She smiled ruefully. "I learned something about character from Charles Melton, and they are simply not the type to kill. Noel and Margo—and I might as well include Lila and Marie and all of us—we're all much too civilized.''

"All right; assuming a thief broke in and shot him, why would he make off with a few pages of manuscript? Any of Paul's possessions would appear to be more valuable.''

"We're only assuming those pages are gone, aren't we? What if Paul had moved them to a new hiding place and happened to drop one? Come on, Hank, it's perfectly possible that they're still in his room somewhere.''

"Which brings us back to the undeniable fact that he stole that page from you, along with the rest of your inheritance.''

Millie slumped dejectedly, but Hank got to his feet and pulled her up, saying, "We have to get it together if I'm going to make my flight.''

The sun had fallen lower in the sky. A light breeze tossed shreds of mist up from the valley to float before their faces as they carried the remains of their picnic to the roadside where they had left Millie's car.

They climbed in, but instead of starting the car Hank turned in his seat and gazed solemnly at Millie. "I have to be careful how I put this so you won't see it as an attack on your friends, but I'm not going to rest until you're out of that house.''

"Damn it, Hank...''

"Wait, just give me a chance, Millie. It's not that I'm jealous of your closeness with a group of people I don't understand all that well, though that may be part of it. And it's not that I want to get you to New York so I can take charge of your life.''

She tried to speak, but he touched her lips with his finger.

"I'm scared, Millie, and that's the truth." His voice was low and slightly husky. "Something weird is going on here and you're in the middle of it. If anything happened to you I'd..." He stopped for a deep breath. "How about giving it one more week and then cutting out? What do you say?"

Millie had been sitting with her arms tightly folded, stiff and defensive. Now she relaxed and gently pulled Hank's face close to hers.

"I'll think about it, darling, that's the best I can do. You see, I think I know how to take care of myself. I only wish you could believe it."

With a gusty sigh Hank drew away and started the engine. He thrust the car into gear and the little blue Fiat began its descent down the curving mountain road.

From Carrie Porter's journal, dated May 12, 1989:

Yesterday the atmosphere at La Rêverie was so emotional, between the death of Paul Clifford and the discovery that he had stolen Millicent's manuscript, that Ben and I escaped right after lunch and awarded ourselves a couple of hours of pool time at the hotel. Not that Ben was able to relax: he was much too busy going over his notes and muttering about the sinister signals he's been picking up.

While I drowsed in the sun he tried out his ideas on me—even though I responded with no more than an occasional "uh-huh." His chief notion is that someone among Charles Melton's heirs is determined to possess the complete manuscript at any price. He pointed out that the book will probably never be published otherwise, so although the obvious motive is greed, in the mind of the perpetrator this could be disguised as artistic altruism.

His theory fits Paul Clifford, who was desperate enough to steal; but I find it hard to believe that Margo or Noel or Millie could have murdered him. Margo and Millie were genuinely fond of Paul, I think, and Noel isn't the type. (I *think!*)

Jeanette Melton is another matter—within five minutes of meeting her I decided she is capable of anything: yet she's the only one of Melton's heirs who couldn't have killed Paul.

Another part of Ben's theory is that Charles Melton might have been an evil-minded scamp, who set up the whole devilish scheme in a spirit of revenge. (If so, for what?) Or, and I liked this one better, he did it simply to make all these people reveal their true natures. This in turn would demonstrate his own brilliance as a character analyst, showing them that he'd been on to their secret motives all along. (Then he must have believed in an afterlife, or there'd be no fun in it.)

Around 4:00, when it began to cool off, we went in from the pool and dressed. Jeanette Melton was due at La Rêverie in time for dinner—being met by the sexy chauffeur of Margo's friends, the Marchands—and both Millie and Lila had urged us to be there and help everyone get through the evening.

Before we left I insisted on telephoning home to talk to the children, and the sound of their little piping voices made me frantically homesick. I could tell that Brooke had a cold, but according to Mrs. Duffy, no fever. Terry could hardly spare two minutes for us because Cabby Dillon had come over to play. We still have a week before we go home, assuming—scary thought!—that Ben can be pried away without solving the manuscript mystery.

Given a few more days, I may also have trouble prying him away from Jeanette Melton. God knows it was instant attraction on her part. Though Ben says I'm imagining the whole thing, he can't keep from looking quite stunned with pleasure when I tease him about it.

I really don't blame him, because Jeanette turned out to be a powerhouse of a woman. She'd arrived only about an hour before we got to the house, but already everyone was hopping around, Lila working on electrical connections for her computer, Marie pressing her clothes, and Millie taking phone messages while Jeanette took over Melton's study and used what had been his private line.

Noel looked quite grumpy when he met us at the door, and when Marie came panting through the hall with a

steaming pot of tea she was taking upstairs, he asked her to
please remember that dinner was to be earlier than usual
because he expected many of Paul's friends would be coming by. I felt sorry for her and would have offered to pitch
in and help if I hadn't thought it would make things worse.

Jeanette, when she finally appeared, looked like the
movie version of a career woman: tall, with long, gorgeous legs nicely set off by high heels and a tight, thigh-high
black skirt. She has masses of healthy-looking auburn hair
swinging to her shoulders and one of those clean-lined faces
with a crisp, short nose and big, flashing brown eyes and
what's called a mobile mouth—beautifully made up, of
course. She wore a wonderfully cut blouse made of heavy,
heavy ivory silk, and a thick gold chain and big gold hoop
earrings.

She strode—it's the only word for her walk—up to me
and ran a quick head-to-toe appraisal while we shook
hands. Then, apparently having filed me under "suburban
housewife," she moved on to Ben and in two seconds had
him chortling happily while they compared notes on the
thrilling world of journalism.

I had to admire Ben's aplomb in pitting his reminiscences of a very brief and low-level tenure in the news-
room of the *Times* against Jeanette's escapades as features
editor of *World Beat*. He didn't dare talk about Porter
Publishing, of course, since Millie had quite rightly sworn
us to secrecy, so he embroidered the truth, and did it very
imaginatively, I thought.

They were a pair of ink-stained adventurers all through
dinner—I thought of Hemingway and Gellhorn—while the
rest of us looked on from remote, quotidian shores. By the
time we got to coffee on the terrace Ben had progressed to
his career as a painter, and Jeanette was longing to see his
work and sighing over her own unrealized ambitions in the
graphic arts.

When the callers began arriving to extend sympathy over
Paul's death, Millie and Noel left us and, so instantly that
I knew she'd been waiting for the chance, Jeanette brought
up the subject of Melton's legacy. (Margo had not come for

dinner, and Lila was helping Marie, so the three of us were alone.)

Jeanette was dying to know how everyone had reacted to the terms of the will—especially Noel. She was stunned when we told her about Paul Clifford having stolen Millie's pages, then became defensive and blamed his behavior on his being exploited over the years by both Melton and Noel Wright.

Whether it was her anger, or fatigue, or all the wine at dinner I'll never know, but when Noel came back out Jeanette immediately announced that she'd had the most wonderful idea: she was going to print her three chapters of Melton's novel in *World Beat*! Didn't Noel think that would cause a sensation—besides giving priceless publicity for the completed novel?

Well, of course Noel was absolutely outraged. He was spluttering, falling over his words as he tried to explain why that was the worst idea he'd ever heard of in his life. The scene would have been comical: that tiger of a woman reducing Noel Wright—no helpless bumpkin, let us remember, but one of the sharpest literary agents around—to incoherence. It wasn't funny, though, because of the very real anger that ran between them like an electric current.

He had her, it seemed, when he pointed out that she could print none of it, not one sentence, without a copyright that she did not possess—and, if he had anything to do with it, never would.

Now, Jeanette must have known that, which makes her continued taunting of the man puzzling to me. Anyway, perhaps just to make sure she had completely ruined Noel's evening, she turned to Ben and ever-so-sweetly begged him to read over her pages of Melton's manuscript and tell her what he thought of running them in *World Beat*. His professional opinion would mean more to her than she could possibly express, etc.; so would he consider taking just a couple of hours to read it and then tell her what he really, *really* thought?

Ben answered, need I say, that he would be really, *really* glad to. (He did add that Noel certainly appeared to be right about her chances of using the material, but he said it rather softly, I noticed, and Jeanette paid no attention.)

Noel was so affronted he could hardly contain himself. I was the only one who received a civil goodnight as he left us, although he must have seen that Ben had been dragged into the situation and could not be considered an ally of Jeanette's. I only hope there won't be any unpleasant repercussions tomorrow. Meanwhile I'm keeping very quiet because Ben has started reading the manuscript, and I get to have it when he's finished.

NINE

SHORTLY BEFORE 1:00 P.M. Margo Honeywell stepped through the front door of her villa, intending to walk to the gate to welcome her visitor. She was wearing a full skirt in a black-and-ochre Provençal print and a loose white cotton blouse—the costume having been selected to contrast, rather than compete, with whatever New York chic Jeanette Melton might be featuring. In the doorway Margo paused, gazing down at the clogs on her feet. She'd gone too far there. The things were authentically rustic, but they tortured the foot with every step. When she saw that a black Mercedes was already nosing between the stone entrance pillars, she slipped out of the clogs and waited in bare feet, enjoying the warmth of the stone doorsill beneath her toes.

The car drew up, with Jeanette Melton peering out from behind the wheel through huge, horn-rimmed sunglasses. She slumped for a moment in exaggerated relief before pushing the door open and stepping out of the car.

"Whew! What a responsibility!" Jeanette shook the creases out of her tan linen trousers, then pushed the sunglasses up into her hair. She said, "You can imagine what Lila will do to me if she finds one scratch, one minuscule dent..."

"I wouldn't be caught touching a fender of that car in my best kid gloves. How did you get to drive it? Steal the keys?"

"I'm family, darling, remember?" Jeanette bent to peck Margo on the cheek, then straightened and with her eyes half-closed drew a deep, ecstatic breath. "What heaven, after horrible, gray New York! God, the smell, the sun, this soft, wonderful air! Let's go to the beach, can we?"

But instantly she was frowning as she looked at her watch. "Hell, there isn't time. I've got to be near the phone when the office opens, and that gives us exactly one hour. Listen, Margo, I have a great idea to discuss with you." Jeanette tucked her hand beneath Margo's arm and drew her toward the garden, but Margo resisted.

"Hold it a minute," she said. "Let's have some wine and—I suppose you're dieting, as usual?" Jeanette nodded and Margo went on, "That's lucky. There's nothing in the house but fruit and cheese."

The two women went into the house and crossed the shadowy, tiled foyer to get to the kitchen. There, on the pine table, a bottle of white Bordeaux stood chilling in a crock of melting ice. Beside it was a shallow basket of nectarines and apples, and a small round of goat cheese on a wooden board.

"We do have bread, of course, if you want it," said Margo, lifting out the dripping wine bottle and wrapping it in a red-and-white linen towel.

"No thanks," said Jeanette, "but a plate would be nice."

Carrying the fruit and cheese, she crossed the narrow kitchen to the open door that led to the patio. Margo followed with plates and glasses, holding the wine bottle in the crook of her elbow. She frowned as she stepped out into the hot sunlight, but Jeanette, having set their lunch on the stone table, was stretching herself out on a chaise.

She looked so contented that Margo stifled her protests and began awkwardly rolling an iron umbrella stand to that end of the patio. "No sun for me," she said firmly. "You can imagine what my skin would look like by now. I'm surprised you don't worry about it."

Jeanette looked up in time to see the envy in Margo's face as she studied her younger friend. Without smugness, she said, "You've done amazingly well, Margo, considering that you couldn't always get the sunscreens they make now. I'm wearing Number 35. It's impervious to everything except laser beams."

She unbuttoned her blue linen shirt and pulled it open, exposing a white lace bra and an expanse of pale skin; then, without sitting up, she fumbled in her bag until she came up with a bottle of lotion. Applying it to her chest and arms, she said, "Don't you want to hear my idea?"

"I do, I do; right after I pour us some wine. I'll bet it's about Sonny Devere. You've thought of some new way to trap him."

Jeanette laughed, sitting up to take her glass from Margo. "No, I've put Sonny on hold for a while. Something told me I was being a teeny bit too aggressive."

"Well, you don't get a crack at forty million every day. I wouldn't let any grass grow if I were you."

"Maybe I don't need forty million. Maybe two or three would be enough if I had them all to myself, without the bother of Sonny."

"Jeanette . . ."

"Tell me something, Margo. How do you feel about your legacy from my revered uncle?"

"Three chapters of an unpublished novel? What's to feel?"

"Oh, come on. I know you must be seething. Which pages did you get?"

Before answering, Margo stood up to change the tilt of the umbrella, then pushed her chair into the patch of shade and set the wine bottle beside it. She offered the basket of fruit to Jeanette, and when she had selected an apple, took one for herself and sat down again.

"I guess there's no reason not to tell you," she said at last. "I have pages 116 through 256. How about you?"

"Mine are 1 through 115, the first three chapters. And, incidentally, the title, which is *Mirror Image*."

Margo said, "I wonder what that signifies. Mirror Image. Maybe it's about Melton, his life, though I didn't see any of that in the part I read."

"Now that you mention it, the book opens with Robert de Laine, the protagonist, I gather, in a homosexual episode with someone named René de Cendre. It's hot stuff, Margo. Uncle Charles was never that explicit before; I wonder if he meant it as a confession."

Margo chuckled in her hearty, peasant manner. "More likely he was fantasizing about the good old days. Either way it would be sensational—if we could ever get it published.''

"That's why I'm here, my friend. If you help, I think there's a chance.'' Jeanette picked up her pouchy straw handbag and pulled out a black object in the shape of a paperback book. She said, "This is a pocket copying machine—brand-new on the market. To use it I'll have to do a bit of snooping around; that's why I need you.''

"Jeanette Melton, you're as scheming as your uncle, God rest his soul.'' Margo wore an admiring smile as she reached for the machine.

Handing it to her, Jeanette said, "You see, I don't believe for one minute that Paul took Millie's pages. Noel's got them, I'll swear to it, *and* Paul's, *and* his own. Do you see what that does to us?''

The astonishment on Margo's face was genuine, as was her immediate feeling of chagrin, remembering how she had treated Noel, when possibly...

She said, "Jeanette, you're not suggesting that Noel shot Paul?''

"Why not? And then set it up to look as though Paul had stolen from Millie. You know how he hated him.'' Jeanette's lips were parted; her brown eyes flashed with impatience while she waited for Margo to come around to her view.

"But Noel wouldn't murder for money. He must be quite rich after collecting Melton's commissions all those years. Some thief killed Paul—everything points to it. Someone who read about Charles Melton's death and wanted to get in before the estate was broken up. The Riviera's crawling with them.''

"Maybe Noel didn't kill Paul; maybe you're right about that. But no thief would take pages of manuscript, and that means someone else did. Somebody found Paul's body before Marie did and seized the opportunity to steal his part of the novel. It has to be Millie or Noel...''

"I can't believe it of Millie.''

"...and everything's happened so fast I'm sure those pages are still in the house. We have to hurry up and find

them and copy them before they get carried off to some safe
deposit box. There'll be no sign anything has happened
until—*voilà!*—we turn up with the copyright!"

"You're indulging in some very wishful thinking, I would
say. Do you expect to find Noel's manuscript pages waiting for you on top of his desk?"

Jeanette said, "Obviously not; but I'm good at finding
things. Don't look so skeptical, Margo, it's true. I really
have a talent for figuring out where something's lost, or in
this case, hidden. It's like an ear for music, I've always said.
Of course I won't have a lot of time, and I agree the odds
are against me. But since this is our only chance it's worth
a try, wouldn't you say?"

"Sorry, my friend, I'm having no part of it."

"Come on, I know you better than that." But both
women had heard the tremor in Jeanette's normally confident voice, and she went on, "I'm uncomfortable about
the skulking around; I can't hide that from you. It will be
embarrassing as hell if I get caught, but considering what's
at stake, I'm willing to risk it."

"Embarrassing. That's putting it mildly. Have you ever
seen Noel in one of his icy rages?" Margo shivered dra-
matically. "I wouldn't want to face it, and I've never been
thought of as lacking in nerve."

"Well, we have to see that I don't get caught, that's all."

Jeanette pushed herself out of the chaise and carried her
empty glass to where the wine bottle stood in the shade.
Margo watched as she filled both of their glasses, sipped
from her own, then set it on the table and began buttoning
her shirt.

"Look, Margo, I'm going to do it whether you help or
not. Wouldn't it be silly to cut yourself out when there's
practically no risk for you?"

"That's the problem." Margo smiled slowly, looking like
a wise old cat. "What you really need from me is my part
of the manuscript."

"Well, sure, eventually."

Margo managed to sip from her wineglass without
changing her expression. "So before you expose yourself

to Noel's wrath, you'd like to make a copy of my pages. Well, darling, I'm afraid I can't allow that.''

"Margo, I am not stupid enough to think you would. But that's the great thing about my plan: your pages are your insurance. I don't get a look at them until I've collected all the rest. You're last; that guarantees I have to do my part. Until I do you keep yours in the bank—along with the contract I've had drawn up, which gives us equal shares in the copyright.''

"After it has been awarded to one of us, to meet the terms of the will?''

"Right. That formality is covered in the contract.''

"I'm impressed, Jeanette; I really am. You're as creative as your uncle—in a rather criminal style, if you'll forgive me. I find I'm tempted after all.''

"Well then, let's work it out. It'll be your job to get Millie and Noel out of the house so I can search their rooms. Then if I can't find anything we'll have to dream up some other way to get a look at their pages, possibly by way of that nice Ben Porter. I made a point of lending him mine to set an example.'' Jeanette narrowed her eyes thoughtfully. "What about that marriage, Margo? Is it solid?''

"Does Carrie Porter look like the kind of wife men run out on? Not to me.''

"You never know.'' Jeanette was sliding her feet into her sandals. "I've got to get to work. Thanks for lunch.'' She picked up the copier and weighed it in her hand. "What do you say, Margo? Are you with me?''

Margo rose from her chair. "Give me a day to decide,'' she said. "I have to think of all the angles.''

"Think of this one then. Noel must want your pages and mine just as much as he wanted Paul's. Delay could be—I hesitate to use the word—fatal.''

The two women were unsmiling as they gazed into each other's eyes for a moment; then Jeanette turned away and hurried through the house and out the front door.

THE TOWN OF Beaulieu-sur-Mer is built around the natural harbor formed by the peninsula of St.-Jean-Cap-Ferrat.

The beauty and convenience of its situation—midway between Nice and Monte Carlo—have made it a favorite stopping place for generations of wealthy and fashionable travelers. Those who disdain the crowded promenades of Cannes and Nice feel at home in Beaulieu, where the staffs of the select hotels seem as well bred as the guests; they enjoy gambling in the small, jewel-box casino and shopping in the exclusive boutiques.

In a bay on the north side of the town is a large marina, where at almost any time of year yachts flying flags of the world's most desirable ports can be seen bobbing sedately in their slips. As in most European marinas, the broad cement quay is dotted with restaurants and shops; in Beaulieu the latter are notable for their elegance. Few would be out of place on Bond Street or Place Vendome, and if a guest on one of the yachts has forgotten something—her favorite Hermés silk blouse, for example—she can usually find a replacement there on the dock.

The restaurants are sprawling, open-air cafés offering a wide choice of international cuisine. Each has a theme; the one into which Ben Porter led Carrie and Millicent that night was called Key Largo and featured photos of Bogart and Bacall on the walls and on the waiters' T-shirts.

When they had been seated and had ordered drinks, Ben took some papers from his jacket pocket, unfolded them, and began to read:

. . . they were following, but too sure of overtaking him to hurry. Robert de Laine could hear their low voices somewhere behind him, as ominous as the rumble of approaching thunder, but he could not tell exactly where they were. He heard a stab of harsh laughter and stopped running, spinning around so quickly that he almost fell. He saw shadows flickering across the elevated walkway a hundred yards back; yet the voices seemed to come from the level of the road.

What would they do to him when they caught him, as they would, without question? He could not keep going much longer; the panic that propelled him was

ebbing with each moment, subsiding beneath a
mounting wave of self-loathing.

They could kill him; he wouldn't care. After those
moments with René he had no further reason to live.

He remembered watching an eclipse of the sun when
he was a little boy. In his mind the scene with René was
similar: a majestic force blocking out light, life, the
world, in one cataclysmic instant. But the eclipse had
ended, restoring the day to its normal shape. Robert de
Laine's world was changed forever.

Carole would know. From the first touch she would
know that he was changed. Standing there in the
darkness, shivering as the icy river wind slashed at his
bare arms, he pictured her grave, beautiful face as re-
alization struck. He seemed to hear her speak one
name, René de Cendre, then turn away from him forever.

He was shuddering now with shame as well as cold.
The fear was gone, and with it the taunting voices of
his pursuers. Perhaps they had been a product of his
hysteria. He suddenly felt conspicuous in his bare-
chested state and, squinting through the darkness, saw
a tipped-over wire trash can spilling its contents over
the hard-packed mud of the riverbank. He went over
and began picking through the cans and bottles and
mashed remnants of food, feeling no revulsion as his
fingers became soiled with the foulest kind of leav-
ings, feeling instead as if he belonged there on a cold,
dark riverbank, searching for a shred of cloth to cover
his body.

Millie said, "Ben, don't stop."

"That's all I managed to copy; Jeanette didn't give us
much time." Ben moved the papers to make room for the
drinks the waiter had brought. "I made notes on the rest of
it, though."

"So did I," said Carrie. "Robert de Laine is running
away in a frenzy of self-hatred because of a homosexual
encounter with a man named René de Cendre. All he can

think of is cleansing and punishing himself, so he starts out by slaving in an African diamond mine, in horrible conditions, of course. To protect himself from his bestial companions he learns to fight and kill and steal. He also figures out some ingenious ways to smuggle diamonds. That's as far as it goes.''

Ben said, "What went on in your section, Millie? Other than the strangling of..." He paused to consult his notes. "...of Abu Sahid. What was that all about?''

Millie removed a swizzle stick from her glass without noticing that it was carved with a tiny replica of the Maltese Falcon. She said slowly, "The page we found in Paul's bathroom is apparently near the end of de Laine's adventures in some Middle Eastern kingdom where he has overthrown the evil tyrant and been rewarded with a fortune. He has also rescued a pal he met in the diamond mines, a fellow named Claude Dépouille, who had been enslaved by Abu Sahid and turned into a drug addict. It's time then to return to New York and take over Wall Street. He soon has one of those power setups: the plush office in a towering skyscraper, the corps of worshipful retainers, the best tailor, biggest house, most gorgeous wife, etc., etc.''

"A familiar figure. Not Melton's usual type, though.''

"No, that struck me right away. *But* there are hints that tumult seethes beneath the glossy facade. He has a scheming secretary named Helene Rocher...''

"Rocher?'' Ben spoke up. "Spell that for me, please, Millie.''

After Millie had obliged him Carrie said, "The name that gets me is de Laine. For some reason that sounds familiar; I can't think why.''

"Well, anyway, this Rocher woman is secretly in league with de Laine's beautiful but nasty wife, Carole. The two are preparing a major dirty deal that will unseat the boss, but Dépouille is spying on them and keeping de Laine informed.''

"He's cured of his addiction?''

"Yes, but de Laine knows some secret that binds them together.''

The waiter had returned and was staring at them with hostility. Looking up at him, Ben said, "You must be Bogart's brother. *Etes-vous le frère de Humphrey Bogart? Quel resemblance!*"

The waiter frowned and shrugged, pointing to the menus, until Millie explained in her more comprehensible accent that the American gentleman had remarked on his resemblance to the famous actor. Instantly the man broke into a beaming smile and, without being asked, hurried off to get them a second round of drinks.

"Now, where were we?" said Ben.

Millie resumed her recollection of the story. "De Laine is fully aware of his wife's treachery, but his years of hardship have schooled him so that he can hide his feelings and smoothly plot her downfall, while still enjoying a fabulous sex life with her. Which, by the way, is carefully detailed."

"Then his lapse with René de Cendre was an isolated episode? He's not a true homosexual?"

"That's not spelled out. He's so disciplined, however, that he can play any part he wants to, and of course he's immensely attractive and simply mows down the women."

Ben grinned across the table at Carrie. "It may not be the Charles Melton we're used to, but oh boy, wouldn't it sell?"

"No question."

Their waiter was bringing the drinks, threading his way between the crowded tables with a smile of anticipation on his swarthy face. When he reached them he fixed his eyes on Ben and snarled in the style of Bogart, "Lishen, shweethot, I 'ave bring your cocktail!"

He beamed as they laughed and praised his talent; then Ben began reading from the menu and the waiter repeated the order as he wrote it down. *"Pissaladière des moules, oui; le thon cru à la mode Japonais, oui; le biftek saignant avec les pommes frites, oui."*

When he had left them, Ben consulted his notes and said, "So in the first part, Jeanette's, we have Robert de Laine fleeing from a possible homosexual entanglement and resolving to purge and ennoble himself. After that . . ." Ben looked up at Millie. "How many pages did you have, Millie?"

"I'm not sure. Around 150, ending with page 401."

"So you must have started with 250-something. Jeanette's end on 115. I wonder if Noel and Margo will tell us their page numbers, at least; then we'll know which were Paul's."

Carrie said, "Robert de Laine; what does that mean to me?"

Millie smiled. "You see it on labels, Carrie. *Laine* is the French word for 'wool.' Maybe that's what you're thinking of."

"Of course: de Laine. Of wool—that's what the name means."

Ben was frowning thoughtfully as he added the word to his page of notes. But the waiter was approaching with their dinner, making his way between tables that had suddenly become crowded and noisy. The Key Largo had begun to throb like a disco; it was a place for people-watching now, not for serious talk. Ben put away his papers and ordered a bottle of Bordeaux.

TEN

MILLIE HAD CHOSEN the chapel of St. Sulpice for Paul Clifford's memorial service because of its size; it was so tiny that the group of people she expected would come close to filling it. She couldn't bear to think of delivering her eulogy in a large church, facing row upon row of empty seats.

Still, as she waited beside the door in her black silk suit, she silently apologized to Paul for not giving him a grander send-off. She hadn't really applied herself; she knew that and thought he probably did too. There were many who would have made the effort to come if she had added her appeal to the prestige that still clung to any close associate of Charles Melton. But she had been tired and distracted, and now it was too late.

A car pulled into the small parking area, immediately followed by another, which she recognized as the Marchands' Citroën, and Millie brightened. Maybe it wouldn't be so bad; especially after the people she thought of as family had arrived. Poor Paul. Not one blood relative had bothered to make the trip, not even the schoolteacher niece who lived in Duluth and might be expected to jump at an excuse for a trip to the south of France. Millie was glad the selfish girl wouldn't get much of an inheritance.

The Delaneys were coming up the walk, Michael red-faced, as always, and looking as if he were about to burst out of his dark blue suit. The cuisine of the Riviera had that effect on many newcomers, though it appeared that his wife, Marge, disciplined herself. She was thin and tanned and athletic looking, like so many middle-aged American women. While Millie greeted the Delaneys and thanked them for coming, she imagined Paul groaning in dismay. But they liked you, Paul, she told him silently, even though you were such a snob; maybe *because of it*.

Claude and Loulou Marchand came on the heels of the Delaneys, and Margo was with them, as Millie had known she would be. She was wearing a beautiful new *tailleur* by Givenchy, in dark red-and-amber silk, and a wide-brimmed hat of shining, dark red straw.

"Margo, you look perfectly stunning," said Millie as they embraced, and instantly Margo's eyes glistened with tears.

"I wanted to make myself beautiful for Paul," she said. "Do you think he would be pleased?"

"Paul would love our Margo today, would he not?" Claude Marchand kissed Millie's cheek, then stepped back to beam approvingly at all three women. "And you, Millie, as well, and of course, my Loulou."

Loulou Marchand combined the good fortune of being able to spend anything she liked on clothes with the bad luck of having inherited a short, unmistakably solid body. On Loulou, with her shape and her impatient, bustling walk, her expensive dresses looked as if they had come from a thrift shop, Paul had once lamented, instead of being on their way to one. He had loved her, though, as they all did. Loulou's warmth and generosity made her irresistible.

She kissed Millie and said, "I will miss that dear man dreadfully. *Dreadfully,* Millie!"

They all went into the chapel, where the organ had begun playing softly. It was ten minutes before 11:00.

As if they'd been waiting for a signal, all the household arrived at the same time. Noel came up the walk with Lila, who for once was wearing a dress, of dark blue linen, and high-heeled pumps, in which she looked as self-conscious as a young girl. Marie followed, wearing her usual black dress, with the wide lace collar she added on Sundays, and a black straw skimmer. Her nose was pink, Millie observed, and she held a handkerchief wadded in one large hand.

Jeanette had driven over in the Mercedes with Ben and Carrie Porter, and as they approached, Millie decided not to tell her that Sonny Devere had arrived ten minutes earlier. It would be a nice surprise for her.

But when they walked in together, Jeanette held back. As
Noel led the way to the front pew, she whispered, "You go
on, Millie. I'm feeling shaky."

This was so out of character that Millie turned in astonishment and saw that indeed Jeanette was extremely pale.
She would not have Millie stay with her, however, but
pushed her ahead, saying, "I'll be OK. Go on or they'll all
start buzzing," and reluctantly, Millie left her.

The priest entered and the service began, all of it to be
conducted in Latin except for the brief eulogies that would
be given by Margo and, because decency demanded, by
Noel. Seated between Lila and Marie, Noel listened to the
ritual drone on and wondered why he had allowed himself
to be trapped into such a false display. Surely his underlying insincerity would turn his words to mockery. And yet
there had been a time when he would have meant them.

Marie was sniffling into her handkerchief, and Noel
shifted in his seat, hoping she would take it as a signal for
quiet. He glanced at his watch; the Catholic service was
endless and seemed such a waste when he knew Millie had
picked the church solely for its size and location. Paul had
been no churchgoer, any more than the rest of them, even
though he had looked like a choirboy when he came to La
Rêverie.

Lulled, perhaps, by the gentle voice of the priest, Noel,
for the first time in years, allowed himself to remember
when Paul had first come to work for Charles. Had he
known what he was doing? Noel had always wondered; not
that it mattered to the outcome, which was predictable from
the moment the slender, golden-haired boy stepped into
Charles Melton's drawing-room.

They'd been happy days, with the three of them working together, Paul so perfect for the job and so impressed
by his famous employer—and his employer's worldly-wise
assistant, as Noel had been then. They had included him in
everything from the first, enjoying his fresh perceptions
and puckish humor. For at least two years they had known
harmony; and then Charles and Noel had begun to compete for Paul, and everything changed.

Noel shifted in his seat again and fancied he saw the priest look at him critically. I'm not a Catholic, he thought, you can't hurt me; then he smiled at his own childishness. That was part of what drew him to Paul, he remembered. Paul had a sense of fun, of innocent mischief, that had been supremely refreshing to both Charles Melton and Noel after years spent among the literati of Europe.

Noel glanced at his watch again, trying to estimate how soon he would be called upon. Surely the service was winding up; the priest was swinging the censer with what looked like finality, and, glancing over his shoulder, Noel saw that Millie was fidgeting nervously.

In a moment the priest fell silent and stood peering under his brows at Millie, who rose and stepped to the front and delivered what Noel assessed as a charming tribute to Paul. She finished and made her way back to her seat wearing an unmistakable look of relief, and Noel stood up to take her place.

He began speaking the words he had rehearsed: Paul's role would never be fully appreciated by the world of literature, his professional talents had been equal to the exacting demands of genius, his diplomacy made him indispensable in a complex culture; his loyalty...

His loyalty had been put to the supreme test by Noel Wright, and he had hated Noel Wright ever after because it had failed the test. Amen.

Noel hoped he had not actually spoken the words; the placid expressions of the congregation told him he had not. He glanced from face to face as he delivered his final phrases. Everyone he would have expected was there, with a few surprises, such as Sonny Devere. Looking for Jeanette, no doubt. Jeanette. Where was she? An alarm went off in Noel's mind, and he ended his speech abruptly and strode back to his seat. There he bent to whisper to Lila, then walked swiftly to the side door of the chapel, opened it, and slipped out.

WHEN JEANETTE MELTON quietly left the chapel at the beginning of the service, it was with a well-thought-out plan in mind, one she rehearsed on the brief drive back to La Rêverie in order to calm herself.

Her small copier was basically an electronic camera that could be connected to a printer for later reproduction of the documents it photographed. Jeanette figured she would need between five and ten seconds to record each page; therefore, presuming Noel possessed roughly 150 pages, as she and Margo did, she should allow twenty-five minutes for the job of copying. Obviously she first had to find the pages, wherever they might be hidden, and find them quickly.

So, she told herself, she should allow fifteen minutes for the search, making a total of forty to do the whole job— unless she found Paul's and Millie's pages as well as Noel's. That stroke of luck could throw everything off. Still, Paul's service would certainly last for an hour, and she could safely count on another thirty minutes for leaving the chapel and returning to the house. As far as time went, she appeared to have a safe margin; confidence was another matter.

Pulling into La Rêverie's drive, Jeanette found herself slowing nearly to a stop. She forced herself to continue into the garage, but her hands were trembling as she switched off the ignition and fumbled for the door handle. For one delicious moment she considered giving in to her weakness; her scheme was crazy; it would never work anyway.

Then anger took over, as usual at such times, anger at her own softness, and she drew a deep, shuddering breath and, with a quick glance at her watch, stepped out of the car and strode across the gravel to the house.

By the time she reached the front door she felt sufficiently composed to observe the reproachful expressions of the saintly faces carved into the ancient wood. If you're telling me I'm nuts I already know it, she thought, as she pulled the door open.

She hurried up to the second floor and went directly to Paul Clifford's room, where she was pleased to find that the curtains had been left open. Paul's room was in the front of the house, and Jeanette planned to bring Noel's manu-

script there for copying so that she could keep watch for
unexpected arrivals.

Across and down the hall Noel's door stood ajar, and
when she reached it Jeanette hesitated, feeling again that
tempting inclination to give up. In a moment she stepped
inside, however, and once there gave herself utterly to the
task of finding what she had come to find.

The door opened into the area Noel used as his office, a
small but well-lighted space containing his desk, a walnut
file cabinet and, beside it, a work table piled with ledgers
and reference books. One wall held bookcases and a small
fireplace, and the two soft leather chairs placed before it
suggested cozy evenings of literary discussion.

The filing cabinet was locked, so Jeanette tackled it first,
using a thin steel wand she had been given by the paroled
convict who had worked as night maintenance man at
World Beat until he was found drunk one morning in the
publisher's office. The average file cabinet lock opened
easily under Jeanette's skilled manipulations; Noel's was no
exception, and in ten minutes she had rifled through his
orderly files and relocked the cabinet.

Before moving to the desk, Jeanette darted across the hall
for a quick look from the front windows. She returned,
swiftly went through the desk drawers, then stepped into
the center of the room and stood perfectly still, putting her
imagination to work.

She imagined she was Noel, with Noel's mind, so orderly and devious, and that he was thinking of a hiding
spot. As well as concealment he would want easy access to
the manuscript, and Jeanette concentrated on that re-
quirement as she gazed around the office area, then walked
slowly into the sleeping part of Noel's room.

It would be there, she decided at once. He would keep it
near him, where he could hear any nocturnal intruder. Even
by day few would be inclined to disturb the stern, almost
monastic, arrangement of Noel Wright's bedroom and
Jeanette felt a twinge of admiration as she realized that
Noel must be fully aware of that.

The walls were white, the curtains were made of heavy white linen, and the bedcover was a thick piece of hand woven white cotton. The bed itself, of old wood painted a faded, rusty red, provided the only note of color aside from the books piled on the round table beside it. More books were stacked on the floor beneath the table, and Jeanette went over them all, being careful to replace them exactly as they had been.

She was kneeling there on the rug when a faint sound caused her to stiffen, straining her ears to identify the source. Holding her breath, she silently rose to her feet and moved to the shadowed corner of the room. Again she heard the sound, and now there was no mistaking the creak of the hall floor beneath a cautious tread.

Jeanette edged along the inner wall, working her way toward the door that opened into Noel's office. She swore at herself for forgetting that Sergeant Clement was watching the house. No doubt he had seen her car and would feel duty bound to check on the unexpected arrival. Still, everything would be fine if she could get into the corridor, where she had a perfect right to be.

She reached the door and slipped behind it. Flattening herself against the wall, she fixed her eyes on the inch-wide opening and prayed that in her black dress she would be invisible to anyone who peeked from the other side. But what if her gaze should suddenly meet the startled brown eyes of Sergeant Clement? She fought hysterical laughter, forcing herself to concentrate on listening for the sound of footsteps.

The crack of light widened as the door was pushed back against her, and in a moment she heard Noel Wright say, "It will be less embarrassing if you stop cowering behind the door, Jeanette."

JEANETTE STEPPED OUT, holding her head high and her chin at a defiant tilt, but she made no effort to hide her chagrin.

"I might have known," she said. "You've always been able to read my mind, haven't you?"

Noel silently held out his hand for the copier, which she gave him with no sign of reluctance.

He examined it and said, "Let's see. You would have photographed the manuscript, I suppose, page by page. But I can't believe that would work."

"I'm a jump ahead of you there, Noel. That's not just a camera; it's a sophisticated copying machine that can be plugged into a printer." She grinned into his face. "Get the manuscript and I'll show you how it works."

"Aren't we the saucy little tease." Noel balanced the machine in his hand. "I'll just relieve you of this, for your own good. It might go off in your hand."

Jeanette sighed. "I suppose I deserve some punishment. Now may I go?"

"First I want to make you understand what you have accomplished with your greediness. You've guaranteed that Charles's last work will never be published."

"I don't see why."

"Sit down and I'll explain." Noel gestured toward one of his easy chairs, and Jeanette sat down, giving a little sigh as she sank into the soft leather.

"We've had some pleasant evenings here," she said, "you and I and Uncle Charles."

Noel's thin face was grim as he settled opposite her. "Don't bother dusting off reminiscences of happy days gone by. Your uncle understood you as well as I did. I've often wanted to tell you that, but it seemed too cruel."

"Anything goes, of course, now that you've caught me snooping."

"Isn't *snooping* rather a childish word to describe a crime? Several crimes, if you make it illegal search in order to steal, in order to defraud. But I have no desire to torture you, Jeanette. I merely think you should know that until you announced your plan to exploit your uncle in your cheap magazine, I had intended to ask you to join with me in assembling the manuscript, to our mutual benefit."

"Noel, that makes so much sense!" Jeanette leaned toward him eagerly. "And if we're together I'm sure the others will listen to reason."

"It's too late for that, foolish girl. There has been a murder. Do you think the murderer will come forward now and produce Paul's part of the manuscript? And Millie's?"

Jeanette sat back in her chair and dropped her hands helplessly in her lap. "Can't we do anything, Noel? Isn't there some way...?"

"What I suggest you do, my dear, is leave this house. Get yourself back to your office in that hideous skyscraper, where you may be safe." He smiled as he saw her begin shaking her head stubbornly.

"It kills you to give up," he went on. "I knew it would, so I'm prepared to sweeten the pill. Leave your pages with me, Jeanette, it's the only hope."

She stared at him incredulously. "Are you insane, Noel Wright? I should hand it all over to you and go meekly back to New York with no evidence that I ever owned a single page of my uncle's work?"

"No, no, no, of course I'm suggesting no such thing. You'll copy your pages first—possibly with this machine." Noel glanced at the copier as if surprised to find it still in his hand. "You'll give me the copy and get safely out of here with the original. Then if the killer is found, and Paul's and Millie's pages as well...."

"You'll have all but one section. Margo's."

"*We'll* have all but one section. You and I. And I feel certain Margo will cooperate if there's a chance of getting the book published."

Jeanette's face was solemn as she said slowly, "I have to think about it, Noel. I don't want to do something I'll regret."

Noel got to his feet and stood looking down at her. Finally he said, "Will you feel better about it if I let you copy my part, after all?"

Jeanette's mouth dropped open, but she quickly closed it and watched in bemused silence while Noel went into his sleeping area, then after a moment returned with an inch-thick sheaf of papers held together with a rubber band.

"Don't get any creative ideas now, Jeanette. I hardly need tell you this is a copy of the original, which is safely tucked away. Nevertheless I want this back by dinnertime this evening."

As she took the manuscript he covered her hand with his and said, looking intently into her eyes, "I do hope you'll accept my suggestion, Jeanette."

She studied his face, with its bladelike cheekbones and tightly stretched, pale skin, wishing she could see through to the thoughts behind the mask.

She said, "I imagine I will. Probably, that is. Now shouldn't we go down, Noel? Everyone seems to be coming back from the service."

From the front of the house came sounds of car doors slamming and voices speaking in both French and English. Lila's rose above the others as she scolded Sergeant Clement, who apparently had been watching the front of the house when she arrived. The mere sight of the man infuriated her, and she was doing her best to make his assignment into a sojourn in hell.

Noel said, "Yes, we must join the others. But I'll expect your answer before the end of the day."

He strode through the door, leaving Jeanette to follow when she was ready.

INSPECTOR FOCH SWUNG his Peugeot around a sharp curve, and Carrie Porter slid across the slippery leather of the back seat to collide with Ben.

"Do you think we'll get out of this country alive?" she whispered, retrieving her bag from the floor.

Before Ben could reply the car swerved again, sending both Porters to the opposite corner.

"*Pardon!*" Ben shouted. "*Monsieur Inspecteur! Est-ce qu'il est possible à propeller votre voiture...* Carrie, what's 'slowly'?"

"*Lentement,* I think." She raised her voice. "*Lentement! S'il vous plait!*"

The car slowed to a crawl, and in the rearview mirror Carrie met the baffled gaze of the inspector. "*Avez-vous malade?''* he inquired anxiously; then with a swift turn of the wheel, he pulled the car to the side of the road, stopping short of a deep, rock-filled gully.

"No, no, no." Smiling and shaking his head, Ben flipped his hands in a forward direction to indicate carrying on. *"Ma femme... elle a petit peur."* He looked meaningfully at Carrie, and the inspector's face cleared.

Wagging his head in a kindly, understanding manner, Inspector Foch started up the car and continued the trip at a cautious speed, with frequent glances in the mirror to make sure Carrie was all right.

Carrie was convulsed. "What did you say I had? A little purr? Really, Ben, I can't see that that's any business of the inspector's!"

"I'd say he thinks you're pregnant, from the way he's driving."

"With my figure? Oh well, who cares what he think as long as he gets us home in one piece."

"Or two, more accurately. Carrie, what happened in the church? Have you any idea why Noel cut out like that?"

She shook her head. "He was going along fine with his eulogy, and then he wound it up in an awful hurry, it seemed to me."

"And slipped out the side door and left. Now what triggered that, I wonder?"

Carrie said, "When did Jeanette leave, did you notice?"

"No, but it was early in the ceremony, I think." Ben leaned forward to say, *"Inspecteur Foch, à quelle heure Mlle Melton est-elle departe de la chapelle?"*

"Pardon?" The inspector tipped his head like a deaf man, moving his lips to follow Ben's tortured pronunciation.

"Never mind, Ben," said Carrie. "The point is, Noel couldn't have seen her leave because she sat at the back. Then while he was speaking he suddenly noticed her absence and lit out after her."

"Do you think we'll find them here? Alive, that is?"

They had reached La Rêverie, and Inspector Foch was turning into the driveway. He nodded triumphantly into the mirror, then stepped out of the car and hurried to open the door for Carrie.

The drive was nearly filled with cars, apparently parked under Sergeant Clement's direction, for he immediately came over to move the Peugeot to a better spot.

He climbed in, then twisted in the seat to pull a letter from his hip pocket. "One moment, Monsieur!" he called after Ben, who had started for the house. "I have a letter for Mlle Melton. If you do not mind to give it to her..."

Half out of the car, the sergeant smiled apologetically as Ben turned back. "It arrive when everyone was in church, but when she came home I forgot it."

"Mlle Melton came home early, *n'est ce pas?*" Ben took the letter and added, "And Monsieur Wright *aussi*. Tell me, Sergeant Clement, did they come together?"

"No, Monsieur, first the lady. I see her, but she did not see me." Sergeant Clement glanced at Inspector Foch for approval. "It was later for Monsieur Wright."

"And did he see you?" Carrie asked it with a teasing smile, as if they were playing a game.

"*Oui,*" replied the sergeant, grinning into her eyes. "But he did not speak, so I did not. He went in very quietly, to surprise, I think." The sergeant shrugged. "So once again I forgot the letter!"

"Very understandable," said Ben. "I'll give it to Mlle Melton."

He and Carrie turned and started for the house once more.

ELEVEN

In her own room Jeanette scanned the first pages of Noel's manuscript:

"…then I will ask Charles Tremont to come along. And strongly suggest that his associates should not be told of the meeting." Marc Mielmont smiled, his face lighting up with what appeared to be innocent pleasure. "That means, as you know, Robert, that not only will his colleagues be informed, they will be provided with a transcript of the proceedings."

"I'll see that Yannick makes that easy to obtain. He must also place a large block of shares on the market that morning, wouldn't you say? Or the day before?" Robert de Laine was smiling too as he poured cognac from a crystal decanter into the glass Marc Mielmont held in his hand.

"I think the preceding day is the time for the stock offering. Give them time to develop as many conflicting theories as possible." Marc Mielmont sipped from his glass, then sighed and got to his feet. "If you don't mind, Robert, I'll add soda to my cognac; a sin, I know, but I must coddle my fragile digestion these days."

Robert jumped up, his face filled with concern for his friend. "Let me get it for you," he said, "or perhaps, Marc, you should have nothing. We are both under a strain just now; I feel it myself."

"Thank you. I can still handle a drop of cognac, I should hope. And if you're worried about my heart, let me assure you I have no intention of popping off until we've completed our current undertaking. I haven't enjoyed anything so much since we took over International Cosmic, and that was almost twenty years ago."

Focusing her copier on the page, Jeanette pressed a button, then moved the page aside to disclose the next:

"When we were young and fresh," added Robert de Laine.

"And greedy. There's nothing to equal the greed of the young, is there, Robert? I miss it sometimes, do you? The hunger for more than money: for power, for love, for the thrill of the game."

"I still have it. I've hung on to it carefully, because the greed, as you call it—I think of it as a drive, an energy—is more important than money or power or even..." Robert de Laine stopped, and Mielmont saw that his face had taken on a look of naked sorrow. "I was about to say, more important than the possession of a deeply loved woman, but in my case that would not be true."

Marc Mielmont turned away from the emotion in de Laine's face. He walked to the hearth, where a few embers still smoldered from the fire they had lit earlier in the evening. The tall clock in the far corner of the room sounded its silvery chime and, listening, Mielmont counted to eleven with one part of his mind while with another he fought the anger that rose in him whenever he allowed himself to contemplate the treachery of Carole de Laine.

Drawing a deep breath, he swung around and began, "Robert, I know you are unable to look beyond your passion and grasp the reality of Carole's intentions. But as your trusted advisor—more important, your closest friend..."

He stopped. Robert de Laine was watching him with the dutiful attention of a bored but courteous listener. A wall had gone up in his mind, the impenetrable barrier that shielded him from an awareness he could not tolerate.

As if his friend had not spoken, de Laine said, "It's time to bring Yannick into this, wouldn't you say, Marc?"

Marc Mielmont nodded, then crossed the room to set his glass on the boulle cabinet where drinks were made. Robert pressed a button on his desk and stood for a moment frowning down at the slim leather folder that contained the agenda for the most ambitious undertaking of his career.

"Let me just say, Marc, that I appreciate your concern for me. But you must understand that I can't talk about Carole with anyone, least of all with you." He looked up then, and on his face Marc Mielmont saw the expression of candor that had drawn him to Robert years ago when they had first met.

Robert went on, "I don't want you to think I'm an idiot, though; you have too much invested in me for that. So I'll tell you this much: I have set a plan in motion that will take care of your worries. If it succeeds, that is. If it doesn't, your funds will not be affected, only mine."

"And you, of course, feel confident you can make another fortune if you have to." Suddenly Mielmont felt choked with resentment. Against his will, the piquant face of Kay Tourette flashed into his mind. If Robert had confided his plan to anyone it would be Kay, for it was clear that as she grew to maturity he took increasing delight in her keenly perceptive mind. Since childhood she had brought lightness and laughter into his life, and as his own hopes for children had dwindled, he had come to love her as a daughter. Marc imagined himself the only person, however, who guessed that Robert had also begun to look upon her as his heir. He placed the blame for that squarely on Carole and her selfish vanity. If she had given Robert a child he would have kept his empire secure against encroachment by any outsider, however talented, however winning.

Silence fell while the two men faced each other in the dim, elegantly furnished room. Between them stretched the weight of their shared years, like a length of priceless fabric.

Robert de Laine said slowly, "I can make another fortune, or ten; it isn't important. I can never make another friend like you, Marc. Please trust me."

Before Marc Mielmont could reply there was a gentle knock on the door. Robert de Laine did not speak or move, however, but kept his eyes on Mielmont's face until some unspoken signal passed between them. The tension left him then, and he turned away saying, "Come in, Yannick."

The heavy, polished door opened silently and Yannic de Laine entered the room, glancing from his brother to Mielmont with his usual defensive air, as if he had come armed with excuses for any accusations they might make.

Watching Robert de Laine, Marc Mielmont sensed the discouragement he felt each time he recognized Yannick's envy and suspicion. Though there were only four years between them, Yannik had no understanding of his older brother; he knew only that on the day Robert returned from his years of self-imposed exile he was cloaked in an aura of power and mystery that left the twenty-five-year-old Yannick permanently dumbfounded.

The brother he had carried in his mind was like those of his friends: alternately bullying and protective. Yannick had looked up to Robert, but he had not felt the overwhelming, crippling awe inspired by the returned adventurer. He longed to have Robert tell him everything that had happened, but any reminiscences were brief and sketchy, leaving the younger man with more questions than, it soon became apparent, would ever be answered.

A CAUTIOUS KNOCK sounded on her door, and Jeanette felt her heart leap up in fear that it might be Noel. She wasn't ready; he hadn't given her enough time.

The knock was repeated, then the door slowly opened and Lila Baines peered into the room. Her lively brown eyes were wide with concern as she said, "Sorry, Jeanette, but we're all worried about you. Are you all right? Can I bring you something to eat?"

Desperately trying to remember why her health should be a matter of interest, Jeanette replied, "Of course I'm all right, Lila. I'm perfectly fine."

She was sitting at a table placed before the window, and when she heard Lila's knock some instinct had made her place the copier beside her on the seat of the chair. As Lila came into the room she carefully shifted her body to hide it.

"Well, you looked pretty shaky at the church, and then when we found you'd left right after the service started..."

"Oh, of course you wondered. But it was just business. I'd no sooner gotten to the church when I remembered that today was the deadline for an important piece I had to phone in." Jeanette shook her head helplessly. "The time difference—I never get used to it."

On Lila's face, guileless as a Girl Scout's, disbelief shone forth as clearly as if she had called Jeanette a liar.

She said, "What, after all these years? Well, anyway, I'm glad you're OK."

With the door open they could hear the hum of voices from below, mingled with the clink of ice and the hurrying footsteps of Marie and her helpers.

Jeanette said, "I'm coming down in a few minutes. I hope I'm not being rude."

Lila shrugged. "Most of them don't know you're here. But I imagine Millie could use some help." She was peering curiously at the manuscript stacked on the table. "Looks like a long article. What's it about?"

As she approached for a closer look, Jeanette gathered up the pages and slipped them into a manila envelope.

She smiled up at Lila and said, "It needs a lot more work before anyone sees it. But you're right, I should be helping Millie, so I'll pull my face together and come right down."

"Good idea. Maybe you can do something about those blasted policemen. The inspector follows me around like a puppy."

Jeanette laughed. "He has designs on you, Lila, and who can blame him?"

"Oh, God, what a grotesque idea!"

Lila departed, leaving Jeanette fuming with irritation. She would have to go downstairs and waste valuable time making small talk; there was no way out of it.

She pulled a suitcase out from under her bed, opened it, and placed the manuscript and copier inside, then locked it and pushed it back.

Five minutes later she strode onto the terrace, where people stood in the sunshine drinking wine and eating food brought from the buffet set out in the dining room.

Margo Honeywell called to her from where she sat on the stone steps leading to the garden. The Marchands were with her, and Sonny Devere was dragging a rickety garden chair across the lawn to join them.

Jeanette took a glass of wine from the table, and as she turned away to join her friends came close to colliding with Ben Porter, who held a plate of food in each hand.

"I've been looking for you for hours," he said, peering around for a spot to put down the plates. "Sergeant Clement gave me a letter for you. Here, it's in my pocket." He lifted his right elbow, and Jeanette plucked an envelope from his blazer pocket.

"Thanks, Ben," she said. She glanced at the return address. "La Hospitaliere de Ste. Jeanne. Probably another charity appeal. Would you give it to Millie, Ben? She's in charge of the paperwork now." She slid the letter back into Ben's pocket and turned away. Sonny Devere would not be likely to stay for lunch.

"He said it came by messenger." As Jeanette began threading her way to the steps, Ben attempted to follow, awkwardly juggling his burden of food.

"I guess they're desperate," Jeanette said over her shoulder as she slipped past a knot of chattering guests. Ben gave up and went in search of Carrie.

> *. . . and because it has been very disturbing for Mrs. Rowan, I must ask you to come and advise her about what to do with this manuscript, or whatever it is. Mrs. Rowan's mental health is precarious, the slightest stress overwhelms her, and she has not had a moment's peace since receiving her legacy, if that is the proper name for it. The mention of Charles Melton's name is enough to send her into a fit of weeping; still, she will discuss the manuscript with no one but his bona fide representative.*
>
> *Therefore I beg you to come as soon as possible and clarify this matter as best you are able.*
>
> *Sincerely yours,*
> *Anne Rouffet,*
> *Nursing Staff,*
> *La Hospitaliere de Ste. Jeanne*
> *Eze-Village*

Millicent Girard looked up from the letter in her hand. "So there is another section of the manuscript," she said, "and he sent it to Celia Rowan. That is so touching . . ."

"You mean it's a touch!" Jeanette Melton exploded. "The woman is planning to hold us up; it's perfectly obvious. Give me that letter, Millie."

Imperiously Jeanette reached out for the letter, but instead of giving it to her Millie said, "Just a minute, Jeanette. If Celia Rowan has part of the manuscript it's because Melton wanted her to have it. Our responsibility is to explain to her that those pages may be of great value some day."

"But she's crazy. Of course the nurse wouldn't say so, but why else would she be in that place?" Again Jeanette reached for the letter. "Come on, Millie, let me read that thing again. It was addressed to me, after all."

They sat in a shaded corner of the terrace while Marie and her hired helpers cleared away the glasses and plates and crumpled napkins used by the luncheon guests. Though it was only three in the afternoon, it felt like midnight to Millie. Her head was throbbing from the wine she'd drunk, and she was in no condition to deal with strong personalities. She glanced at Ben Porter for help as Jeanette took the letter from her fingers.

Clearly Ben was itching to get his own hands on the suddenly fascinating piece of mail. He jumped up from his chair and paced restlessly while Jeanette studied the letter. "Will one of you tell me about this Celia Rowan?" he said. "What did she have to do with Charles Melton?"

"Ah, that's a good question," Jeanette muttered. Her mind was teeming as she tried to work out a way to get Celia Rowan's pages for herself. It was no help to realize that it would have been easy if she had taken the letter when Ben tried to give it to her. The rest of them might never have known a sixth section of the manuscript existed.

Millie said, "All we can do is speculate, Ben, but I think Celia Rowan could have turned the tide for Melton—sexually, that is. He told me once that she was the only woman he ever loved."

Jeanette looked up. "I heard the same thing from my mother. She said Celia Rowan broke his heart, and that's why he turned into a 'fairy,' as she called it—whispered it, I should say. Mother was so horrified she wouldn't let me anywhere near him. I never met Uncle Charles till after she died."

"But she must have been proud to be the sister of Charles Melton, the great author."

"She was torn between pride and embarrassment. You can imagine, in a small town . . . it amused me a lot when I was old enough to understand." Jeanette grinned. "Of course, at college Uncle Charles was a burden. I never got a fair shake in English; the teachers expected me to be a genius too."

"There was a good deal of mystery about Celia Rowan," Millie said. "When their affair ended Melton disappeared for a couple of years. He wasn't famous yet, so nobody noticed at the time, but his biographers have never been able to account for that period.''

"What period?"

Noel Wright stepped onto the terrace, followed by Carrie.

Ben beckoned to her, saying, "Come and sit, Carrie. There's been an interesting development."

Noel stood blinking at them in the sunlight, looking, with his pale skin, like some antediluvian creature stepping out of its cave. Jeanette studied him with a quizzical smile forming on her lips; then she rose and sauntered over to him, dangling the letter in her hand.

"Remember Celia Rowan, Noel?" she drawled. "It seems she's practically a neighbor of ours—though not in the best of health, apparently."

"What are you talking about?" Noel took the letter and rapidly scanned the lines, pursing his lips and slowly shaking his head as he read. He finished and looked up to meet Jeanette's level gaze.

He said slowly, "You and I must go and see this woman, Jeanette, and make it clear to her that she has no claim on Charles's estate, none whatsoever."

"*I* must go and see her. Her letter was addressed to me, so I'll take care of it." Jeanette glanced at her watch. "I suppose it's too late to go today."

Noel's expression did not change, but his voice held a steely ring as he said, "I will call the nursing home and ask permission to visit Celia Rowan tomorrow. I would like you to come along, Millicent, as well as Jeanette. Your interests are very much involved here."

For a moment he stood watching Jeanette, waiting for her reaction, and when she gave a helpless shrug and said, "Oh very well, Noel, I suppose that's the best way," he turned abruptly and strode into the house.

MARGO HONEYWELL answered her telephone on the first ring. She was about to leave for cocktails at the Delaneys', who were entertaining a visiting American novelist, and she had promised to arrive on time and dine with them later at La Reserve.

At Jeanette Melton's first words, however, she regretfully gave up all thoughts of *loup en croute* or *jarret de veau à la menagere* and began composing an excuse for the Delaneys.

"Whatever you're doing tonight, cancel it," Jeanette ordered crisply, "and that goes for tomorrow morning as well. I'll be there in twenty minutes to explain—unless Noel locks me in my room."

"And just why would he do that? Have you been naughty?"

"Yes, actually. And had the bad luck to get caught. I don't think he'll go that far, though, especially if I promise to come right home after I keep my long-standing date to have drinks with you."

"Well then, I don't have to cancel my plans, just tell them I'll be a bit late." Mentally Margo re-placed herself in the elegant dining room of La Reserve.

"Right, but listen, Margo, I've just had a thought. Noel has reason to keep an eye on me for the next twenty-four hours. He just may decide to come along and chaperone. If he does . . . let me think . . ."

"Noel is expected where I am, at the Delaneys'." Margo paused, then said, "Where are you calling from, Jeanette?"

"Don't worry. I'm on Uncle Charles's line, but I can't stay long. If I suddenly start talking business jargon it's because dear Noel has looked in to see if I'm all right."

"Can you give me a tiny clue as to what this is all about?"

"I can't take time to spell it all out, so here's what I'll do if Noel insists on coming with me: I'm going to write you a note, explaining, and put it in an envelope with some papers you may need in the morning. I'll wrap it up with . . . what? Think fast, Margo."

"How about that beach towel you borrowed from me the other day?"

"I did? Oh, of course. I remember, now that you mention it. I'll see you shortly—*alone,* with luck!"

They hung up, and after a moment of silent speculation Margo dialed the Delaneys' number.

TWELVE

THE VILLAGE OF EZE perches on a mountaintop all its own, commanding a magnificent view of the surrounding hills and the blue Mediterranean far below. From a distance the town resembles a child's sand castle punctuated with the deep green of fir trees and the rusty tones of ancient tiled roofs. It is reached by a narrow road carved into the rock in a spiral that ends at the town square. On the steep slope beyond the square stand ancient stone buildings, so tightly clustered that the narrow lanes between them must be traversed on foot.

The lanes are paved with uneven stones and centered with a smoother strip of bricks to carry off rain water. They climb and angle between the old houses, many of which are now used as shops selling ceramics and paintings by local artists and the printed cotton fabrics and pungent herbs of Provence. The buildings have arched wooden doors set into their facades, some reached by stone steps on which stand pots of growing herbs. Grapevines finger their way around niches and passageways and wood-shuttered windows. Tiny gardens are tucked into every available space: the bend of a stairway, the well-space behind a fountain, the angle of a wall. There is whimsy in an iron torchère leaning from the entrance to an *auberge,* in the red-and-yellow cock painted on a wooden door, in the round, staring eyes and plump breasts of a statue, suggesting that the occasionally besieged inhabitants retained a sense of humor.

Near the top, on a ledge facing the sea, there is a charming inn with a vaulted, wood-beamed tap room and a porticoed terrace where huge pots of oleander surround a small swimming pool. Not far away, a Romanesque church with a tall, square steeple looks inland toward a panorama of

tree-strewn hills dotted with the white stucco houses and
terraced gardens of small farms.

After World War II one of the larger farms was turned
into a nursing home, La Hospitaliere de Ste. Jeanne, spe-
cializing in the treatment of patients with chronic nervous
diseases. The facility's main building peers over the valley
from a narrow shelf of rock. One-story wings have been
added on terraced levels like those of the surrounding
vineyards, producing the effect of a rustic retreat rather
than a sanitarium.

At three o'clock on the afternoon following Paul Clifford's memorial service, Noel Wright pulled the black
Mercedes into the graveled parking area. He climbed out
and opened the rear door for Millie as Jeanette stepped out
of the front passenger seat. Then, as they approached the
entrance, where a small brass plate bore the name *La Hospitaliere de Ste. Jeanne,* he could be seen to draw himself
up defensively.

Noel preferred to have nothing to do with hospitals. If he
recognized their existence it was as a repository for everything that repelled him: sickness, mutilation, nasty smells.
He would have liked to flick away such frightening re-
minders of mortality with the silk handkerchief he wore in
his blazer pocket.

La Hospitaliere should be better than most such places,
he told himself, for it was unquestionably expensive; the
delicate sensibilities of Celia Rowan would demand the
highest possible level of care.

Indeed, he failed to detect even a faint trace of unpleasantness in the atmosphere as they were shown to a small
salon to wait while the receptionist confirmed their ap-
pointment. The director of the sanitarium, a thin, dark man
with a nose that appeared as finely tuned as Noel's, then
joined them for "a brief chat," as he put it. His first words
made it clear that visitors were carefully screened.

"I gather none of you is related to Mrs. Rowan." He
smiled, not wishing to sound accusing. "But you are good
friends, perhaps?"

"In a way."

"Not exactly."

Noel and Jeanette spoke together, then stopped, and with assumed courtesy Jeanette deferred to Noel.

"Miss Melton is the niece of the late Charles Melton, the author. Surely you are familiar with his work?" The director nodded, and Noel went on, "Miss Girard and I were his close associates, as at one time was Celia Rowan. That would be a good number of years ago, you understand."

"Yes, I see."

"Yesterday Miss Melton received a letter from Mrs. Rowan's nurse requesting that she retrieve some papers sent to Mrs. Rowan by the executors of Charles Melton's estate."

Millie said, "Do you have the letter with you, Noel?"

"I brought it along, yes." Noel took the letter from his pocket and handed it to the director. "It seems Mrs. Rowan was disturbed by the strange nature of this legacy—that's what it is, you see—and we felt obliged to explain it to her. If that is possible."

"Pages of manuscript, are they? How interesting. And I should think any writings of Melton's would have great value." The director's expression was gently questioning.

Jeanette shrugged. "The value is mainly sentimental," she said, "since the manuscript is incomplete—merely a fragment of an unpublished novel. We all have such bits of my uncle's work. In their present form they are quite worthless."

The director sat in silence for a moment, staring at the letter in his hand; then he said, "Mrs. Rowan's condition is rather difficult to describe. She fits into no single category of mental illness, which is not surprising considering her complex nature and brilliant mind."

Jeanette bent forward eagerly. "I always wondered what sort of woman she was. She apparently had an enormous effect on my uncle. He was madly in love with her and . . ."

Noel interrupted. "We have no proof of that, Jeanette; rather the contrary, I should say."

"You never heard my mother's stories, Noel. She was convinced that Celia Rowan was the only woman Uncle

Charles ever wanted. She was so beautiful and fascinating she spoiled him for any other."

"A romantic theory, but one that hardly holds water, I'm afraid. You were aware of your uncle's proclivities, were you not?" Noel's voice was full of scorn, but an underlying tremor suggested some deeper emotion. The director glanced at him curiously.

Jeanette snapped, "Don't treat me like a child, Noel." Then, seeing the director's keen gaze turn to her, she smiled apologetically. "Mr. Wright and I are like brother and sister, aren't we, darling?"

"I'm afraid so." Noel managed a brief chuckle. "But we're basically in agreement. That's why we have come. We feel, all three of us, an obligation to reassure Mrs. Rowan about these manuscript pages. If you think best we could keep them for her."

"Let me speak to her nurse before we decide anything," the director replied, rising to his feet. "I'll call her now from my office, if you'll excuse me."

He left the room, closing the door behind him, and Millie whispered, "Do you two think this is the place to air your differences? I'll be surprised if we're allowed anywhere near Celia Rowan today."

Noel looked at her in surprise. "Why, Millie, you sound rather agitated yourself."

"I've wanted to meet this woman ever since I first heard about her. I have a feeling she is crucial to any real understanding of Melton." Wearing a faint smile of apology, she added, "Sorry. I didn't realize I felt so strongly."

The door opened and the director entered the room, but instead of sitting down he grasped the back of his chair and looked around at them with an expression of bewilderment.

"I don't quite understand what is taking place here," he said carefully, "but it seems that Celia Rowan has had another caller today: a woman who called herself Jeanette Melton." He fixed his eyes on Jeanette, who sat rigidly staring back. "She was admitted after identifying herself to the receptionist."

"But that's impossible," Jeanette whispered huskily.

Noel looked stunned. He was stammering as he said, "You never left the house this morning, I know that."

"Then it was an imposter, someone carrying Jeanette Melton's credentials."

Millie said, "Jeanette, are you missing anything? Look and see," but Jeanette had already begun searching through her handbag.

"Everything seems to be here," she said. She held up her passport, then pulled out her wallet to display her driver's license. "I can't imagine . . ."

The director's face was solemn as he continued, "I understand the visit was cut short because Mrs. Rowan became overexcited. When the woman left, however, she took with her the pages of manuscript Mrs. Rowan had received from Charles Melton's estate. Mrs. Rowan was then given a sedative. I'm afraid you will not be able to see her today."

"MARGO? HOW COULD SHE possibly pass herself off as Jeanette? There was a passport, remember, with a photograph. No, a new element has been added to the puzzle."

Noel looked white and exhausted, alarmingly so to Millie, who got up to pour him a fresh cup of tea, then added milk and stirred it for him as if he were an invalid.

"Thank you, Millicent," he breathed, summoning a wan smile. "The strain is beginning to tell, I'm afraid."

Carrie said, "Celia Rowan was a new element too. A figure from Melton's past, that's who you have to look for."

"There was no other woman he cared about." Noel was vehement; the tea had energized him. "Celia Rowan was absolutely the only one. By the time I met him, Melton was well recovered from that brief episode and had found his true affinity."

Ben said, "You've gone into this quite thoroughly with Jeanette, haven't you, Noel?"

Noel made an explosive sound that might have started as a chuckle. "You might say so, Porter. I'm afraid she was in tears when we finished, and Jeanette Melton is no weakling, as you may have observed.''

"And Margo? Have you questioned her?''

"Margo was as astonished as the rest of us. I know her very well, and I'm certain her reaction was genuine.''

Ben said, "You know, it really doesn't matter who took Celia Rowan's manuscript.''

"What are you saying, Ben?''

Noel spoke up. "Let me see if you're thinking what I am—that there can be only one of two outcomes to this crazy puzzle Melton has contrived. The entire manuscript may be assembled by the most enterprising of the heirs—but that will be impossible without my pages, which are safely locked up, and yours, Millie, which may already be in the possession of that person.'' He looked around at their intent faces. "So it doesn't matter who performs this task of gathering; he or she can't succeed without coming to me.''

Millie said, "What is the other possible outcome, Noel?''

"Why, obviously, that the novel is never put together at all. We all go to our graves with our three or four chapters, and Melton's final work is lost to the world.''

"Unless *your* heirs do a better job.'' Ben grinned at Noel. "You may be handing them a fortune, tax-free.''

Noel looked insulted. "I suppose you're implying that our heirs will be cleverer than we are? Thank you very much, Ben, but you haven't met my pudding-faced nephew.'' He sighed. "One of the most wrenching things about departing this earth will be the certainty of enriching that little toad.''

Carrie laughed in delight. "Your heirs couldn't be smarter, Noel, but they might manage to join forces if it meant making a fortune; that's more than you've all been able to do.''

Millie said, "Is it too late, Noel? I would be willing.''

"But you have nothing to offer now, have you, Millie? And whoever stole your pages and Paul's can never come forward without being accused of Paul's murder.''

"Unless his murder is solved.''

Noel looked startled. "Of course there is that possibility," he said.

Ben said, "Carrie and I are getting an inkling about what you call Melton's 'crazy puzzle.' We think the manuscript is loaded with clues that will explain a lot about Melton and his relationships with all of you."

Carrie said, "Look at the name of his hero, Robert de Laine. In French *laine* means 'wool.'" She uncrossed her legs and bent forward to peer into Noel's face. "What is melton cloth, Noel?"

"Why, it's a wool fabric," he said slowly. "You mean de Laine represents Charles Melton? What a bizarre notion!"

"With every page of the manuscript it gets less bizarre." Ben got up and crossed the room to where he had tossed his jacket on a bench. He took his sheaf of notes from the pocket and brought them to the group around the tea table.

"Jeanette let us read her pages, and Millie described what happened in hers," he said, spreading his notes before him on the table. "And so far Carrie and I have noticed two striking parallels, besides the names de Laine and Melton. Robert de Laine leaves his country to recover from a disastrous love affair and stays away for two years or more. Yesterday Millie mentioned that Charles Melton did the same thing, for the same reason."

"Only Melton's lover was a woman," Carrie put in. "That difference bothers me."

Millie said slowly, "Both men became hugely successful, de Laine as a financier and Melton as one of the world's most renowned authors. Another parallel."

"And how about this one? Remember when you told us de Laine has a disloyal secretary?" Millie nodded and Ben stabbed the page of notes with his finger. "Her name is Rocher, right? Helene Rocher. Well, in French, as you two know very well, *Rocher* means 'cliff.' What was the name of Melton's secretary?"

Noel said slowly, "Paul Clifford. I see what you're getting at, Ben, but it could well be coincidence."

With a glance at her watch, Millie got up from her chair. She said, "Hank will be calling soon; I can't wait to tell him about this. He'll love it!"

"You're reaching for it, all of you," Noel said wearily. "Why would Melton make a disloyal female secretary the counterpart of a loyal male one? Why would he do any of this? To tell us what?"

"Was Paul Clifford always loyal to Melton?" Ben saw a flicker of something in Noel's expression that warned him not to press. "I'm not implying...that is, I know you and Paul were not friends in recent years, Noel. Perhaps he once let Melton down. You may not want to tell us, of course."

"If Paul was ever less than faithful it was a long time ago. There was perhaps one lapse in judgment over a twenty-year period. That's all I am prepared to say, except that Charles never found out; I'm certain of that."

The last words were barely audible. As Noel's voice faded into silence they all looked away from the pain so evident in his face.

After a moment Ben said, "You ask why Melton would do this, and I say we have to remember what he was: a wordsmith. Language was his life; his playthings were words, not golf clubs or tennis racquets. His greatest pleasure was putting words together in original ways."

"And what could be more original than this?" Carrie pulled her glasses off impatiently. Her blue eyes shone as she glanced eagerly from Millie's face to Noel's. "He's constructed a fabulous puzzle, and whoever solves it makes a fortune!"

"Noel, what Carrie and I need now is something I'm almost afraid to ask for: a look at your pages of the manuscript."

Noel immediately began shaking his head stiffly from side to side, but before he could speak Carrie said, "Please don't refuse, Noel." She rose and went over to sit beside him. Taking his hand in hers, she said, "I know you're a man who despises violence, so I don't have to be told that you were horrified by Paul's murder. I also have a feeling..." Her voice dropped to a husky whisper. "I sense in spite of whatever came between you, Paul was your dear friend. You lived and worked together for a long time; you must feel his loss very deeply. Surely you want to find the answer as much as we do.''

Carrie stopped. Noel's face was working as he struggled to control his feelings. His eyes were wet, and as he gently drew his hand from Carrie's and got to his feet, he pulled a handkerchief from his trouser pocket.

"You're right, of course," Noel mumbled, dabbing at his eyes. "We must work together to solve this terrible crime. I'll be glad to do anything…" He paused to blow his nose. "Come with me, Ben. I'll get the manuscript for you now."

THIRTEEN

CARRIE PORTER climbed out of the pool at the Hôtel des Fleurs and reached for the beach towel she'd left on her chaise, being careful to avoid dripping on the envelope beside it. Her eyes crinkled in a smile as she read the names printed in pencil on the back: *Terry Porter,* and beside it in larger, less uniform letters: *Brooke,* followed by a giant X.

Her longing for her children was at that moment a physical sensation, like pain or hunger. Only three more days, she thought, and as she picked up the letter to read it again she could not keep from humming a buoyant little tune, although she'd been keeping quiet for the last hour so Ben could concentrate.

He looked up from Noel's manuscript and smiled at her; in his eyes, shadowed by the brim of his rough straw hat, she saw complete awareness of her mood. He reached up to squeeze her hand.

"Getting homesick?" he said.

"I've been homesick ever since we got here," she said, "even though it's the most beautiful place in the world."

"And possibly the most interesting." Ben clutched at the pages that were about to slide off his lap. "I'm going to have trouble leaving if we haven't found any answers. How about you?"

"I feel kind of schizoid about it; I'm crazy to get home to the kids, but, like you, I'll hate to leave so many questions unanswered."

"Well, it's your turn to read this, while I think."

"Think about lunch, while you're about it."

"I don't have to; it's all planned. Lobster salad followed by Charentais melon."

Carrie had settled on her chaise and was applying sun lotion to her arms and legs. "You know what I really want, don't you?"

"Yes, but you can't have a hamburger till we get home. We agreed on that." Ben stood up and handed her the pages of manuscript. "Here, do your homework. I'm going for a swim."

She watched him stroll to the end of the pool, noting that he barely glanced at the half-naked women he passed on the way. Either Riviera life had inured him to the sight of bare flesh or, more likely, he was totally caught up in the puzzle presented by Charles Melton's unpublished novel.

She picked up the manuscript and began to read.

"Don't worry about Yannick; he will do whatever we say, as long as we convince him it is to his advantage."

Carole de Laine put down her hairbrush and began to wind her lustrous blond hair into a skein which she would pin up in a French twist. Helene Rocher watched, fascinated, as the shapely, red-tipped fingers flashed skillfully among the golden strands. Carole's satin dressing gown slipped from her shoulders as she worked. She paused and was about to pull it back, when her eyes met Helene's, reflected in the looking glass with an expression of avid curiosity.

Carole slowly smiled and instead of gathering the robe around her body, allowed the folds of satin to slide to her waist, exposing her naked breasts. In the mirror she saw Helene's fair skin redden as her eyes traced the flawless symmetry of the body so casually, so insolently, displayed.

Feast your eyes, you pathetic, envious creature, thought Carole; though I can see how you despise me for my coarseness. See why the man you worship worships me—vulgar, unworthy me. You're longing to tell him what you know, but you don't dare because he would throw you out; it would be the end for you. Robert de Laine loves me utterly, blindly. Beside that adoration your cleverness amounts to nothing.

Helene said, "You are an amazing woman, Carole." Then, as she saw the smile in the mirror broaden with satisfaction, she added, "I don't mean amazingly beautiful, though that is certainly true; I mean you are extraordinary in your ruthlessness. You see that gorgeous body as a tool, don't you? You use it to manipulate your husband with about as much feeling as you use a key to unlock a door."

"Or a safe deposit box. Isn't that comparison more apt?" The smile had stiffened; the wide blue eyes had lost their self-contented glow. Carole de Laine pulled her robe up over her shoulders and tied the sash at her waist.

Glancing at her watch, she said, "Now let's go over it again. The board meets at ten next Tuesday, right?" Helene nodded, and Carole continued, "Two million shares will be offered over the preceding three days. You'll have to give me the list of how they're broken down; I can't possibly memorize that."

Helene's eyes filled with alarm. "You know how I feel about giving you anything in writing."

Stiffly perched on the edge of a fragile boudoir chair, Helene in her black gabardine blazer and pants might have been an actor who had wandered onto the wrong set.

"For God's sake, you must know you can trust me by now!" Carole had tossed the satin robe onto the foot of her bed and was fastening her bra. "In a week it'll be all over. We'll be rich and, best of all, independent. Don't lose your nerve at this point."

"It's Claude who worries me. I know he's watching me, and probably you too. Haven't you noticed how he's around all the time? He used to be too busy to pay any attention to us." Helene Rocher got to her feet abruptly, tipping the little French chair off balance.

Carole stepped over and caught the chair before it fell. She said, "Honestly, Helene, you may be fantastic on the tennis court, but you're like a Great Dane in my bedroom.''

"It's true; I'm sorry." Swallowing her discomfort, Helene watched Carole stride to the mirrored door of her closet and pull it open. "You're right, I do seem to be losing my nerve. At the same time, I think you're entirely too sure of yourself. I can't seem to make you see that Claude Dépouille is a greater threat than Yannick could ever be. And he has Kay on his side, remember that.''

"Kay, yes. I agree she's one to be watched because of her influence on Robert. But Claude Dépouille? He's a self-important joke—bustling around with his lists and ledgers, as if being Robert's major domo were a sacred calling. Certainly the man's efficient; God knows he keeps everything running smoothly, but he has no comprehension of what goes on in the business world.''

From the closet she took a black wool dress with a wide gold zipper running from neck to hem. She unzipped it and pulled it on, saying, "I wear something easy to get on and off when I go to fittings." She grinned at Helene as she pulled up the zipper. "Especially my fittings at Romaine's. Madame is such a perfectionist she makes me try things on over and over.''

Helene Rocher sighed as she ran her fingers through her clipped brown hair. "I wish you wouldn't be flippant, Carole. Come on now, let's go over those figures again.''

She looked around for a place to sit and settled on a brocade hassock, saying, "It would be nice if you had some grown-up furniture in this room instead of all this poufy, movie-set stuff.''

"You sound a little waspish this morning, Helene." Carole was back at the dressing table, bending toward the mirror as she applied mascara. "If I were in your position I think I'd try to be more tactful.''

"My position was a good deal more comfortable before you decided to improve it, thank you. Now can you spare me a few minutes of your valuable time to concentrate on the work at hand? Amalgamated Motors, 45,000; White Industries, 10,000; Cerulean Dye and Chemical, 50,000..."

"Bendorf Capital Management, 100,000; Isotherm International, 25,000. I can reel them off as fast as you can; that's what kills you." Carole had not taken her eyes from the mirror. She put down the mascara and blinked experimentally, then picked up a tiny brush and used it to smooth and separate her lashes.

There was a knock at the bedroom door, then it was pushed open, and a fluffy Lhasa Apso puppy bounded into the room, followed by a long-legged girl dressed in jeans and a thick black sweater.

"Cherie! Tu viens ici! Vite, vite!" the girl ordered, laughing as she scooped up the dog and held it in her arms. "Carole, Robert said you're taking the car, so maybe you could drop me off in midtown." The puppy tried to wriggle free, but the girl tucked up its legs and kissed it on the nose, her long black hair falling over both their faces.

"If that animal makes one spot on my rug..."

Carole was on her feet, her eyes flashing as she examined the pale pink carpet.

"What a knockout dress, Carole!" Clutching the puppy under one arm, the younger girl swept back her hair to gaze at Carole, who was immediately distracted.

Turning to display the figure so spectacularly outlined by her tight, broad-shouldered costume, Carole said, "Praise from Kay is praise indeed. But you might as well erase that covetous gleam; I've only worn the thing once."

"So you can't have it till next week at the earliest," said Helene. She pushed herself up from the hassock and consulted her watch. "Your fitting is at twelve, Carole? You'd better get started."

"I'm ready. Want to come along?"

"No, not unless you need help making decisions,

which I imagine is unlikely."

"I don't anticipate any problem there." Carole walked to the window and pushed aside the filmy curtain to look out at the sky. Seeing that it was filled with rolling gray clouds, she went to her closet, took out a shiny black raincoat, and tossed it over her arm. From a nearby dresser she picked up a black crocodile handbag, opened it to check on the contents, then snapped it shut and strode to the door.

"Give that beast to Helene, Kay, and let's be on our way."

When the two women had left the room Helene closed the door behind them and shut the frantically wiggling dog in the bathroom. Then she picked up the telephone and dialed Madame Romaine to report that Mrs. de Laine was on her way.

In Robert de Laine's study a beep indicated that a message had been recorded by the sophisticated listening device that monitored certain of the household's private telephone lines.

De Laine's face was empty of emotion as he played back the brief message. At the end he turned off the machine and pressed a button on the keyboard beside his telephone.

Speaking into it, he said, "Noon. The usual place."

He released the button and turned his leather chair toward the fireplace and the portrait of his wife that hung above it. Against the painting's shadowy background the contours of her beautiful face appeared three-dimensional. Her red lips curved in a smile that might have conveyed a saintly compassion if not for the mocking glint in the slightly tilted, wide blue eyes.

As he studied the portrait Robert de Laine's own face softened in a look of ineffable sadness. As he had done a thousand times, he searched every brushstroke, looking for what he knew he would not find: a trace, a subtle hint, of tenderness.

His search ended as it always did; he swung his chair around to his desk again, and by the time he faced it, he was once more de Laine of de Laine et Cie, the feared and respected manipulator of fortunes. The other de Laine, the one who vainly yearned for love, had disappeared.

Carrie glanced up to find Ben watching her over the silver-covered dishes that had been brought to their poolside table.

"I didn't hear that arrive," she said.

She marked her page with a paper clip and placed the manuscript in her beach bag, then lifted the cover from her plate. The lobster salad had been arranged on a bed of endive and watercress like a delicate pink-and-white bouquet. Accompanying it was a crystal sauceboat of freshly made mayonnaise, as well as a baguette of bread and a saucer of butter carved into rosebuds.

A bottle of white wine stood in a cooler beside the table, and Ben lifted it out and poured their glasses half full.

"What do you think?" he asked her as he replaced the bottle.

"I think it's the prettiest lunch we've had yet."

"For once I'm not talking about food. I mean the manuscript. Are you getting anything out of it?"

"I'm having fun trying to match up the characters, and I'm beginning to agree that Helene Rocher could represent Paul Clifford, in spite of the difference in sex. Noel did hint at some disloyalty on Paul's part. Still, I find it hard to think of that gentle man as a schemer."

"Me too. I should think any betrayal of Paul's would be quite different from what Helene Rocher is cooking up with Carole. However, if you think about Carole and the person who matches up with her..." Ben peered at Carrie over a forkful of lobster. "Well, come on, who would that be?"

"A woman Melton loved? According to Jeanette, Celia Rowan was the only one."

"Not a woman, Carrie, but someone who might have meant as much to Melton as Carole to de Laine. Think about the title for a minute."

"You're ruining my lunch, do you know that?" Frowning, Carrie took a sip of her wine. "Let's see. *Mirror Image*. That means a reflection of reality."

"And?"

"And what? Stop being enigmatic, Ben. It's extremely irritating."

"An image in a mirror is reversed, isn't that right? So we reverse the sexes, making Helene Rocher stand for Paul Clifford, and Carole de Laine..."

"Carole, de Laine's wife, would represent someone, some man, in a wifely relationship to Charles Melton. That would be... Noel Wright, wouldn't it?"

"Noel—Carol. Christmasy, isn't it?"

Carrie was staring at him across the table. She put down her fork and pushed her sunglasses up into her hair.

She said, "Ben, you may have hit on the key to the whole thing. What are some of the other names? Let's match them up."

She pushed back her chair, preparing to get the manuscript from her beach bag, but Ben stopped her.

"I have the list right here." He took a piece of paper out of his shirt pocket and unfolded it on the table. "In the order of appearance we have: René de Cendre..."

"I'd forgotten about him," Carrie put in.

"Then Carole de Laine, Marc Mielmont, Yannick de Laine, Helene Rocher, Kay Tourette, Claude Dépouille..."

"Marc Mielmont. Let's see, he is Robert de Laine's trusty old advisor and confidant and, I gather, business associate. That takes us right back to Noel."

"Flip it, Carrie; switch the sex."

"Oh, right. That gives us... who? Millie? That doesn't seem right."

"You know our biggest problem, don't you? Linguistics. We've got to get our hands on a French dictionary *tout de suite*!"

"Why? We're surrounded with people who can help." Carrie slid her sunglasses back in place and peered around the deck, looking for their waiter.

Ben said, "I don't know that we want to share our thinking quite as freely as that." He carefully cut a sliver from his translucent wedge of melon and slipped it into his mouth. After a moment he said, "I wonder how places like this get everything at the peak of ripeness; it doesn't work that way for us."

Carrie pushed her plate away and reached across the table for Ben's list of names. She studied it, murmuring the words to herself, then she looked up and said, "Some of these associations may be from Melton's past, have you thought of that? Mielmont, for example, certainly isn't Millie. Maybe he stands for her predecessor."

"That's a possibility."

Carrie said slowly, "There's only one person who can help us—if she's willing. Celia Rowan."

Ben grinned at wife. "I happen to know you've been dying to see that woman ever since she came into this. But she may not be capable of telling us a thing. She's sick and confused, and anyway, I can't imagine why they'd let us question her."

"If they thought we could put her mind at rest about the manuscript they just might."

"I don't know. After yesterday, the director of the place is likely to be extra careful."

"Let's give it a try, Ben. I want to see Eze anyway, and Millie says there's an excellent restaurant. Le Chat d'Or, or something like that. We can have dinner there."

Ben's face brightened. "Right. We'll plan our strategy on the way up." He signaled the waiter to bring their *addition,* then sat back and said thoughtfully, "The lever to use may be the truth, Carrie. We are publishers, after all. And since we've also become acquainted with the other heirs, who could be in a better position to advise Celia Rowan?"

"I have another suggestion. If we ask the concierge to call and say we're coming, they won't have a chance to turn us down."

Ben said, "Same goes for the restaurant—I hope."

FOURTEEN

From Carrie Porter's journal, dated May 16, 1989:

WE DID IT. Ben and I got to meet the legendary Celia Rowan, and even though it's nearly 11:00, and I'm exhausted, I have to put down every detail of our visit before I forget.

We drove up to Eze this afternoon, scheming all the way about how to get in, then found it surprisingly easy, thanks to the fact that the director of La Hospitaliere de Ste. Jeanne had gone out, and the woman in charge was busy admitting a new patient. She readily accepted us as consultants in the matter of Charles Melton's legacy, though to me our credentials seemed pretty vague. She then called Celia Rowan's room to check on her condition and announce us to her nurse.

The nurse turned out to be Anne Rouffet, the one who had written to Jeanette, and she seemed slightly surprised to see us, since as far as she knew Celia Rowan's manuscript was now safely in Jeanette's hands. She was a young woman with a sweet, anxious face, who was obviously afraid we were going to get her patient stirred up again; but we assured her we would do no such thing and had come only to gain our impressions of a famous literary figure. I'm afraid we implied that this was part of the publishing process, along with Ben's desire to do a quick pencil sketch of Mrs. Rowan.

Anne Rouffet seemed intrigued by this idea, though she was quick to say that if the suggestion alarmed Mrs. Rowan it was to be dropped at once. She hoped Mrs. Rowan would cooperate, she said, as she would make a beautiful subject, and she, Anne, would dearly love to have a copy if the drawing turned out well. She turned a skeptical eye on Ben as she said this, almost as if she had seen the wildly abstract portraits he loves to paint, and I stifled the impulse to giggle and assured her that Ben was certain to do a fine job.

We walked down the corridor, our feet making little sound on the rubbery floor, and I noticed that the doors to the patients' rooms were widely spaced and had handsome brass knockers and numerals. We stopped at number twenty-five, and Anne Rouffet looked at us with an expectant smile as she lifted the knocker. Again I had the feeling that she cared for her patient beyond the requirements of duty, and I was so eager to meet the woman who inspired this devotion that when a silvery voice called, "Come in!" I had to restrain myself from bursting into the room.

Instead, Ben and I followed Anne through the door, then stopped when she moved aside, both of us struck by the beauty and strangeness of the scene. The room was high-ceilinged and spacious, its outer wall lined with tall, arched windows that overlooked a stone terrace. Beyond was a garden that shimmered like an emerald in the afternoon sunlight, placing a haze of green on the white surfaces of the room like a wash put on by a watercolorist: green shadows in the folds of a white linen table skirt, a pale hint of green in the sheer muslin canopy hanging over the bed at the far end of the room, firm green strokes in the leaves and stems of the white flowers that stood all around in glass bowls and pitchers.

It was like stepping into a watercolor, especially that first instant when nobody moved, including the occupant of the room, who sat on a small white sofa with her back to the light, so that we could not quite make out her features.

Then Anne introduced us, going to Celia Rowan as she spoke and holding out her hand to help her to her feet. I started to protest that she shouldn't get up for us; then she turned her face to the light and I stopped—not only because of her extraordinary beauty but because it was instantly clear that she was the one in control of the situation, not I.

She said, "I'm delighted to meet you, Carrie Porter, and you, Ben. Please come and sit down and tell me about yourselves."

Her voice had a melodious quality I've heard only a few times, usually on the stage, with an undercurrent of amusement that suggested we should all be careful not to take ourselves too seriously.

I could see that Ben was captivated. He stood so long beaming down into her upturned face that it might have been awkward, except that there was no possibility of awkwardness around this woman. In seconds we were all seated and talking and laughing as if we'd been waiting months to get together, and I'm sure Ben and I were saying anything that popped into our heads just to hear Celia Rowan respond in that entrancing voice.

Ben's idea of sketching her turned out to be just the thing, giving us a chance to question her without seeming impertinent, as if we were on a professional assignment. Of course she understood such procedures very well, having always been a part of the literary world herself, not only through her acquaintances, as it turned out, but as a translator.

"Fetch the Roublais, will you, Anne?" she said. "I'd like the Porters to see the result of my most recent labors."

Anne crossed the room to a wide bookcase and searched the shelves onto which books had been stuffed at every possible angle, spilling over to be piled in stacks on the floor. I saw titles in French, Spanish, Italian, and German as well as English, and asked Celia Rowan if she worked in all those languages.

"I prefer to keep to French," she said, reaching for the thick volume Anne had brought to her. "But this tome—here, feel the weight of it, Carrie—this one nearly undid me. M. Roublais loves to show off by using obscure words. It's probably his fault that I have to stay in this place. Not that I mind, you know," she added, smiling at her nurse. "As long as I have my friend, Anne, to care for me, and this charming room to stay in. It is so like an apartment I once had in the Bois . . ."

Her voice trailed off, and the hand with which she had gestured fell into her lap while she gazed toward the open terrace door. The angle, with her profile outlined by sunlight, would have been difficult for most women of her age; for Celia Rowan it emphasized the perfection of her fine straight nose, high cheekbones, and rounded chin. Her lips curved in a faint smile, and I saw a dimple come and go. Her eyes crinkled, and she turned to us to share the thought that amused her.

"Melton used to visit me in that apartment," she said, "and I'll never forget how impressed he was. He was so young, you know, and Paris was a wonderland to him. Even the creaking of the old floors enchanted him, and he would spin fantasies about the figures who might have worn down those boards: Balzac, Flaubert, Baudelaire, George Sand and Chopin. The building was very old, an *hôtel particulier* that had been converted to flats, and he peopled it as the *salon* of his dreams."

Ben had his drawing pad ready and he said, "Mrs. Rowan, if that position is comfortable for you, it's very nice for my sketch."

"Oh yes, the sketch! Well, remind me if you need to. I'm not terribly good at sitting still."

Her hair was still mainly a deep brown with only a scattering of gray streaks—astonishing for a woman who must have been in her seventies, though some brunettes are lucky that way. Her eyes, set deep in her oval face, were a dark, lustrous brown, almost black, with the warm glints of color you see in an opal or the very richest sort of black velvet. She reminded me of someone, and on the way home I realized it was the actress Claire Bloom, whose beauty has that same combination of strength and allure.

She was slender, I could tell, though her figure was camouflaged by a flowing negligee of soft white crepe, trimly buttoned and belted, with a wide collar and cuffs of lace-edged white satin. On her feet she wore white pumps with flat, tailored bows; her slim fingers were bare except for a gold-and-diamond ring that set blue-red glints flashing when she moved her hands.

I said, "I'd love to hear more about Charles Melton when he was young. Was he very handsome?"

Celia Rowan seemed to have trouble deciding how to answer. "I guess he was handsome," she said finally, "but when people are close to me I don't appraise their looks. Charles was tall and he moved gracefully, and of course he had that well-bred, clean look and he dressed well." She paused. "The main thing about him was his ferocious mental energy. He was animated by it, by his talent, I suppose it was, though none of us realized that at the time."

"Had he started writing when you met?"

"Oh yes, in an amusing way. He was helping to edit a small literary magazine, and he often got so exasperated with the quality of the submissions that he would completely rewrite the pieces instead of patching them up. They'd get so unrecognizable he would have to make up a new name for the author, and he found himself writing under five or six *noms de plume.*"

At this point Anne Rouffet, who had been hovering nearby, interrupted to invite us to have some tea or a glass of wine. We all agreed on tea, and then as I started to ask Mrs. Rowan another question, Anne interrupted again, inquiring about milk, sugar, lemon, etc., in a lot more detail than seemed necessary. Later, of course, I understood what she was trying to do.

Finally she left the room, and I said carefully, "From what other people have said, I gather your romance with Charles Melton was a turning point in his life. Would you mind telling us a little about it?"

"No, I love to talk about Charles. The time when we were lovers was the richest, most exciting chapter of my life. When it ended—when it had to end—I felt bereaved; I don't think I ever recovered. And Charles..." She stopped and turned to face me, and there was so much sadness in her eyes that I felt tears come to my own.

Ben had stopped drawing when she turned, and he quickly flipped to a fresh sheet and began sketching her full face. She paid no attention, however; she was too caught

up in recalling the doomed love affair that I now realized
had been as important to her as it was to Charles Melton.

I said, "What a shame it was, when you clearly meant so
much to each other..."

"That was the reason, my dear. An ordinary love affair
could have run its course. With us there was an intensity, a
desperation..." She threw up her hands, and shards of light
glanced from her diamond. "We never resolved it, but we
never stopped trying. All our letters—thousands of pages,
it must have been, over the years—were attempts to understand what it was between us."

Ben said, "You kept in touch with Melton? I don't think
anyone knows that."

"No, isn't that fun?" She chuckled happily; her eyes
were sparkling with mischief. "We had the best time keeping our correspondence secret. Maybe that's why we kept
it up: we so enjoyed the conniving." She stopped and shook
her head. "No, the truth was, we couldn't do without each
other. We had to share our thoughts, even though it was
impossible to share our lives."

I thought this was the most romantic tale I'd ever heard,
and Ben obviously did too. He had stopped drawing and
was staring at Celia Rowan, transfixed by all the new pos-
sibilties.

He said, "Then you never married?"

"Oh, of course I was married—more than once!" She
was laughing again, as if her marriages were merely part of
the prank she and Melton had played on the rest of the
world. "I had two lovely husbands—one at a time, you
understand—and quite a nice, interesting life, actually. One
of them died, and I divorced the other, but we're still good
friends—better than when we were married."

"Like you and Charles Melton."

"No, nothing in my life was like that; and nothing in
his."

Mrs. Rowan went on to tell us how Melton wrote his first
novel and about the creative agonies she saw him through
during the process. She seemed to love remembering all
this; she became quite animated as she talked and laughed

in her lovely, melodious way. Our interview was doing her so much good I began to wonder if her therapist had thought of the same approach.

Anne came back with the tea tray, and when she had served us she asked Celia Rowan if she felt at all tired. Mrs. Rowan said no, no, she was having a delightful time, but I saw that her hands trembled as she picked up her cup and that her reassuring nod was slightly too emphatic. I was about to say we would leave and hope to come back the next day, when Ben spoke up.

He said, "Mrs. Rowan, I wonder if you read the manuscript pages Melton's lawyer sent to you? That is, maybe you'd rather not say..."

He was faltering because his question had clearly upset Mrs. Rowan. She held out her cup so abruptly that Anne Rouffet jumped to take it; otherwise it would have crashed to the floor.

"I can't talk about that story," Mrs. Rowan said, and her musical voice quavered with what I was amazed to recognize as fear. "That story is dark and false. It was very bad of Charles to tell those lies. It's gone, isn't it, Anne? I don't want to find those pages here anywhere."

Suddenly she was on her feet, and again Anne prevented disaster by quickly moving the tea table out of her way. With her long white skirt swirling, Celia Rowan hurried across the room and began pulling books out of the bookcase and throwing them on the floor, muttering broken phrases in French and English.

Ben and I jumped up, but Anne got to her first. She took her by the shoulders and said, "No, Celia, don't throw your nice books on the floor. Charles will be angry."

Celia Rowan stopped and turned to look at her, and I saw that her eyes were huge and black and that her beautiful face was twisted with anxiety.

"I must find his manuscript, Anne, you know that! I promised to read it. He won't go on till he knows what I think. And he wants to work, he needs to, Anne! I must help Charles with his work!"

"He told me the publisher likes the story, Celia. He wants you to rest now. His letter will come today. Come and lie down now, and when you wake up his letter will be here."

With one arm around her waist, Anne was gently pulling her away from the books, but Celia Rowan suddenly twisted free, a button flying from her robe, and ran to her desk a few feet away. She wrenched a drawer open and bent to rummage through it, searching for something, with her hair tumbling into her face and the front of her robe falling open.

Ben started for her, but Anne called out, "No! Stay back!" and hearing this, Celia Rowan looked up sharply and fixed her eyes on Ben while slowly baring her teeth in a distorted grin.

Ben didn't move, thank God. Mrs. Rowan didn't move either, just stayed bent over the desk with that horrible, challenging leer on her face, until Anne slipped up behind her and something flashed—a hypodermic syringe—and Celia Rowan cried out in rage and then began to tremble, holding stiffly to the desk while she fought the effects of the drug.

It was awful to watch the madness leave her, to be replaced by the most pathetic helplessness. She looked pleadingly at Ben, weakly reaching her hand out to him, then she whimpered softly and slumped into Anne Rouffet's waiting arms.

Afterwards, when Celia Rowan had been put to bed, with an aide called in to keep watch, Anne Rouffet came out to the lounge, where Ben and I were waiting. I think she wanted to assure us that we were not responsible for what had happened, but I knew we were, and I felt ashamed of causing such a lovely woman—possibly the most extraordinary creature I'd ever met—to change in a flash into a disheveled lunatic.

Ben and I were so shocked that we left her room clinging to each other's hands like two children in a fairy tale. We must have looked distraught too, because a nurse came up and suggested we sit down right away and have some hot tea until Mrs. Rowan's nurse could join us. We were only too willing to obey her.

When Anne came in we all embraced like mourners, which we were.

"She was so charming to us..."

"She seemed perfectly rational..."

"I feel so guilty..."

We were whispering; we couldn't talk about it out loud, and yet we had a thousand questions to ask Anne. We wondered, for instance, whether Mrs. Rowan would remember our visit, and Anne assured us that she would. Apparently her mental balance is very precarious, but when her mind functions it's on an extremely high level.

Anne said her intelligence is part of the problem, that in translating she exhausts herself trying to meet her own high standards.

"She attempts to catch every subtlety, every nuance of the author's meaning," she said, "and of course it is draining. So we limit her to what seems a comfortable amount of work. But we also run into trouble if she gets bored, so you can see it's a problem."

Ben said, "I noticed that you promised she'd have a letter from Charles Melton waiting for her. How do you manage that?"

Anne smiled sadly. "I simply produce one out of the hundreds I've collected over the last five years—that's how long Mrs. Rowan has been in my care. I keep them filed in chronological order, so they make some sense, but I don't know what I'll do when they wear out and start to fall apart."

I asked her how she could get away with this if Celia Rowan had such a brilliant mind, and again she gave that regretful smile.

She said, "Mrs. Rowan loses her rationality when it comes to Charles Melton. That tie is so strong that she allows herself to believe he is alive and communicating with her. You should see her face when she's reading one of his letters. She looks like a child on Christmas morning."

Ben said, "I imagine she writes a reply, doesn't she?"

"She starts to," Anne said. "She starts scribbling notes to herself while she reads, and then she sits down at her desk and begins writing furiously. A strange thing has happened though. In the months since Melton has been dead Mrs. Rowan has not finished a single letter to him. She writes for a while, then gets up and wanders away, and that's the end of it. I put everything out of sight, and the subject is not mentioned again."

"But you did tell her when he died?" I was fascinated by the hint of mysticism here.

She said, "Yes, after conferring with her doctor, and we were surprised at how well she took it. It turned out, obviously, that she didn't take it in at all—except perhaps subconsciously."

"And that's why she doesn't finish those letters." Ben sighed, and I could tell that he felt, as I did, that we had discovered a wonderful new friend only to have her snatched away from us.

He had also noticed that poor Anne Rouffet was quite worn out. Though she answered all our questions willingly, without cutting us short, her face was pale and her white uniform suddenly looked too big for her, as if she had shrunk.

We both jumped up and thanked her profusely for her help. Ben said he hoped it wasn't presumptuous to thank her as well for her loving care of Celia Rowan.

He said, "The woman we met today wouldn't exist at all if it weren't for you. I hope you realize how important you are to her."

Anne looked pleased, but she was too tired to smile. She just said, "I'll never leave her," and then we said goodbye and left.

FIFTEEN

THE BLACK POODLE, Finesse, objected to baths on several grounds. Being wet was a condition he enjoyed no more than being cold, and a bath was apt to combine both, with the additional unpleasantness of soap stinging his eyes and making a bitter taste when he licked his muzzle. The only part of it he considered fun was the preliminary chase, when Lila Baines tried out the new strategies she'd devised to catch him. Finesse was clever at sensing an approaching bath, however, and that afternoon, when a certain sound woke him from the nap he was taking beside the open kitchen door of La Rêverie, he instantly stiffened.

It was the sound of water running into the big tin tub; there was no way they could fool him, even by running it slowly to keep the noise down, as they were now doing. He sighed, but lay still, waiting for Lila to come stealthily through the door to grab him. If he had to go through with the experience he might as well have the pleasure of bounding up with a loud bark just as she reached for him.

Falling into the trap, Lila tiptoed across the grass, and as Marie and Sergeant Clement had been standing by to lend a hand, the garden was quickly transformed into a pandemonium of running, calling, barking figures. Finesse was basically a cooperative soul, however, and he allowed them to corner him after only a few minutes' chase.

Standing at the window of the drawing room, Jeanette Melton and Inspector Foch laughed at the sight of Sergeant Clement carrying the big dog across the grass with his long black legs dangling and his muzzle resting resignedly on the policeman's shoulder.

"Poor Finesse, he lost again," said Jeanette, turning away. She looked at her watch and frowned. If the inspec-

tor would only give in, she had a good chance of catching
the evening flight to New York.

But Inspector Foch felt duty bound to examine every
angle of the situation before allowing any resident of La
Rêverie to leave the country. Even though they had agreed
that Jeanette would post a bond to guarantee her return if
it should prove necessary, the inspector required permission from his superior in Nice before granting his own.

He had placed the call, but the man had 'stepped out of
his office,' which Foch was fairly certain meant they must
wait for the end of a leisurely lunch.

In the meantime the inspector also hoped to elicit certain assurances from Noel Wright, who could be expected
to join them at any moment. Inspector Foch shuddered in-
wardly when he thought of Mlle Melton's reaction to that
restriction. Knowing she would not take it well, he had said
nothing about M. Wright, but soon he would appear, and
then...

Jeanette was running out of patience already. "We
agreed that you can't hold me without charges," she said.
"So I don't understand your problem here."

"There has been a murder, Mademoiselle." Inspector
Foch glanced nervously at his wristwatch, then forced
himself to face Jeanette again. Nothing in his experience
had prepared him for dealing with such a determined
woman. He stiffened his posture and said sternly, "Perhaps in your country murder is not a grave offense, but I
assure you it is taken very seriously in France."

"Surely, Inspector, you aren't confusing me with the
characters you see on American TV? I'll match my morals
against yours any day." There Jeanette stopped. She dared
not allow the man to see how his hesitance was infuriating
her. She said more gently, "You are a working man, Inspector, so I'm sure you can imagine how it bothers me to
be kept away from my responsibilities at home. I could lose
my job, you see; that is why I am getting so anxious. I support myself, just as you do."

She tried to smile companionably, mentally comparing his probable salary with hers and hoping he had no way of finding out the discrepancy.

Her job. Inspector Foch could not imagine why a young woman as rich and beautiful as Jeanette Melton would work at a job. Many men would be happy to keep her supplied with those tailored linen trousers and silk shirts she seemed to live in. Even the Comtesse de Blaise, who ranked highest among the local nobility, looked dowdy beside Mademoiselle Melton. The comtesse, on the other hand, understood the inspector's devotion to duty and respected him for it.

He said, "Mademoiselle, I have no wish to detain you one moment longer than necessary, and as soon as I receive permission...ah! Perhaps that is Captain Giroux now."

Inspector Foch snatched the ringing telephone from its cradle, saying, "Allo, allo," then handed it to Jeanette.

"It is for you, Mademoiselle," he said, "Monsieur Devere is calling."

After a moment's hesitation she took the phone and greeted Sonny, who claimed to have been devastated when he heard from Margo that Jeanette was on the point of departure. She would change her plans, he was certain, when he finished describing the unique adventure he was inviting her to share: a week in Morocco as the guest of Pierre Demarchelier, the cosmetics tycoon, who was launching a new perfume called Caprice. The company would be glittering—Sonny rattled off celebrity names—and because he so admired her work, Pierre was offering exclusive coverage of the event to *World Beat*.

Jeanette's mind functioned with its usual efficiency as Sonny babbled on. She had no idea how large a bond Inspector Foch might ask her to post, but Sonny's resources were inexhaustible and hers were not. His desire to publicize his friend's product might turn out to be a godsend, though she had no intention of actually going on such a deadly junket.

Carefully, charmingly, she stalled, affecting the manner of the vague, slightly helpless females Sonny probably fancied. She pattered on about what divine fun it would be if she could only juggle her dates and somehow, miraculously, assemble an adequate wardrobe.

She rang off without committing herself to anything more than a possible drink with Sonny later in the day and saw that Inspector Foch was standing in the doorway talking in low tones with Noel Wright.

They fell silent as Jeanette walked over to them, but she saw something in Noel's face that put her on guard. He looked pleased—secretly pleased; he could not hide it behind his severe expression.

He said, "Inspector Foch tells me you have asked permission to go back to New York, even though Paul's murder is still unsolved."

Before replying Jeanette moved up the two steps that led to the tiled hallway, and the two men stepped back to make room for her.

With her eyes fixed on Noel's, she pushed up the sleeves of her white silk shirt and slipped her hands into her pockets. She said, "Yes, I have to get back to work. Do you have any objections, Noel?"

He shook his head, no longer bothering to conceal his cheerfulness. "No, indeed, my dear. In fact, I thought it would be helpful if I explained what a very important job you have, something modesty would prevent your doing yourself."

Jeanette's brown eyes narrowed, and the inspector said quickly, "If you will please come and sit down for one moment, Mademoiselle, and you, Monsieur Wright, there is another matter."

They all stepped down into the room and seated themselves in chairs grouped around a low table where Inspector Foch had earlier placed his notes. He picked up the folder and took out a paper, which he briefly scanned, then he looked up at Jeanette, who sat frowning into space with her arms folded across her chest, and Noel, who appeared to find the situation more amusing with each passing moment.

The inspector said, "I can tell you that we are becoming convinced that M. Paul Clifford was shot by a thief whom he surprised in his room. We are quite prepared to accept that explanation, and have, in fact, an important lead as to the identity of the intruder."

As his two listeners exclaimed in surprise, Inspector Foch held up a warning finger. "There is, however, the question of M. Clifford's pages of manuscript to be resolved. We believe these were not taken by M. Clifford's killer, but by one of his fellow heirs, probably at the same time Mlle Girard's were stolen."

"The day before," said Jeanette. "But why wouldn't Paul have told us they were missing?"

"Think, Jeanette." Noel's voice was harsh. Clearly, the inspector's news had unsettled him.

"You mean because he had stolen Millie's? But I don't see . . ."

"It is probable that both sections of manuscript were taken together from M. Clifford's room," said Inspector Foch.

"How can you be so certain of all this?" said Noel.

"We have the testimony of one in whom M. Clifford confided," said the inspector. He added ponderously, "I fear that is all I can say at this time, except that the source is highly reliable."

"Why in the world haven't you told us this before?" Jeanette was on her feet. "If what you say is true, there's no reason to suspect any of us of Paul's murder."

"I said it was probable, Mademoiselle. We do not make public statements until we are absolutely certain of our facts." Jeanette stood so close, looming over him, that the inspector had to push his chair back in order to get up and confront her.

Noel regarded them coolly. "You both appear to be missing an essential point here," he said. "And that is the fact that any one of us could say that Paul told us his manuscript was stolen. There is no way to prove it, however."

Inspector Foch said, "The person who told us has no reason to lie, Monsieur. That is almost as good as proof."

"Now what in the world do you mean by that?" Jeanette felt like picking up the inspector and shaking his silly secrets out of him.

"Please control yourself, Jeanette," Noel cautioned. "Inspector Foch doesn't have to tell us a thing if he doesn't wish to."

"Clearly Mlle Melton is nervous, Monsieur, and I do not blame her." The inspector spoke with dignity, ignoring the fury that emanated from Jeanette. "It is to relieve her anxiety that I am telling you these facts. The person who told me of M. Clifford's manuscript is not one of Charles Melton's heirs, thus has no reason to conceal the truth."

"Not an heir, but close to Paul . . . who would that be?" Jeanette stared at Noel. "Lila, Marie, Loulou Marchand—he loved her . . ."

"Millie's friend, Hank Stovall? He and Paul were getting very cozy, I noticed."

"I guess they had something to get cozy about if Paul's pages were stolen too. Hank was very concerned about Millie, you know."

"And possibly motivated by greed as well as love. He has a good business head on his shoulders; he would be well aware of the profits at stake here."

Inspector Foch interrupted. "Excuse me, but there is also concrete evidence that points to an intruder. I do not wish to say more about that at this time. What I do need before allowing Mlle Melton to leave the country is some assurance regarding the manuscript which appears to be so crucial to this case. I would not care to assist in, how shall I say . . . ?"

"Embezzlement? No, not exactly." Noel glanced in amusement from the inspector's embarrassed face to Jeanette's, which had turned livid.

She said, "I will ignore your insinuation, Inspector Foch, in view of the fact that Monsieur Wright and I have reached an agreement regarding the manuscript. I don't know that we need to tell you any more than that." She regarded him haughtily for a moment, then turned to Noel. "Do we, Noel?"

"I think we should be as candid as the inspector has been with us, Jeanette, especially if you hope to be on that six o'clock flight." He smiled, but she saw the warning in his eyes. "It is true that Mlle Melton and I have decided to collaborate," he went on cautiously, "but I would like that information to be held in confidence. Is that possible, Inspector?"

Inspector Foch sighed. He turned away and stared unhappily out the window, then faced them once more and said, "The manuscript is a baffling matter. I have never had such a complication before. So you two have decided to work together; so?" He shrugged. "So what of the interests of the others? Am I expected to protect them?"

"I certainly don't see that as your duty," Noel replied. "Any more than you could protect us against them. Let's face it, Inspector, even if Paul was not killed for that manuscript, someone did steal two sections of it: his and Millie Girard's, though to what purpose I can't imagine."

Jeanette looked startled. "You're right. The only possible profit is in assembling the whole novel, and no one can do that without our parts."

"May I suggest another reason for stealing the manuscript, Mademoiselle? Perhaps to prevent publication. Perhaps, in fact, to prevent anyone ever reading more than a few pages of it." The inspector paused, enjoying their reaction to what was clearly a new concept. "You may ask why," he went on, "and I say, I do not know. Perhaps, as M. Porter has suggested, you should look within your own pages. Perhaps the reason is hidden there."

"You mean you agree with Ben Porter? You think Melton disguised some shocking message in that story?" Noel looked at Jeanette. "Can you believe this, Jeanette?"

She said, "I'm afraid Inspector Foch has a liking for melodrama. Perhaps that is why he is such a brilliant detective.'' She bared her teeth in a sugary smile, which Inspector Foch made no effort to return.

The telephone rang and Jeanette darted across the room to answer. She picked it up, said a few words, then, once again wearing a grin of insulting sweetness, cooed, ''It's for you, Inspector Foch, from the Prefecture in Nice,'' and held out the phone to the inspector.

As soon as she had received permission to leave, Jeanette called the airline, but her disgruntled responses made it clear to Noel and Inspector Foch that she had missed out on the evening flight. Observing the way her brown eyes raked over him while she talked with the reservations clerk, the inspector decided to take his leave. He had had enough of American career women for one day. He prayed Jeanette would be able to leave on a morning flight, at the latest, and would take her time about returning to La Rêverie.

Noel hovered only long enough to hear Jeanette accept a seat for the following morning at eight o'clock, then he too departed, with the idea of paying an impromptu call on Margo Honeywell. He could not telephone her first without going upstairs to the private line, and he was too impatient for that.

The session with Jeanette and Inspector Foch had left him with a throbbing head. No one, except possibly Margo, had any idea how stressful such scenes were to a person of his sensibilities. Even if Margo happened to be out he needed at that moment to escape the atmosphere of La Rêverie, which suddenly seemed to reverberate with hostility and suspicion.

He left the house, as he nearly always did, by way of the kitchen so he could tell Lila of his plans. It was somehow comforting to know she cared about his whereabouts and would worry if he were late getting home for dinner.

Nearing the kitchen, he heard the laughter and splashing that accompanied Finesse's bath. He forced a good-natured smile as he pushed the door open, but he resented having to compete with a dog for Lila's attention. Finesse looked particularly unworthy standing in the tub of soapy water, trembling like the coward he was, while Lila and Marie and Sergeant Clement fussed over him.

"I'm going over to Margo's, Lila." Noel spoke loudly to be heard above the merriment, but she did not acknowledge his presence until Sergeant Clement alerted her with a nod of his head in Noel's direction.

She turned her flushed face to him then and said, "Give us a hand, Noel. First we couldn't get this fellow into the tub and now we can't get him out!"

"I'm afraid that's your problem, Lila, yours and your husky helper's." Noel glanced at Sergeant Clement with distaste. "I have no desire to get wet at the moment."

"All right, run along to your fine friends." Lila pushed herself up and, holding her dripping hands before her, stepped to the table where she had placed a stack of towels. "You'll be home for dinner?" she asked. She dried her hands and blotted at her soaked jeans, grinning at the hopelessness of it.

"I'll be back at my usual time," Noel replied, "and Jeanette will be with us, after all. She's not leaving till tomorrow."

"Oh? She couldn't get on the flight?"

"It was too late by the time the inspector was willing to let her go, so she booked the 8:00 A.M. instead. I'll see you at dinner."

Looking past his shoulder, Lila squealed at the sight of Sergeant Clement lifting the wet dog out of the tub. She snatched up a towel and hurried to help, crying, "Don't let him get loose, Jean! He's slippery, be careful!"

Noel was smoldering as he let himself out and crossed the drive to the garage. 'Jean,' was it? He'd had no idea Lila and Sergeant Clement had become such chums. Now that he thought of it, he recalled seeing them together with unnecessary frequency, usually laughing in that common way Lila sometimes affected. Well, she was approaching an interesting age for a woman, he reflected as he climbed into his car, and the sergeant was virile and good-looking, some might think, in a coarse, earthy way.

Noel backed out and deliberately left the garage door open. Let the jolly poodle washers take care of it; he had more important matters on his mind. He only hoped he wouldn't start encountering the sergeant at the dinner table. *There* he would have to draw the line.

SIXTEEN

MARGO ANSWERED HER DOOR wearing the costume that meant she'd been giving herself a facial and a pedicure: a faded pink cotton caftan, nothing on her feet, and a white chiffon scarf wrapped around her head.

"What have you been up to, you rascal?" She embraced Noel warmly and seized his wrist to pull him into the house. She closed the door firmly and turned to face him. "I've been going mad over here by myself. No word from you, no word from Jeanette, and I can't very well call up and ask questions with God-knows-who listening in. Really, Noel, you've been very neglectful!"

"Not because I've been enjoying life, Margo, no indeed." Noel was so glad to see her, so pleased at the prospect of pouring all his complaints into a sympathetic ear, that he almost forgot his purpose in coming.

"Poor darling," she murmured. Her amber eyes looked soft without their usual rim of makeup; they glowed with a concern he could only describe as motherly. Noel suppressed a smile, imagining Margo's indignation if she could read his thoughts.

"Let's have some tea, shall we, while you tell me your troubles?" She started for the kitchen and Noel followed.

From the doorway he said, "First, my dear, I have to tell you that I am perfectly certain you are the one who so cleverly collected Celia Rowan's manuscript." As she whirled to face him, her face full of outrage, he held up a hand in warning. "Don't bother; please don't tell any more lies that in the long run will only embarrass you."

"Has Jeanette claimed that I went up there and impersonated her? If she has..." Margo banged the kettle onto a burner and turned on the gas with a vicious twist of her fingers.

"Jeanette has made no accusations. She doesn't need to. I'm just a little hurt that either one of you thought I wouldn't figure out such an utterly obvious scheme."

"But you said . . ."

"Oh, I know I pretended to believe you both. What was to be gained by making you look foolish? And I rather enjoyed everyone else's confusion, especially since I knew you or Jeanette, probably both, would have to tell me eventually."

"Oh?" Margo started to say more, then abruptly clamped her lips shut and began setting the tea tray. She opened the china cupboard, saying, "Shall we use the Limoges? It is sort of a celebration, after all."

"What are we celebrating, pray tell? Our reunion or my catching you out?"

Noel's eyes were twinkling affectionately, and Margo ran to hug him.

"Oh, Noel, there's no one like you!" With her lips touching his ear she murmured, "There's no friendship like ours, is there, darling? The understanding, the honesty . . ."

"I wouldn't say too much about honesty at the moment." Noel shook his head gravely. "No, you wounded me, you really did. I expect such behavior from Jeanette, but not from you."

The kettle was humming, and Margo broke away and went to fix the tea. She said, "You have to realize that I was acting in your interests just as much as mine. I couldn't very well spell it all out though, could I? Not until Jeanette went home, when of course I intended to explain the whole thing to you."

She picked up the tea tray, and Noel preceded her into her cozy drawing room and made room for the tray on a table before the hearth.

"I haven't seen this, Margo, it's charming," he said, examining an enamel figure of a monkey dressed in eighteenth-century breeches and waistcoat.

"I went antiquing with Lulu, and you know what that's like. She throws money around with such abandon I begin to feel rich myself." She sat down and squinted at the little figure appraisingly. "Actually, I'll probably make money on that. The dealer practically gave it away, he was so ecstatic over what Lulu bought."

Margo poured them each a cup of tea, adding a drop of milk to Noel's and placing a sliver of lemon on the saucer. He took it carefully and held the cup before his eyes for a moment, admiring the translucence of the old porcelain.

"Exquisite," he murmured, then took a sip of the fragrant tea and set the cup and saucer on the table. He smiled happily at Margo and took a vanilla wafer from the plate she offered him. "All your sins are redeemed by moments like these," he said.

Margo looked cheerfully affronted. "I'm not the only sinner in town," she said. "I have a strong suspicion that you had searched Paul's bedroom quite thoroughly before we all went up there the other day."

"Margo! What in the world would make you think that?"

"Never mind, it doesn't matter now. I just wanted you to know you're not the only one who sees through people. I'm curious about one thing, though." Margo sipped her tea, made a face, and reached for the hot water pot. "Why have you decided to accuse me of taking Celia Rowan's manuscript? Yesterday you seemed quite willing to believe me."

"I put in an instructive hour with Jeanette and Inspector Foch today, and I have an idea that man is not as thickheaded as we've been assuming he is." Noel squeezed a few drops of lemon into his tea and wiped his fingers on his lace-edged napkin. He said, "The reason I tolerated your disloyal action was that I knew you would have to share Celia Rowan's pages with me eventually, hers and all the others. There's no other way to get the novel published and make some money out of it."

"Quite true."

"But this morning the inspector suggested another reason for gathering up as much of the manuscript as possible, one I hadn't thought of." Noel peered solemnly across the table at Margo, who held her cup suspended in midair while she waited.

"Concealment," Noel intoned, then sat back to study her reaction.

Margo looked disappointed. "I don't get it," she said flatly.

Noel said, "I guess you weren't there when Ben Porter suggested a connection between the characters in Charles's manuscript and the people who had figured importantly in his life."

"No, but Jeanette mentioned some such theory. She thinks the Porters are fantasizing, and I'm inclined to agree."

"That was my opinion at first; then I read my section over and you know, Margo, there may be something to it." Noel took a scrap of paper from his trouser pocket and smoothed it out. "Last night I jotted a few notes, let's see. Ah yes, some of the names link up: Paul Clifford and Helene Rocher, both secretaries to super-successful men, Charles Melton and Robert de Laine." He looked up at Margo. "Do I have to explain that both *melton* and *laine* mean 'wool'?"

"Good God, you're right." Margo's cup rattled in the saucer as she abruptly set it on the table. "And *rocher* means 'cliff,' I know that."

"I put it down to coincidence—mostly because the sexes don't match up—and then I thought about the title." Noel smiled enigmatically.

"The title." Margo's eyes widened. "I never gave it a thought. What is the title anyway?"

"*Mirror Image.* Does that suggest anything to you?"

"Well, I suppose that could mean the story reflects real life. Is that what you're getting at?"

"And perhaps reverses certain things, as images are reversed in a mirror." Noel held out his cup for more tea. "The sexes of the characters, for example."

"Not de Laine and Melton." Margo filled the cup and handed it back to Noel. "Unless there's some twist. Tell me, does de Laine seem to be heterosexual?"

"Yes, *but*—get this, Margo, I feel it's very significant—he's had one homosexual affair, with a man named de Cendre. Charles had one hetero affair, with Celia Rowan." Wearing a satisfied smile, Noel sat back to watch her reaction, and indeed Margo responded most obligingly. Her jaw dropped and she gave a gasp of amazement.

"My God, Noel! You could be right." Margo got to her feet and strode across the room and back. She did not sit down but stared down at Noel and said, "Then the whole story could be stuffed with secrets Charles had kept to himself all his life?"

"It could be stuffed like a Christmas pudding, yes, with deliciously scandalous morsels—about any of us." Noel kept his eyes fixed on Margo's expressive face; he couldn't remember when he'd enjoyed himself so much. "Or it could contain just one big secret, one so earthshaking that it's worth killing to keep it quiet."

Margo sank into her chair, limp as a rag doll, her bare feet with their glossy pink toenails sticking out under the hem of her caftan. "What's the name of that lover—Descendre? That means 'descent'—hardly the same as Rowan."

"It's de Cendre, Margo. *Cendre* means 'ash' or 'cinders.'"

Margo said slowly, "Noel, we've got to read every word of that thing over again. I never thought..."

"Neither did I. Of course Ben Porter may be dead wrong, but his theory is certainly worth exploring."

"For many reasons, old friend." The shock had left Margo's face, but her eyes were bleak as she stared at Noel. "Supposing we're involved somehow in this fearful secret—one of us or both? Our lives could be in danger, have you thought of that?"

"I suppose that's at the back of the urgency I feel, though I hadn't spelled it out." Noel's expression was as somber as Margo's as he set down his cup, then sat back and crossed his arms.

He said, "What has become very clear, my dear, is that I cannot allow any further plotting between you and

Jeanette. The possible consequences are far too serious. Instead, we must all share any insights that come to us as we read over that manuscript. The thing suddenly seems to me as threatening as a grenade with the firing pin pulled out."

"Why in God's name would Charles cook up such a conundrum? Revenge for something he fancied one of us had done?"

"*Fancied* we'd done? Is your conscience perfectly clear, Margo? Search your memory."

"You know, I'm not enjoying your visit as much as I usually do, darling. I hope that doesn't hurt your feelings." Without looking at him, Margo poured the last drops of tea into their cups.

"I'm not concerned about my feelings right at the moment. All I want is your promise to stick to the agreement I thought we had made."

Margo glanced at him sharply and said, "I'm a little tired of being scolded, Noel. Apparently it hasn't occurred to you that without me you had no chance of getting anything out of Jeanette. You had completely antagonized her, you know."

"True enough." A slow smile came to his face as he studied her. "I suppose you're a more dependable ally than Jeanette, at that, though it's not much of a choice."

"Damn it, Noel..."

Ignoring her indignation, he said, "I'm curious about one thing. How did you get yourself identified as Jeanette when you went to the nursing home?"

Margo sighed. "No reason not to tell you now, I guess. We cut my photograph out of my passport and stuck it into hers—using rubber cement so we could peel it off afterwards. There's no date on the photo, you know, just the seal pressed into it."

"I suppose they didn't examine it very closely."

"No, they had no reason to be suspicious, especially since I also took along the letter from Anne Rouffet, Celia Rowan's nurse, asking Jeanette to come and get the manuscript."

"Jeanette probably delivered both items to you while I thought she was safely asleep in her room. What a pair you are!"

"Yes, we were very pleased with ourselves until you caught on." She gazed at him beseechingly and said, "Can you forgive me, Noel? I felt kind of shabby about the whole thing, I might as well admit, even though I fully intended to share everything with you eventually." She grinned, struck by a new thought. "Maybe because of that."

"Of course, the role of double agent imposes a strain— even for one as experienced as you."

Margo said, "Hmm. When I figure out what you're implying I don't think I'll like it."

"Possibly not, but we've got to stop sparring for a while and devote our energies to combing that manuscript for hidden meanings. I presume you have Celia Rowan's pages here in the house?"

"No, not yet. Jeanette's making a copy—she has a neat little machine...oh, you've seen it? She's going to keep the copy in her machine and bring me the original before she leaves."

"She's leaving on the morning flight, has she told you?" Margo nodded and Noel continued, "Meanwhile I had better read your part. I trust you have no objections?"

"None at all."

"You should read it too, if you haven't already. But Margo—I'll tolerate no more tricks, is that quite clear?"

"I'm no longer in the mood for tricks, Noel; to tell you the truth, I'm rather scared." Her fingers clutched his arm for a moment, then she gave a nervous laugh and left the room to get her manuscript.

NOEL ARRIVED BACK at La Rêverie to find that Hank Stovall had arrived unexpectedly from Paris and was having a drink with Millie on the terrace.

"My meeting in Lyons was postponed," Hank explained, "so it seemed only logical..."

"Of course." Noel shook his hand, aware that Millie was looking on with an absurdly happy smile. She was wearing a long black cotton skirt with a raspberry linen blouse that gave her skin a soft rosy glow.

"You look quite radiant this evening, Millie," Noel said to her.

"Do we credit that to Hank's arrival or my departure?" Jeanette wore a sardonic grin as she stepped out on the terrace to join them. She strolled to the table and poured herself a drink, first pushing up the sleeves of her cream silk shirt in the habitual gesture that allowed her heavy gold bracelet to slide to her wrist.

"The prospect of your departure stirs mixed emotions," said Noel, and Jeanette turned and raised her eyebrows inquiringly.

"Though you will be desperately missed," Noel continued, making a polite little bow, "we could not otherwise expect the kind of dinner Marie has cooked as a farewell gesture. Fricassee of lobster. When did she last give us that?"

Jeanette sat down in one of the wrought-iron chairs, saying, "It's true, you should all be grateful. Especially Hank, who wasn't even expected."

"Marie has a generous heart," said Hank, "but I hope you'll forgive me if I take Millie away after dinner. I have to leave in the morning."

"I'll be disappearing after dinner too," said Jeanette. "I've a mountain of paperwork to get through this evening."

"And I too have work to do," said Noel. He looked pointedly at Jeanette. "An interesting manuscript has turned up, one I must evaluate very carefully."

"Really? Who's the author, Noel?" Jeanette peered at him over the rim of her glass. "You haven't discovered any more of my uncle's works, have you?"

"Nothing you haven't seen if you've been in touch with Margo."

"Well, we've all been in touch with Margo, haven't we?" Jeanette managed to sound only faintly defensive.

"What is this about?" Millie frowned, looking from Jeanette to Noel. "Aren't we sharing everything we find? I've certainly been open with you two."

"There's no skullduggery afoot, Millie," Noel said. "I've thought of a new interpretation of the manuscript, that's all. But it's too early to test my theory on you."

Jeanette said, "Not for me. If you have any bright ideas, I'd very much like to hear them before I leave."

"You'll be informed, Jeanette, and you too, Millie, if I make any progress. You see, I am convinced that our only chance of solving Charles's riddle lies in working together. As a team. Rejecting any temptation to strike out on our own." Noel spoke each phrase with exaggerated clarity, keeping his eyes fixed on Jeanette.

She, meanwhile, affected an air of indifference, glancing idly around at the others as he spoke, and even stifling a yawn when he had finished.

"I don't know what you're implying with that portentous statement," she said, "but I'd like to suggest that we have dinner served a trifle early tonight. What do you say, Millie?" She rose to her feet and set her glass on the table. "If it's all right with the rest of you I'll ask Marie to get it under way." In the doorway she turned to add, "And please try to cheer up, Noel dear. I'd like to enjoy what will probably be my last really good dinner in quite a while."

Before he could reply she had swung around and disappeared in the direction of the kitchen.

SEVENTEEN

MARIE'S FRICASSEE of lobster was a triumph of tenderness and flavor and was followed by an ethereal raspberry soufflé accompanied by fresh raspberries soaked in Kirsch. The remarkable food could not give a festive air to that particular evening, however, with Hank and Millie obviously impatient to get away by themselves and both Noel and Jeanette preoccupied with their own concerns. When the last crumb of soufflé had been consumed, coffee was served at the table—no lingering over brandy that night—and everyone drank it quickly and excused themselves. It was left to Lila to rhapsodize over the dinner with the enthusiasm Marie had anticipated.

On his way up the stairs Noel could hear the two women's voices as they cleared the table, Lila's reassuring and Marie's distinctly querulous. He felt only a slight twinge of guilt, however.

Nor did he experience any strong emotion when he said his adieux to Jeanette, whom he encountered in the doorway of her room. If he felt anything it was relief as they exchanged a perfunctory salutation, and when he stepped back to look into her face he saw that she was similarly unmoved.

"Keep me posted, won't you?" she said, and he nodded.

"I think we understand each other." He shrugged and threw up his hands. "There's not much more to say, is there?"

"Only, *bonne chance* in your efforts, Noel. May they prove rewarding to us both." A smile flickered briefly, then she turned away.

"*Bon voyage* to you, my dear." Noel continued down the hall to his own room.

Once inside, he took off his jacket and hung it up, put away the foulard he'd worn to dinner, and, placing a pencil and paper in reach for note-taking, settled in one of his easy chairs with Margo's manuscript pages 116 through 256.

. . . coughing in the acrid air of the room that brought hot, stinging tears to his eyes.

From a brazier beside the bed a plume of sweet incense pushed upward, forming a dense mat of smoke that hovered beneath the low ceiling. When he came near to the bed, Dépouille understood the purpose of the burning incense, for the smell of decay would have been unbearable without it.

He clenched his fists, trying not to breathe, deliberately driving his nails into his palms for the distraction pain could bring. He dreaded the sight that would meet his eyes, but he could not allow Katerina to see his revulsion. Should she have even the slightest awareness, he would try to show her the face she had so often seen filled with love. No matter now that she had rewarded that love with scorn and mockery; it would be his final gift to her.

The woman was pushing him closer while with one hand she clutched a faded red scarf against her nose and mouth. Above the dirty cloth her black eyes shone with the curiosity that might have been expected as the lover of the *quartier's* most notorious whore approached her deathbed.

Dépouille could summon no indignation for her or the others who pressed forward in a stifling mass, shutting him off from any chance of escape. He could only stare in amazement as his eyes traveled over the doll-sized form that took so little space on the rumpled bed.

This could not be Katerina; the limbs that formed so faint an outline appeared no thicker than a bird's, and the mass of tangled hair was an ugly, gray-streaked brown, where Katerina's, as everyone knew very well, was a glossy skein of black, like a length of rich satin.

He was on the point of swinging around to accuse them of playing a crude joke when the frail legs moved and a soft whimper brought two women pushing forward, reaching out to gently turn the patient so Claude Dépouille could look into the eyes of his love.

He did not need to force himself then. He sank to his knees, his soul immersed in the gaze that passed between them like an electric current. Her face was ravaged, unrecognizable; all that lived of her lived in the brown eyes that glowed now with the same light he had seen when she teased him into her bed.

"Katerina," he breathed, and at the sound of his voice her eyes softened and her parched lips trembled, attempting a smile.

As cautiously as he would touch a newborn baby he touched the thin hand that lay on the pillow beside her face. He caressed it lightly, watching her face, willing the smile to remain, though it flickered as weakly as the light of a guttering candle.

"Your skin is soft as velvet," he murmured, and saw the light leap up in her eyes.

Her lips moved, but the sound was too faint, and he bent closer until his cheek brushed the point of her chin. His heart pounded with the excitement of possibly hearing her speak.

"Liar." The word was spoken firmly, but the effort caused her to close her eyes, and Dépouille turned frantically to the women.

"Do something! She's dying!" he said, but they merely glanced around at one another, murmuring and nodding.

Only the one with the red scarf moved closer, and as she bent over the bed Katerina's eyes flew open, startling the woman so that she jumped back.

At that a whispery chuckle rose from the bed, and Dépouille found himself grinning, sharing the joke as they had shared so many bawdy ones in the past.

Suddenly, from the darkness beyond the knot of

women, Dépouille heard a child's voice, a shocking sound in that chamber of death. He turned his head and saw the women moving back to open a path for a ragged little girl who had entered the house. The child, who looked about five years old, was carrying a small basket containing two oranges, holding the basket with both hands as if it were very precious. As she approached the bed her smile of anticipation widened and her dark eyes sparkled as if she were bringing a birthday present.

"Mama," she said, "I have a surprise to make you well," and before Dépouille could stop her she had taken an orange from the basket and placed it in Katerina's limp hand.

Amazingly, her fingers curled weakly around it, but only for an instant. As the orange rolled away Dépouille reached out and caught it, watching Katerina's face, seeing her struggle for the strength to speak to her daughter.

The child watched too, waiting to be thanked, and Dépouille realized that she was not shocked by her mother's condition. To her the change had been gradual; to her Katerina was not a dying woman, but her sick mother who would soon get well. Everyone did eventually, except the beggars in the streets, whose entire existence was a terminal illness.

Again there was a faint sound from the bed. Katerina whispered, "Thank you, Mimi," and Dépouille saw how she fought the weakness, willing her eyes to stay fixed on her daughter with heroic concentration, as if to engrave the child's image on her very soul.

Then he saw a thought strike her, and she slowly shifted her gaze to him. He caught his breath. Was she about to tell him what he had longed to know during all the years since Mimi's birth? Dared he ask again, or would she laugh scornfully, weak as she was, and leave him to wonder forever?

She was thirsty, he saw; she was attempting to lick her parched lips, and he looked up at the woman with the red scarf that never left her face and growled, "Get her some water."

Again a murmur passed among the women, and in an instant someone handed him a brass cup filled to the brim. Impatiently, he tossed half the water to the floor—couldn't they see it was too full?—then carefully held the cup to Katerina's lips.

Beside him the child spoke. "You do like this," she said, and leaning forward on her stomach, she used both hands to lift her mother's head so she could drink.

Tilting the cup as Katerina swallowed, Dépouille saw how she watched the child over the rim, and how the little girl smiled encouragement while she propped her elbows to keep Katerina's head steady. He felt his throat thicken with tears—the first time that had happened since the night of Mimi's birth, when Katerina had come close to dying.

The water dribbled, Katerina's eyes had closed, and Mimi gently lowered her head to the pillow. She did not move away from the bed, however, but began to stroke her mother's hair very lightly, looking up at Dépouille with a mischievous smile, as if she were indulging in a forbidden treat.

It was too much for him, and he whispered, "Mustn't wake her," and gently drew the child away.

He felt his arms trembling as he let her go, and glancing at his watch, he was horrified to see the hour. The morning had gone by; the time he needed to find money had been spent in this fetid room, and soon the need would be upon him.

Now his mouth was dry. He looked at the cup in his hand, but he was afraid to drink from it after Katerina. His heart had begun to pound and he could feel his face turning hot. Were they all watching him?

He turned anxiously to the child, but she was staring at her mother, whose face, Dépouille realized, had undergone a profound change. The flesh, thin as it was, now appeared to rest against the bones like putty.

Katerina's nose, once piquant, stood forth imposingly; the hand that had held the orange lay limp and gray against the wrinkled sheet.

Dépouille seized the little girl's hand and pushed himself to his feet. "Come with me," he whispered hoarsely, but she resisted, keeping her gaze locked on the still figure on the bed.

Dépouille was swaying. His need to escape, to find money, to find de Laine, to find help somewhere, was overpowering.

The child clung to his hand unthinkingly, but she would not look away or move, so Dépouille shook her hand loose as roughly as if it were a snake. Then he turned and headed for the door, plunging between the close-packed women like a charging bull.

His head seemed to vibrate like a gong as he dashed into the street. The pain would come soon, then the sickness. He could not allow it.

He stumbled across the filthy pavement in the direction of the canal. De Laine might have gone to the dock; that was his only chance. He began to run. With the searing heat of noon burning into his back, he ran, and with every pounding step he cursed the name of Abu Sahid, the monster who was responsible for his agony.

In a foul cavern somewhere beneath these very streets, Sahid and his men had turned him into an addict. Once he became their captive, Dépouille had no means of resisting the techniques they employed with scientific precision. Yet the purpose of this unspeakable deed was not his destruction—that was a mere side benefit—but to force him to act as the bait that would accomplish the downfall of Robert de Laine. Sahid's gamble: that de Laine would risk his life to save his friend, trusting him in the face of what looked like certain treachery.

Sahid had guessed rightly. What he hadn't foreseen was the outcome: that de Laine would pluck his friend from his grasp so smoothly, Sahid was hardly aware it was happening.

But there was one miracle de Laine could not accomplish. Even he, with all his brilliance, could not rescue Dépouille from the grip of the drug...

Noel stopped reading and reached for his pencil to note down the names of the characters. Abu Sahid, Katerina, Claude Dépouille, Mimi. He could get no French meaning out of any of them except Dépouille—spoil, or plunder. Had Charles used it in the sense of treasure, he wondered, or as ruin? The latter, despoil, seemed closer to the French, but he could not immediately connect the name to anyone in Melton's life.

He gave up and resumed reading, but a sound distracted him, and he cocked his head to listen. It was a car on the gravel driveway, whether arriving or leaving he could not tell. He rose with the sheets of manuscript in his hand and reached the window in time to see two red taillights winking as someone pulled away. Probably Jeanette, he thought, turning back to his chair; she was slipping over to see Margo, no doubt, and feeling very pleased about putting one over on him.

He smiled to himself as he sank into the leather cushions. Tomorrow would see the end of all this silliness; yet in a way he would miss Jeanette. She had great entertainment value, after all.

JEANETTE MELTON DROVE slowly along Avenue de Verdun and stopped when she reached Boulevard du Général-de-Gaulle. She could turn back here, the sensible thing to do; go home and get a good night's sleep before her flight. She turned the wheel to the left, then the excitement welled up again and she abruptly swung the car to the right, the direction of Margo's house.

Such vacillation was foreign to Jeanette; her practice was to make speedy decisions, preferably well-informed, and stick to them. She despised wavery, wishy-washy people and had pretty well eliminated them from her life. So her present state of mind was uncomfortable, almost frightening.

She tried to think clearly as she drove past the stone walls and the looming black shapes of cypress and umbrella pines, but at the moment it was impossible. Instead, her mind whirled with fantastic conjectures provoked by her reading of the final 150 pages of Melton's novel.

Undoubtedly she was making a mistake in rushing to Margo like this; actually, it had been a mistake even to read those last pages, but she hadn't discovered that until too late. Now Margo would simply have to share the consequences and perhaps—this was Jeanette's fervent hope—come up with a more acceptable interpretation.

She reached Margo's driveway and was slightly dismayed to find lights burning in the two stone gargoyles that guarded the entrance. That could mean Margo was out. On the other hand, she might have had people in for dinner, though Jeanette found no cars parked in front of the house when she pulled into the driveway.

The house was lighted, however; the tall rectangles of the drawing room windows glowed softly through the closed linen draperies and, looking up, Jeanette saw that a lamp had been turned on in at least one of the bedrooms.

She sat still for a moment, trying to picture Margo's reaction. She felt strongly tempted to start up the car and drive home after all. Why open a Pandora's box when in a few hours she'd be safely away from the scene?

She turned off the ignition and the car lights, then slowly gathered up the sheaf of manuscript pages, arranging them as fussily as some elderly secretary. Still she dawdled, gazing at Margo's front door, willing Margo to pull it open, making the decision for her.

Suddenly she felt exasperated by her own dithering. She opened the door and stepped out of the car into the gentle warmth of the spring night. The scent of the Riviera came to her, the tang of pine and verbena blending with the floral bouquet wafting from Margo's garden. Jeanette breathed in deeply, wishing she could store the fragrant air in her head and take it to New York.

Approaching Margo's front door, she listened for the sound of voices, but the silence was broken only by the

crunch of gravel under her step. The knocker was a brass
hand clutching a ball, the same one found on doors
throughout southern France. Margo's wore a ring on one
finger set with an evil eye from Greece.

Jeanette knocked, waited, knocked again, then tried the
door, which silently swung inward, surprising her. Was
Margo in the habit of going out and leaving her front door
unlocked? She must be upstairs.

She called, "Margo! It's Jeanette. Where are you?"

There was no reply, no sound at all, except a faint mel-
ody apparently coming from a radio in the back of the
house.

Jeanette peered into the drawing room, which was softly
lighted by two table lamps, one standing on a table near the
hearth, the other at one end of the chintz-covered sofa.
There were no signs of entertaining, no cocktail napkins or
rings from wet glasses. Nor were there any cooking aro-
mas in the air, Jeanette observed as she turned toward the
kitchen.

She pushed the door open, expecting the radio music to
sound louder, but it receded instead. The kitchen was dim
and tidy, bare of food except for a few puckered green apples in a twig basket.

Suddenly Jeanette longed for a drink.

She took a glass out of the cupboard, added ice cubes
from the freezer, and carried it to Margo's liquor cabinet,
where she found a bottle of vodka. She poured herself a
liberal helping, added a dash of soda, and took a sip. Instantly she felt calmer; she had been more wound up than
she'd realized.

Carrying the glass, she returned to the front hall and
peered up the stairway to the second floor. She saw a glow
of light, apparently coming from one of the bedrooms. The
music sounded slightly louder; it was one of the plaintive
folk songs of the Auvergne being sung in a lovely soprano.
Raising her voice to be heard over the radio, Jeanette called
out Margo's name again and this time thought she heard a
muffled response.

Annoyed, Jeanette mounted the stairs. Why didn't the woman come out and speak to her? She was probably on the phone having one of her interminable conversations with Loulou or Sonny or another of her Cap Ferrat coterie. Jeanette suddenly felt glad to be escaping from all those types. Now that she thought of it, she could hardly wait to get back to New York, where people—the ones she saw, at least—had something on their minds.

Margo's bedroom door was ajar—the source of the light that poured into the hall. Jeanette knocked on it loudly, calling, "Margo, are you here?"

She pushed the door wide and stepped into the room. Immediately her spirits lifted, for the cushion-filled pine rocker in which Margo liked to read and watch TV was rocking gently, as if she had just left it, and the door to her bathroom was closed.

Jeanette waited, sipping her drink. In case Margo hadn't heard her, she called out, "I'm here, Margo." Then, as the bathroom door opened from the inside she added, "Didn't you hear me come in?"

A gun barked twice, two shots close together, and Jeanette dropped to the floor. The glass fell from her hand and bounced on the rug, spilling its contents.

Her other hand, the one that held the final pages of Charles Melton's manuscript, crumpled beneath her as she struck the floor. Her heavy gold bracelet bit into her wrist, but she felt no pain.

Jeanette Melton was all through with pain.

EIGHTEEN

AT TEN the following morning the two spots on Margo's yellow-and-white Portuguese rug were still damp. The bloodstains had been scrubbed away and the area covered with one of Margo's bath towels to spare her feelings. Jeanette's glass had landed a few feet away, and the clear liquid had left no stain.

Ben Porter knelt to sniff the spot, then looked up and said, "She must have made a drink and brought it up here with her."

Margo sobbed loudly and mopped her swollen eyes with her handkerchief. "I wasn't even here to make her last drink for her. Oh God, such a lonely death!"

"If only she had been alone," said Noel. In the weak light of the overcast morning his thin face was even paler than usual, with bluish shadows around the eyes. He had slept only an hour or two, all any of them could manage after the shock of Margo's midnight call.

Inspector Foch said, "The liquid is indeed vodka, Monsieur. We were able to take a sample last night."

"Then she fell just about here, is that right?" Ben got to his feet, keeping his eyes fixed on the towel.

"She was lying exactly there, Monsieur. When we have the photographs you will see." Inspector Foch paused as if doubtful whether to continue, then added slowly, "There were two shots. She did not have time to suffer."

Margo had wept herself into a fit of hiccups, and at the inspector's words she emitted a pathetic bleat that brought Carrie to her side.

"You've had enough, Margo." Carrie put her arm around her waist to lead her away. "Let's leave it to the men for a while. You need a cup of tea and a rest."

Margo did not protest, and Ben watched them leave the room with Carrie murmuring soothingly into Margo's ear exactly the way she did when comforting one of the children.

He turned to Inspector Foch and said, "Now about the shots. Do you know what kind of gun fired them?"

"We will not know that until we receive the coroner's report later today. Then we will know much about the weapon, but still, I am afraid, very little about who fired it, or why."

The inspector's face was sad. He did not like thinking that the beautiful American lady had been occupied with cross feelings about him during some of her final hours.

He said hopefully, "Mlle Melton was happy to be going to the States this morning, was she not?"

Noel Wright said, "Oh, I think so, Inspector. Although, like the rest of us, she was still grieving over the death of Paul Clifford. How very ironic it is that she too should have been brutally murdered. Do you see a connection between the two deaths, Inspector Foch?"

"That is certainly a possibility, but at this point I do not have enough information to speculate." He paused, then said to Noel, "Tell me, Monsieur Wright, in your opinion was Mlle Melton's eagerness to leave the country connected in any way with the mysterious manuscript left by her uncle? I ask because if there is a link between the two deaths, I feel it is in some way bound up with that legacy."

After a moment's reflection Noel replied, "I don't think she could accomplish anything in New York that she couldn't do here. Now that I think of it, it's a little surprising that she wanted to leave before we had located the missing parts of the manuscript."

"Which brings us back to a possible motive for the murders." Ben had not moved from the spot where Jeanette had fallen. He stared at the rug, visualizing her body lying there, the glass rolling away from her hand, her handbag nearby, perhaps spilling open. He said, "Did she have a handbag with her, Inspector, or a briefcase, anything like that?"

Inspector Foch replied slowly, "Her handbag was found on a chair in the downstairs hall—a handbag, at any rate, containing her passport and other personal items."

Noel snorted. "Have you checked that out with Mrs. Honeywell? The two of them have been known to borrow each other's documents when it suits their purposes."

Ben looked sharply at Noel. "Oh? Do you know that for certain?"

Noel nodded. "Margo has told me the whole story of the little trick they played on Celia Rowan's nursing home. I could never get Jeanette to admit a thing, however." Ben heard reluctant admiration in his tone as he added, "She stuck to her guns all the way."

Margo's bedside telephone jingled and Inspector Foch went to answer it.

Ben said to Noel, "Do you have any idea why Jeanette was so determined to see Margo last night? She found the house empty, after all..."

"Or so she thought."

"Right. But she must have gone all around, searching for Margo, probably calling her, then carrying a drink upstairs." He paused, shaking his head. He added slowly, "Noel, are you convinced that Margo really wasn't here?"

"What? You mean Margo might have killed her? Oh, heavens, Ben, I can't imagine such a thing!" Noel looked stricken; he stared at Ben in horror.

"I'm not suggesting that, Noel. I merely think it odd that Jeanette would come in and spend so much time in an empty house—unless she was desperate, of course, so anxious to see Margo before she left that she was prepared to wait for her to come home."

"Well, that is a good possibility, as a matter of fact." Relief made Noel feel quite tottery, and he collapsed into Margo's rocking chair and said, "I'm glad you pointed that out to me, Ben; I couldn't stand the thought of..."

"Of course you wouldn't believe such a thing of your good friend. I'm sorry you misunderstood me."

"Well, now that I've gotten my breath again, I can tell you that Margo and I had come up with a new idea con-

cerning that bloody manuscript—one that could tie in with
your theory about the naming of the characters. She was
supposed to be spending the evening reading, in fact, not
out at the Lartigues' dinner party." Noel scowled at the
floor. "It is quite likely that Margo had shared our ideas
with Jeanette, as she had shared so many others." Again he
paused to consider Margo's treachery.

"Which parts were you working on—supposedly?"

"I was reading hers; but you know, Ben, I don't believe
Margo has read one word of that manuscript yet," said
Noel indignantly, "And when I think how much hinges on
it..."

Ben said patiently, "You have read your section, of
course."

"Yes, and Jeanette's, and last night I started on Margo's. She had promised to do the same thing, so that we
could compare notes, but apparently she thought it more
important to go out and have a good time."

"The question is, Noel, where are the pages they took
from Celia Rowan?"

"Didn't I tell you? Jeanette was going to copy them and
then bring the original to Margo. That is why she came over
here, I'm certain."

"Well then, where are they? Where are Celia Rowan's
pages?"

Noel stared at him. "Good God, Ben, I hadn't
thought..."

Inspector Foch had finished his call and was standing
beside the bedroom door, clearly preparing to leave them.

He said, "I must go down now and speak with Madame
Honeywell, but I regret I cannot leave you here. The room
must be locked, you see."

Ben said, "We understand, Inspector, but first I wonder
if you can tell us whether any papers were found in Miss
Melton's bag; specifically, any pages of Charles Melton's
manuscript?"

"Ah, I am glad you brought that up, Monsieur." The
inspector returned to the center of the room and stood
looking down at the spots on the carpet. "There were no

papers in Mlle Melton's handbag; however, the position in which the body was found suggests that she may have carried something like that in her hand."

"What was the position of the body?"

"Well, Monsieur, the bullets entered Mlle Melton's head from the front, that is clear. Therefore, she would most naturally fall forward. We are quite sure she did, I can tell you, due to the fact that her wrist is badly twisted and bruised as if she had fallen on it. However..." The inspector paused, fixing Ben with his round brown eyes. "However, when we arrived Mlle Melton was lying on her back."

"And that implies?"

"That implies, Monsieur, that whoever shot Mlle Melton—presumably from the direction of the bathroom—then turned her body over. I ask you why? Why would a murderer take the time or the risk to move the victim's body? Perhaps to take something from her hand?"

Ben stared at the inspector; he brushed his fingers across his forehead, imagining bullets entering there, his head snapping back, then forward; he looked from the open bathroom door to the place where Jeanette had fallen.

He said, "Noel, I think we must get back to La Rêverie. I presume you will be coming over later, Inspector?"

Inspector Foch nodded, following them out of Margo's room. "Yes," he said, "I must question Mlle Melton's associates. You will wait there for me, M. Wright, will you not?"

"I will be glad to cooperate with you, Inspector."

"And will you please ask of the others that they do not leave?" Suddenly looking anxious, Inspector Foch added, "I think, in fact, I will send Sergeant Clement..."

The inspector hurried to the staircase and began running down, calling, "Jean! Jean! Report to me at once!"

At that point, without saying goodbye to Margo or Carrie, Ben and Noel quietly left the house.

AT LA RÊVERIE they found Millie in the kitchen, weeping in Lila's arms. Marie had been making toast and burning it, and as Noel and Ben entered the room, Lila barked at her over Millie's shoulder.

"For God's sake keep your mind on what you're doing, Marie! You're not helping matters by burning up all the bread in the house."

At that, Marie burst into sobs that shook her large body from head to toe, and began tearing off her apron.

Noel immediately slipped his arm through hers and drew her off to the dining room to soothe her feelings. It was not the first time he had played peacemaker for the two women.

Millie pulled away from Lila saying, "Why? That's what I ask! Why would anyone want to kill Jeanette? It doesn't make any sense!"

"Of course it doesn't, Millie, you're quite right. That's why it had to be an accident." Lila glanced pleadingly at Ben. "Ben agrees, I'm sure. She must have stumbled on an intruder..."

"Oh, certainly, just like Paul! Two murderous intruders in one week? Maybe you can swallow that, Lila, but I can't!"

Through the tears Millie's dark eyes blazed with anger. Glaring from Lila to Ben, she said, "What's happening to this household, anyway? If it's that damn manuscript, let's burn the thing! This is too horrible."

Ben said, "I agree with you, Millie, but right now I have to check on something, so if you'll excuse me..."

He hurried through the dining room, gesturing to Noel to follow, then mounted the stairs two at a time. In Jeanette's room he waited until Noel joined him, then said, only half joking, "I'm not touching anything without a witness."

Noel looked startled, but he quickly nodded agreement. "A sensible precaution," he said, "though I hadn't thought of it."

The two men stood looking around at the neatly made bed; the dresser, which was bare of personal things except for a hairbrush; the luggage rack, where Jeanette's tan, leather-bound suitcase rested, full of her clothes; and the desk, where a brass lamp still burned, as if Jeanette had meant to return to her work after seeing Margo.

The desk had been cleared of the files and papers that traveled everywhere with Jeanette. All that remained was a pottery mug full of pencils, a yellow legal pad, and a calendar turned to the next day, where the time of Jeanette's flight had been penciled. A dark brown leather briefcase lay at one end of the desk, closed, but with its brass buckle unlatched.

Ben walked to the desk, saying, "She'd keep the copier in her briefcase, I should think."

"But should we touch anything, Ben?" Noel had come to stand beside him, and Ben turned to him, perplexed.

"I thought you agreed that we had to find that copier," he said.

"Well, yes, but I feel very strange now that we're here among all her things." Noel's hands were trembling as he gripped the back of Jeanette's desk chair. "It doesn't seem quite right."

From below they heard a car come into the drive and stop before the front door.

The two men exchanged a glance, then Noel went to the window and peered down at the driveway.

"It's the police," he said. "Let's get out of here, Ben."

Ben stood very still, listening as Marie opened the door to admit Sergeant Clement and apparently one other. There was a rapid exchange in French, then the sounds of heavy steps on the stairs to the second floor.

As the voices came nearer Ben reached out and lifted the top of Jeanette's briefcase. There in full view was the copier, a black rectangle that might easily be taken for one of the many varieties of camera that filled the shops.

Smiling ruefully at Noel, who looked as if he might be about to faint, Ben removed the copier just as Sergeant Clement entered the room.

Offering the machine to the sergeant, he said, "I advise you to guard this carefully, Sergeant Clement. It may contain some valuable secrets."

"Yes, Carrie, I can see why the police would have to seal off Jeanette's room. The point I'm making is that Noel Wright must have known that, and realized that they would do it this morning, as soon as they thought of it."

"But what timing, Ben! I can't believe he'd have allowed you to come with him if he really didn't want the copier found. In fact..." Carrie sat up straight as an idea struck her. "In fact, he would simply have gone up and grabbed it himself. Why did he need you?"

"It wasn't so much that he needed me, he *had* me. I was with that guy all morning. I was the one who reminded him that the copier might be important."

Ben slumped in his chair, peering gloomily toward the rain-streaked windows. It was the first bad weather they'd had, and while they had been saving certain attractions, such as the Musée Masséna in Nice, for just such weather, they were too engrossed in the affairs of La Rêverie to enjoy looking at paintings.

Carrie reached for the bottle of very nice Chardonnay that had accompanied lunch, and after Ben had declined with a scowling shake of his head, poured her own glass half full. She took a sip, enjoying the pleasant buzz that resulted from lunchtime wine drinking and regretting that Ben was feeling morose—a condition so rare with him that she had not had much practice in cheering him up.

She said, "Just how important is that copier, Ben? I mean," she hurried on, "the manuscript stored in it is also on paper, isn't it?"

"Yes, as far as we know." Ben tipped his head back and closed his eyes. "But the printouts of half of it are missing. They may have been destroyed by now."

"Ben! What if you printed it all out and found Paul's section in there? And Millie's? Oh boy!" Carrie's eyes were sparkling as she took another sip of wine. "Ben, you've got to make Inspector Foch get that whole thing printed immediately!"

"I imagine he'll think of that himself." Ben sat very still for a moment, then said slowly, "Who else knew Jeanette had a copier? Besides Noel and Margo. Do you remember anyone ever mentioning it?''

He was on his feet, getting his notes, which by now filled a manila folder. As he stood riffling through them, some of the smaller scraps slipping to the floor, Carrie pushed aside his luncheon plate to make room on the table.

She said, ''I can't recall the copier ever being discussed, which seems odd when it's such an interesting little machine. I guess Jeanette kept quiet about it.''

Ben sat down at the table and spread out his papers. ''There's no way to find out who knew now that Jeanette is gone.'' He looked up sharply. ''Except...except that if the killer knew, wouldn't he have made damn sure he got his hands on it?''

''Well, yes. There'd be no point in murdering to get a manuscript that could easily be duplicated.'' Carrie poured the last drops of wine into her glass, wondering how sinful it would be to order another bottle. It was vacation, after all, or had been until these terrible murders occurred.

Ben was looking through his notes, muttering to himself and jotting on yet another piece of paper. Carrie sighed. The rain was coursing down the windowpanes and making a steady thrum on the hotel roof, and she was feeling deliciously relaxed, though not exactly sleepy. She looked across at Ben, still bent over his papers like a schoolboy struggling with his homework.

He looked very boyish at the moment, in fact, with his brown hair disarrayed and his glasses slipping down on his nose. She reached over and tweaked them into place, and he looked up and growled, ''What are you doing?''

She smiled as seductively as possible and got to her feet. She walked around to him and stroked his hair back from his face, saying, ''Wouldn't it be a shame to waste a cozy afternoon in an expensive hotel suite...''

''What are you talking about, Carrie? Oh, I see, but...''

''...with no children around and nothing much to do.''

Standing behind him, she slipped her arms around his neck and began unbuttoning his shirt.

Ben tipped his head back and kissed her, smiling at last, if faintly. He said, ''Noel's going to call when he hears about the coroner's report.''

"Yes? He can leave a message." Carrie was pulling him to his feet.

"And he gave me Margo's section of the novel. We both have to read it today. Carrie, stop it!"

But it was too late, she had dragged him to the door of the bedroom, where she stood smiling up at him, her eyes shining and full of laughter, her cheeks flushed from the wine.

"What do I have to do?" she whispered huskily, "Carry you across the threshold?"

But he made it to the bed on foot.

NINETEEN

By FOUR O'CLOCK Ben had read more than 100 pages of Margo's manuscript while Carrie napped in the bedroom. Time to wake her, he thought, suddenly aware that the room had turned stuffy. The rain had stopped, the afternoon sun was pouring through the windows, and Ben got out of his chair and went to open the French doors to the terrace.

He stepped outside and a fat drop of water plopped onto his head from the eaves above. The air felt fresh and clean on his face, its tangy aroma intensified by the rain. From the terrace below he could hear the voices of waiters who were setting tables and replacing cushions on the wicker chairs; dinner could be served outdoors after all.

The telephone rang, and Ben hurried back into the room to pick it up, but Carrie had answered the call in the bedroom. They both listened as Noel Wright said, "The damnedest thing has happened. We just got a call from La Hospitaliere—you know, Celia Rowan's nursing home—to say she escaped last night. They have no idea where she is!"

Carrie said, "Oh, that poor woman! Something terrible could happen to her!"

"Yes, she is quite helpless . . ."

"Did they say what time?" Ben interrupted. "When do they think she got away?"

"Why, around five in the afternoon, I believe. I didn't pay much attention, I was too fascinated with the way she did it. Apparently she locked up her nurse somehow and simply slithered out through the garden."

"Don't they have an alarm system?"

"An erratic one, apparently, as you might expect in this country."

"In any country," Carrie put in. "You know how ours goes nuts sometimes, Ben."

"Yes, but wasn't she seen by the neighbors, or in the village?"

"Have you ever been in Eze at five in the afternoon?" Noel countered. "The tour buses are leaving, the square is positively teeming with people. Her timing couldn't have been better."

"Of course," said Carrie. "She would have worked it out to the last detail."

Ben said, "Noel, has Margo been informed of this?"

"I just tried to call her, but she's gone out." There was a silence, then Noel said cautiously, "I gather we're thinking along the same lines."

"I'm thinking that Margo's house should not be left empty. Unless you have some objection, I'll run over there now and wait for her."

"That would be prudent, I agree. I cannot leave here until after Inspector Foch's interrogation."

"I understand."

"And, Ben, the inspector has reported that Jeanette was shot by a small-bore pistol, probably a Beretta."

"Was it the same gun that killed Paul?"

"They don't know yet. 'Similar and possibly identical' is the way the inspector put it. I'll let you know when I hear more."

They rang off and, leaving Carrie to shower and dress for dinner, Ben gathered up his manuscript pages and took them along to read while he waited for Margo.

The creature that had washed up to the metal grille was still alive. Dépouille saw its thin legs move as it weakly scrabbled its claws against the force of the water. The fur was black, he thought, maybe brown when it was dry. A river rat. If it did not drown it might crawl to him, and he would welcome its warmth.

A chill shook his body, and he came close to rolling off the curbstone into the churning gutter. Perhaps that would be best: to let himself drown beside the rat.

They would depart this miserable life together. He imagined the rodent's beady little eyes peering gratefully into his, welcoming his company on their final journey.

Now his face burned with fever. He marveled that his emaciated body could generate such heat. It must have been the dying embers of the drug. At the thought a ribbon of pain shot through his limbs, tracing the outline of his bones with devilish accuracy. He opened his mouth to scream, but all that emerged was the feeble moan that might be expected of a dying cat. He writhed, turning onto his back with his face set in a grimace of pain.

"Claude, is it you?"

The voice came from above; was it the voice of God?

A dark figure knelt beside him. His head was lifted up to rest against a man's knee. His face was wiped with a cloth and he moaned again, this time in terror, and then he opened his eyes and looked into the face of Robert de Laine.

He fainted. He floated in a black mist shot through with arrows of pain while men carried him to a car, then after a long time to a bed, where the pain stabbed again and again while they washed him and covered him.

Dimly he knew they tried to feed him, but it could not be done. He felt the warmth of people near him, heard voices that drifted in and out of his awareness speaking words without meaning; finally he felt the prick of a needle, then blessed oblivion.

When Claude Dépouille next opened his eyes he lay still, peering into the dimness of what appeared to be a large room with two tall windows, both heavily curtained to keep out the light. He let his gaze roam about as he identified a massive dresser, a chair, a lamp, and another bed a few feet from his.

Across the room a door was opened, forming an elongated triangle of light through which a man's form stepped. Dépouille closed his eyes again, but only for a moment, and this time when he opened them Robert was there, leaning over him with a worried smile on his face.

Robert said, "Claude? Are you better now? Can you eat something?"

Dépouille managed to shake his head. As he peered up at his friend, he felt a terrible anxiety rise in him. His heart was suddenly pounding, his mouth had gone dry with fear, as if he stood at the brink of some unconquerable peril.

Then Robert spoke and the dark chasm opened.

He said, "Where is Mimi, Claude? Is Mimi safe?"

Dépouille could not escape again. The drug had run its course and now he must look into the chasm.

"She is with Sahid."

He was too weak to lie, and it did not matter now. Let Robert kill him—it was inevitable, he knew his rages—and free him from his shame.

Robert's face had turned to stone, white stone in which his eyes blazed with fury.

"You gave her to him! No, you sold her, to pay for your filthy habit!"

Robert was shaking him like a mastiff shakes a small animal to break its neck. With his head jolting on his shoulders, Claude prayed for the sound of snapping bone. His teeth bit through his tongue and his mouth filled with blood. Robert's steely fingers cut into his shoulders, breaking the skin, and there was more blood. His fingers slipped and he cursed and hurled Dépouille to the floor.

"She is your daughter, Claude! You have sold your daughter!"

Dépouille screamed, "No!"

Relentlessly Robert repeated, "Your daughter, your child, you have sold her to a vile monster!" and Dépouille sobbed and babbled, trying to drown him out. He tried to cover his ears, but his arms were shaking uncontrollably and full of pain.

Robert ran to the door and switched on the lights, then he punched the button that would call a servant, all the while cursing Dépouille in the foulest terms he could summon.

A maid appeared and de Laine pushed her into the room and barked, "Call the rest of the staff. I want them all watching when I prove to this miserable piece of filth that he has committed the most unspeakable of all crimes. Don't leave him!"

De Laine swung out of the room and the frightened girl pressed the button as she had been ordered, meanwhile keeping her horrified gaze fixed on the bloody heap of humanity that was Claude Dépouille.

He writhed on the floor, desperate to get to his feet and escape, but his right arm was broken. He could not push himself up, and the pain was so intense he fell back, afraid he would faint as he had before.

"Help me," he quavered, but the maid stood paralyzed beside the door, terrified of him, but more afraid of de Laine's wrath should she leave the room.

Dépouille fell back and closed his eyes, willing death to release him before Robert returned. He could not bear it. The pain of his broken arm was completely eclipsed by his fear of what Robert would tell him.

Over the thudding of his heart Dépouille heard the whispering and rustling of people entering the room. They were staying near the door, he could tell; no one crossed the room to offer help to the suffering wretch in the corner.

With a part of his mind he enjoyed their fear. He moaned, deliberately, to see if anyone would respond, but though he heard an anxious murmur, not one of Robert's servants came to his side.

Firm steps approached, and Dépouille opened his eyes to see Robert de Laine stride into the room, passing the group of frightened servants without a glance. In his hand he carried a small sheet of paper, and when he reached Dépouille he stopped with the toes of his shoes nearly grazing his bare legs.

He began to read from the paper: *To whom it may concern: I, Katerina de la Tour, declare without doubt or shame that my beloved and only child, Mimi, is the daughter of Claude Dépouille.*

At the first words Dépouille began to tremble, his entire body twitching and jerking in a spasm of despair. He heard a cry of sympathy from the direction of the door, but it was quickly hushed as Robert read on.

I make this statement in order to place my daughter, in the event of my demise, in the care and protection of her natural father.

Robert read the final words in a voice filled with scalding bitterness. He stopped and the room became so silent Dépouille thought the servants must have fled in horror.

Ben Porter heard a car come into Margo's driveway, and he jumped up to look out the window. Stopping in front of the door was Sonny Devere's black Jaguar. As Ben watched, Sonny got out and came around to open the door for Margo.

She was showing her years that day. She climbed out of the car leaning heavily on Sonny, and when she straightened Ben saw that she was dressed in a drab beige linen dress instead of her usual bright silks. She wore a forlorn smile as she lifted her cheek to be kissed, and he felt glad she was not coming home to an empty house.

Hoping not to startle her too badly, he opened the door, calling, "Margo! It's Ben Porter," and stepped out onto the gravel.

"What are you doing here?" she cried, obviously uncertain whether to feel alarmed or pleasantly surprised.

"It's nothing serious," he said, striding over to greet Sonny. "Where have you been? Out having a grand lunch?"

"Hardly that. Sonny and I have been comforting each other." She looked up wearily at the tall young man beside her. "He insisted on getting me out of the house, so we've been drinking tea at his villa."

"Such a tragedy," murmured Sonny Devere. "I am desolated."

"Go home now, darling," said Margo, patting his arm. "I will call you about the . . . the arrangements."

Her face crumpled and she turned abruptly and marched into the house where, after saying goodbye to Sonny, Ben followed her.

In her hallway Margo embraced him tearfully, then pulled away to wipe her eyes. She said, "I can't tell you how glad I am to see you. I was dreading . . ."

She started for the living room, then stopped and turned to him. "How did you get in, come to think of it? I'm sure I locked the house."

"Noel came along to let me in and then take my car to La Rêverie. We didn't want any sign of a visitor in case . . . Well, sit down, Margo. We are a little uncomfortable about having you stay here alone right now."

Margo glanced at him sharply, then sank into a chair, letting her capacious leather handbag collapse on the floor beside her.

"Something more has happened, I can tell," she said; but to Ben's relief, she seemed to have taken charge of her emotions. Perhaps it was going to be easier than he had feared.

He said, "Celia Rowan has run away from her nursing home, and we thought, just to be on the safe side . . ."

"That I'd better get out of here. I couldn't agree more." She sat up and said, "When did she get away? Was it before Jeanette . . . ?"

"Yes, she's been gone since late yesterday afternoon. Not that that means anything ominous. Mrs. Rowan is hardly a murderous type, after all." Watching Margo closely for signs of panic, he added, "I imagine she's drinking tea in somebody's house right now, while they wonder where such a charming lady dropped from."

"I can see she captured your heart, along with hundreds of others, but let's remember why they locked her up, Ben darling. Not because of her charm, I'd say."

Margo rose from her chair and retrieved her handbag. "I guess I'll go to La Rêverie," she said. "Loulou Marchand called from Paris and suggested I move to their house, but I don't want to be alone."

Her voice quavered on the last word, and Ben quickly got to his feet. She stopped him, however, drawing herself up to say, "No, I'll be all right, thanks, Ben. I'll go up and pack a few things." As she started out of the room she added, "Help yourself to a drink," then in the hallway turned back long enough to say, "And make one for me, while you're about it. I can feel my nerves starting to crumble."

TWENTY

BEN COOKED DINNER that night. Noel had sent Marie home to pull herself together, so Ben took over the kitchen and, with Carrie standing by to help him find things, concocted the simple American dishes that all at once appealed to him.

"It'll be comforting, this kind of food," he explained as he shook pieces of chicken in a bag of flour. "Fried chicken, mashed potatoes, apple pie…these people haven't had a meal like that in years. Maybe it will cheer them up."

Carrie agreed. "They'll feel like they're back in Mommy's house. You're a nice guy, Ben Porter." She kissed the back of his neck. "But I'd like to catch you serving up this meal at home. There it would be *poulet sauté Provençale* and *tarte Tatin.*"

"Maybe I'm a cultural misfit. Anyway, it's fun to get a crack at the kitchen again."

There was a light tap at the back door, then the knob was twisted as a man's voice called, *"C'est moi, Jean,"* and Ben opened the door to admit Sergeant Clement.

"Oh, sorry, Monsieur!" The sergeant hesitated outside the door. "I am to stay here tonight," he added. "It has been ordered by Inspector Foch. Because of the shooting, you understand."

"Yes, I see," said Ben. "Have you discovered any evidence you can tell me about?"

"Only the matching bullets, Monsieur, which indicate that Mlle Melton was probably shot by the killer of M. Clifford."

"Probably?"

"That is exactly what I said to Inspector Foch!" The sergeant grinned at Ben; they thought alike. "Then he said to me, but supposing the same gun was used by two different people? Or perhaps it was merely the same kind of gun, if you understand what I mean, and not the same weapon."

"Then you have not received the results of the ballistics tests?"

"Not yet. Perhaps tomorrow morning."

The sergeant turned to leave, but Ben stopped him. "One thing more," he said. "Are you also posting a guard at Mme Honeywell's house tonight?"

Again the sergeant's eyes crinkled affably. "Again we are in accord, M. Porter! Yes, that is being done, for, who knows? Perhaps the killer of Mlle Melton was actually hoping to surprise Mme Honeywell. It is a fearsome thought, but..." With an expressive shrug, Sergeant Clement went off to organize his men.

Ben's instincts had been correct. The novelty of sitting down to simple, once-familiar dishes distracted everyone from their sorrow.

"You must come over more often, Ben," said Noel as he searched his plate for the last crumb of apple pie. "We can always arrange to give Marie a holiday."

Margo mustered a faint smile. "I feel guilty about enjoying that chicken so much, but it did lift my spirits, bless you, Ben."

When dinner was over, the Porters went with Noel and Margo to have coffee on the terrace while Millie helped Lila clean up. This provided Lila with two helpers, or, more accurately, two companions, since Hank would not leave Millie's side even though things were clearly not going well between them.

"Will you talk to her, Lila?" Hank came into the kitchen carrying one butter plate, which dangled from his fingers until Lila took it away from him. "There's no reason for her to stay around here any longer and, damn it, I say she's risking her life!"

"No more than I would be on the streets of New York!"

This was Millie's retort as she came in from the dining room with a stack of dishes. She placed them on the wooden drain board and started back for another load.

"Millie, it's crazy to say that!" Hank caught the swinging door and followed her through. "You're in real danger here, and anyway you promised to go back with me in one week. The week is up."

"You said one week, I didn't; and I'm not ready, Hank. Now will you, for God's sake, stop bugging me?"

While she talked Millie was piling up another load of dishes. She backed through the door with them while Hank followed, empty-handed.

Lila relieved Millie of her burden, shaking her head at Hank. "I can't say much for your helper, Millie. I hope you shape him up before the wedding."

"Wedding—what wedding?" Hank was scowling as he watched Millie stalk back to the dining room. "She's in no hurry, that much is clear."

"Have you asked about her intentions?" Lila said, turning to grin at him over her shoulder. "Maybe you're nothing more than a sex object to her."

"What? Oh, very amusing, Lila. Now how about getting practical and helping..."

"How about you picking up that dish towel, speaking of getting practical? A few rudimentary kitchen skills might help your cause."

The swinging door opened once more, and Millie came through with her hands full of napkins and place mats, which she carried to the laundry basket in the pantry. Taking a towel from the rack, she joined the two at the sink and began drying dishes.

Hank said, "Tell Lila what you told me, Millie, and see if she thinks it makes sense."

"I said I'm in this thing with the rest of you because everyone here has gotten to be my family, and I'm not leaving you in the lurch!"

Millie's eyes were bright with defiance as she faced Hank. She was wearing the raspberry blouse that gave a glow to her skin, and Hank felt a foolish smile come to his face as he gazed down at her.

"But darling, be realistic," he said gently. "You can't help them, you can't protect them..."

"Oh, don't I know that! But we can comfort each other, can't we, Lila? We need each other more than ever while this horrible nightmare is going on, don't you agree?"

Lila's head was bowed and they saw two tears splash one after the other into the soapy dishwater.

Millie threw her arms around Lila's shoulders, saying, "Oh damn! I didn't mean to upset you. Don't cry, Lila, please."

Taking a deep breath, Lila straightened. She turned her tear-filled eyes to Millie and said, "It seems okay to grieve when you've lost two friends in one week."

Millie kissed her wet cheek, then mopped it with the dish towel. "We can grieve for them together, that's another thing."

Hank said huskily, "Maybe some day you'll feel that kind of loyalty for me," and Millie looked at him with a shaky smile forming on her lips.

"I think you're catching on at last," she said.

She gave Lila's shoulders a final squeeze and went to Hank. "Be just a little patient with me, darling," she whispered, "and it will all work out."

He pulled her close, and for a moment the only sound in the kitchen was the chink and splash of dishes bumping around in the sink.

Then Lila said, without turning around, "If you two want references you'll have to look elsewhere," and Millie and Hank laughed and broke apart and went back to their chores.

THEY HAD TAKEN their coffee to the terrace, but when Margo began to shiver they retreated to the warmth and light of the drawing room.

"Pull the curtains, will you, Noel?" she said as she settled into a corner of the sofa. "I can't stand the idea of someone out there looking in at us."

She shivered again, and Carrie sat down beside her and took her hand. "You need to feel cozy and protected tonight, poor dear. You're still reacting to that terrible shock."

Margo smiled gratefully. "I'm not usually such a scaredy cat, so that must be it. Thank God I'm here with all of you and not sitting in that empty house, waiting..."

Noel had closed the draperies, and now he settled in the chair nearest Margo and said, "Margo, darling, you're absolutely safe now. Isn't she, Ben?"

"I should think so. You haven't anything the killer wants, you see. Since Celia Rowan's pages never got to you, all you have are the parts of the novel that are accessible to everyone."

"Maybe so, but I won't get a night's sleep until these ghastly murders are solved—or till Celia Rowan is safely locked up again." Margo paused. "And the two may amount to the same thing."

Carrie exclaimed, "I simply cannot imagine that lovely woman gunning anyone down, I really can't."

"After the scene we witnessed, I'm afraid I can." Ben sighed. "I hope they find her soon so we can scratch that possibility."

Margo drained her demitasse and placed the cup on the table before her. "You all seem to be assuming that Paul and Jeanette were killed for their manuscripts. I happen to know, however, that Celia Rowan was madly jealous of anyone who got close to Charles. I don't have to remind you of that, do I, Noel?"

Noel said, "But not *that* jealous, surely, Margo?"

"Who knows what it takes to make a crazy person commit murder? For a long time Paul was Charles's most intimate companion. I know you hate to admit that, but..."

"I don't mind at all!" Noel protested.

"And when Jeanette started coming over to visit, Charles was delighted with her, remember? He found her so amusing—something Celia could never claim—he wanted her around all the time."

Ben said, "Are you suggesting that Celia Rowan is bent on wiping out everyone Charles Melton cared for? When he's been dead and buried for six months?"

"You keep ignoring the fact that she's crazy!" Margo pushed herself up from the sofa and strode to the cabinet where the brandy decanter was kept. She poured herself a drink, then brandished the bottle, asking, "Will anyone join me?"

"I will." Noel stood up and went to get his own. After filling his glass he put his arm around Margo and said, "Come and curl up with me on the sofa and we'll drink our troubles away."

She kissed his cheek. "I wish it were that easy, you old sot."

Watching them, Carrie grinned and jumped up from her seat. She plumped up the soft down cushions, saying, "It's all yours. Ben and I have to go."

When Ben looked at her in surprise she added, "Yes, we do, darling. We have work to do, remember?"

"True, but..."

Something in her face stopped him, however, and after a few more reassuring words to Margo, the Porters took their leave.

PALE PINK SHREDS of a glorious sunset floated at the edge of the darkening sky, and Carrie stopped in the driveway to peer at her watch.

"It's only eight-thirty, Ben. I wonder if Inspector Foch has gone home."

"Here's the man who can tell us." The figure of Sergeant Clement emerged from the looming shadows of the hedge, and as he came up to them, Ben said, "I wanted to ask you, Sergeant, to speak with Mrs. Honeywell this evening, before it gets late. She is feeling nervous and uneasy, but if she knows you are watching her room especially carefully..."

"I understand, M. Porter. She is to be forgiven, would you not say? In view of the sad events?" Sergeant Clement shook his head gloomily. "I will post a man beside her door, and I myself will watch from outside. I think she should not worry."

"I feel confident that you will take every precaution," said Ben, "but it would be a kindness if you would personally reassure her."

"I will make it a point, Monsieur; thank you for the suggestion."

Carrie said, "And Sergeant Clement, can you tell us where we might find Inspector Foch? I want to ask him a question."

"I don't think we should bother the inspector at this hour, Carrie," Ben began, but Sergeant Clement stopped him.

"It is no problem, M. Porter. Inspector Foch will be staying late at headquarters tonight. The other men are on guard duty, you see, and we are shorthanded."

"I hope it is all for nothing," said Ben, "and that you and your men have an uneventful night."

"I share your wishes, Monsieur."

As the Porters drove away Carrie said, "While you were at Margo's this afternoon I had a chat with the manager of the hotel, M. Piret. They use a computer, you know, for their bookings and accounts."

"Oh, they do?" Reaching a corner, Ben stopped and said, "Before you go on, how about explaining why we're making this urgent call on Inspector Foch?"

"That's what I'm doing." Carrie peered out at the street sign. "Avenue Albert Premier. Turn left, Ben." As he obediently swung the car toward the village, she went on, "I got Mr. Piret's permission to use the hotel's printer if it happens to be compatible with Jeanette's copier."

"You mean, we might be able to print out whatever material she has stored in that gadget? Why didn't I think of that?"

"Well, don't get too excited. If the copier isn't IBM-compatible we can't hook it up to the printer, but the hotel accountant said most computers are made to conform."

"What a break for us if they fit!"

"There's still the possibility that Inspector Foch won't let us borrow it."

"He'll have to be persuaded. Which way here, Carrie?"

They had reached Avenue Denis-Séméria, the road that leads in one direction to the mainland and in the other to the small cluster of shops and cafés that make up the village of St.-Jean-Cap-Ferrat. They followed it around to the right until they reached Avenue des Fleurs, which led to the *gendarmerie*.

Lights shone through the windows of the low stucco building, illuminating the lone car parked in the lot, the black Vauxhall Ben and Carrie had last seen at the door of La Rêverie. Ben pulled up beside it, and in the front window a corner of the venetian blind was twitched up, then quickly lowered.

Carrie grinned. "The inspector must be having a dull evening," she said, reaching for the door handle. "We'll go cheer him up."

"Wait a second, Carrie," Ben said. "Let's plan our campaign."

"It's all planned, love. And we really can't take time to go over it if we want to get the printout done tonight." Hushing Ben's protest, Carrie continued, "Evening is the best time for the hotel, of course, and if we get back there by nine M. Piret will help us hook up the machinery. Come on, darling, trust me."

Carrie stepped out of the car, shook out her blond hair, and, with Ben following somewhat reluctantly, pushed open the door of the *gendarmerie*.

TWENTY-ONE

From Carrie Porter's journal, dated May 19, 1989:

I'M SITTING by the pool, soaking up as much Riviera sun and ambience as possible because we only have two more days, and I gather from Mrs. Duffy's letter the weather is terrible at home. A lot I'll care, I'm so starved for the sight of those children. In fact, I miss them so much I've vowed to become a better mother. I'll read them longer stories at bedtime, cook more hot breakfasts, and never, ever yell at them, no matter what! I hope I get home safely so they can enjoy my improved personality.

Ben is in the hotel accounting office reading the final pages of Charles Melton's manuscript, the ones we printed this morning from Jeanette's copier, which is, by the way, a marvelous little machine. Porter Publishing could put one to good use if we can squeeze it into the budget.

It was difficult to have to wait till today to see if the copier would hook up with the hotel printer—especially since I was scared to death Inspector Foch would have second thoughts overnight and decide not to let us try it, after all. He couldn't have been more agreeable last night, once we had explained how the copier works and how many important secrets might be locked up inside it. By the time we got through he was as excited as we were and was obviously tempted to close up shop and tear over to the hotel with us, even though he had nobody available to stand duty in his place.

The situation is so unusual that the poor man wasn't precisely sure how to handle it, and he obviously wanted to deal with it himself, without letting his superiors make it even more complicated. So, at my suggestion, he put strict limitations on our use of the machine, the main one being to have one of his men monitor the operation, so we would have no opportunity to make extra copies or cheat in any other way.

Ben and I are permitted to read everything that comes off the printer, and we can make all the notes we want, but only in the office, in the presence of the above-mentioned officer. We're not allowed to keep a copy for ourselves, on paper or on another disk. And if we haven't both read it all by quitting time today, it gets locked up until tomorrow morning.

It seems like a lot of fuss over what may turn out to be nothing more than it appears to be: the final work from the pen of Charles Melton and therefore a literary treasure. If Ben's theory is correct, however, and there is a cleverly coded message hidden in the story, we may be on the way to solving two murders.

The suspense is making it very hard to relax. I have to keep reminding myself that in forty-eight hours I'll be en route to reality, to the routine of kids and work, dealing with car pools with one hand and authors' agents with the other. And loving it, let's remember; loving the demands and the certainty I can cope and all the other aspects of the unique life Ben and I have worked out for ourselves. What if I had married an old-fashioned type who believed in all that stultifying role-playing? It's too painful to contemplate.

I think Ben feels the way I do: ready to go home but reluctant to leave this beautiful, intriguing part of the world. Last night when we left the *gendarmerie* we were much too keyed up to go to bed, so we strolled around the little village and the port, soaking it all up.

Everything is small scale, little tea shops and restaurants, most with a patch of terrace for dining *en plein air;* a few craftsmen's studios with tall, handsome wooden doors; a *boulangerie,* of course, and a *charcuterie* with goodies in the window that are never seen at home; shops selling Provençal herbs and fabrics; a flower market with all the brightly painted carts closed up for the night.

It's all built on a ledge overlooking the bay, and there is a tiny park with stone steps leading down to the port. We went down and strolled along the dock, past the cafés, which are smaller than the ones in Beaulieu but feature many of the same dishes: *cassolette de fruits de mer, brochette de poissons, terrine de loup.* (And I've developed an irrepressible yearning for a hamburger!)

People were strolling with us, stopping to read the menus or to buy an ice at the *glacerie.* One girl was training a seeing-eye dog, giving him orders as they walked along: *"Allez, à gauche…non, non, à gauche,"* administering a swift little kick when he got it wrong, which was frequently.

We looked over the boats tied up in their slips, picking out the ones we'd like to own, fascinated by the different homey touches—the flower arrangements, the books and games and pillows with witty messages. It was fun, too, to look in the windows of the marine supply shop at the wonderland of expensive gadgetry, much of it mysterious to us.

We had a drink at one of the cafés and managed to forget the situation at La Rêverie while we watched the people, who were watching us in return, and listened to the conversations around us—a soothing occupation when you don't understand the language. The boats bobbed, creaking and jingling, their masts poking up against the sky, and beyond them we could see the outline of the hills on the other side of the bay—black and rounded at night, without that harsh, scoured look they have in daylight.

Around midnight we climbed back up the stone staircase and were amused when a friendly rat peeked out from a crevice in the wall about halfway up and watched with great composure until we came quite close.

This morning we had another heavenly breakfast on our little balcony and then hurried to the office for the big event. We watched with fingers crossed and hearts pounding while M. Piret hitched the copier to the hotel printer. *Voilà!* It worked! And then it took most of the morning to run off the contents, which did not include the pages stolen from Millie and Paul.

So whatever else Jeanette was up to, she wasn't guilty of that. While I'm relieved in a way, that also lessens our chances of getting this puzzle solved before we go home. I can tell Ben is very apprehensive about that, and I've caught him checking airline schedules and rates, quite obviously with a view to staying a few days longer if necessary—to which I say, nothing doing!

I only hope he finishes his reading soon so that I can get started. I forgot to mention that when we talked to Noel this morning, he said Celia Rowan is still missing. That means there will be no relaxing of the vigilance at La Rêverie or at Margo's—a horrible strain for all these people, of whom, to my surprise, I've become quite fond. I only hope Celia Rowan turns up soon, safe and reasonably sane and, please God, with no blood on her hands.

RAOUL BERNET WAS in his tenth year as head doorman at the Hotel Negresco in Nice. He had started as a porter twenty years earlier and, because he was tall and good looking and tactful in dealing with the extremely varied clientele, had been kept in a position of high visibility that he thoroughly enjoyed.

There couldn't be many better jobs than his, Raoul often thought, especially on a sunny day at the height of the season, when he could hear the shouts of bathers from the beach on the other side of the Promenade des Anglais, watch the cars racing by on the boulevard, and greet the glamorous people who stepped out of shiny limousines, happy to have arrived at what Raoul considered the portals of the Côte d'Azur.

He liked his uniform, too. Each morning when he carefully, almost reverently, put on the dark blue coat with its jaunty red-and-gold-trimmed cape, he felt like a veteran actor assuming his favorite role. The high-crowned blue hat added inches to his height, and the bright red plumes that spurted from its crown tossed cheerfully in the breeze—a theatrical touch that brought smiles to the tourists' faces. It was not surprising that the image of Raoul beneath the glass awning of the snowy white hotel, with the bright flags

whipping overhead, traveled home in thousands of cam-
eras. Secretly, Raoul thought of this as a form of immor-
tality: anonymous, perhaps, but better than none.

A black limousine drew up, the eighth of the day, Raoul
registered automatically, and it was only a few minutes past
noon. The chauffeur stepped out and nodded as he came
around to open the door for his passenger; he was one of
the many hire-car drivers whose faces were familiar to
Raoul. They shared with him the imperturbability required to serve the public while maintaining their personal
dignity.

A lady emerged from the car and stepped toward him,
smiling so infectiously that Raoul allowed some of his own
carefully measured cordiality to emerge. He remembered
this lovely woman—or did he?

"Madame?" He clicked his heels and bowed from the
waist. "Welcome to the Negresco."

"Raoul! You haven't forgotten me, I know you
haven't!" The lady was laughing in the most delightful,
musical way, and smiling into his eyes as if they were old,
close friends.

She turned to her driver and said, "Please bring my little bag and we'll go in and settle things." She swung back
to Raoul, laughing again as if she were the silliest person on
earth. "I came away so impetuously you wouldn't believe
it! I brought nothing, practically nothing, with me. I'll have
to buy out all the shops in Nice!"

He remembered suddenly; her voice, her warm, generous manner brought back a memory of the same woman,
a few years younger, and always before with a man, more
than one—a rich American who was her husband, and another man, a famous face—ah, Raoul had it. Charles Melton, the author. Of course. She was a person of importance.

"Madame . . . Rowan." As usual, the name came to him
when he needed it. "It is a great pleasure to see you again.
You have been neglecting us."

Looking to his left he nodded sharply, and Jacques, the chief porter, instantly came to take his place while Raoul ushered Mme Rowan into the hotel.

"Yes, it has been much too long, Raoul, you are right. And I have missed all of you, truly I have!" She was smiling and nodding at the porters and the concierge and his assistants behind their mahogany counter.

The concierge stepped out to shake her hand, saying, "We are honored, Madame Rowan. It is a joy to see you back again."

While the concierge greeted her, Raoul went to the manager's office to inform him of her arrival, and a moment later M. Vivier appeared in the lobby to escort her to his desk, where they could discuss her accommodations.

"You did not book an apartment, Madame? At this time of year? I am surprised." He shook his head in mock disapproval, but smiling in a way that told her there would be no problem.

She sank into the chair he held for her and folded her hands in her lap while he asked his secretary to get the book of reservations.

"I will be honest with you, M. Vivier," she said when the woman had left the office, "I am getting scatterbrained in my old age." When he began to protest she hurried on, "Yes, it is true, and not a bit surprising, especially in view of the sad shocks I have borne in recent years."

"Yes, Madame Rowan, we were grieved to hear..."

Again she interrupted him. "I did not come to Nice in a mood of mourning, Monsieur, but to enjoy the delights of the Riviera as you and I know they should be enjoyed—from Suite 306 of the Negresco Hotel!"

She beamed at him happily, her beautiful dark eyes shining into his, and M. Vivier was fired with an urgent desire to please her. To disappoint this charming woman would be a despicable act of cruelty; he would not have it on his conscience.

He opened the large leather book his secretary had placed before him, but without turning the pages he said, "Suite 306 is yours, Madame Rowan, for as long as you wish. Now

let us consider what special arrangements might be made
for your comfort.''

"Ah, Monsieur Vivier, you are the most considerate man
in the world, but I don't need special coddling, as you well
know. The only thing I need . . .'' Her hands were busy beneath the flap of her leather handbag—a well-worn
Hermés, M. Vivier observed. "What I need at the moment
is the telephone number of Air France, which I seem to
have stupidly lost, so I can find out if they have located my
luggage.''

"The airline lost your bags, Madame? But they will
quickly find them, I am confident. The concierge will get
in touch with them immediately.''

"Frankly, I would prefer to do it myself, Monsieur. A
terribly nice man was helping me.''

"Of course; but should you have any problem, Henri is
most efficient, as you will remember.'' He shook his head,
frowning. "Such a thing happens very rarely; it is most
surprising.''

"Ah well, the tags probably fell off.'' Madame Rowan
shrugged as if baggage were of minor importance on such
a happy occasion. "I intended to buy some new clothes in
any case. Tell me, M. Vivier, is Mlle Josephine still making
those handsome knits?''

"Unfortunately not, Madame. Her eyesight failed and
she was forced to close her shop, but now we have Grange
& Debreau, and they are just as good, perhaps a little
smarter.''

As he spoke M. Vivier took in some of the details of
Madame Rowan's costume. Her suit, of gray wool flecked
with black, was beautifully made, with self-welting appli-
quéd at the collar and pockets. The shoulders were narrow, however, which dated it, and the fabric appeared a bit
heavy for the season.

She seemed to read his mind, for she sighed and said,
"We have had such a ghastly spring in the States; it has
been more like autumn, and endless! I finally said,
Enough! and simply tossed a few things together—I was in
such a hurry to escape.''

Again her face was transformed by an enchanting smile. M. Vivier watched an elusive dimple come and go; on another woman of her age it would be a wrinkle. She got to her feet and he rose to join her, admiring her slimness and straight posture.

He said, "Madame Rowan, please allow me to compliment you. You look exactly the same as on your last visit to the Negresco, which must have been ..." He glanced at the reservations book on his desk, but she turned to the door and he followed.

"It could not have been as long ago as it seems, Monsieur. Now, I am dying to see my suite. Have you redecorated, or does the sitting room still have that exquisite brocade on the walls?"

Twenty minutes later he left her, reminding himself on his way down the corridor to have flowers sent up and, most important, to ask the concierge to offer his help in locating her luggage.

He stepped into the lift, trying to imagine what his life would be like if every guest at the hotel were as charming and considerate as Madame Rowan.

A SNORE BROKE the silence of the accounting office at the Hôtel des Fleurs, and Carrie Porter glanced up from her reading to see that the young policeman in the corner had fallen asleep. He looked about fourteen, she thought, with his flushed cheeks and his mouth falling open. No doubt he had been on duty for at least part of the night at one of the two houses, and it could hardly be stimulating to watch two people take turns reading a book.

She had been making notes, jotting down the names of the characters as they appeared and summarizing the action. So far no revelations had come to her, and she wondered about Ben. He had barely spoken to her when she came to take his place. He had hurried off, his face tight with concentration, and she knew his head was swimming with connections he'd either discovered or hoped to discover.

If only they spoke French. But surely by now Ben had gotten some help with definitions. She looked at the list: de Laine, Carole de Laine, Helene Rocher; those seemed to match up nicely with Melton, Noel, and Paul Clifford.

Now Marc Mielmont was back in the story; she had forgotten him, but there was something about that name that teased a recollection. So far it eluded her, however, and for De Cendre, Dépouille, and Kay Tourette she hadn't a glimmer.

She went back to the manuscript.

Once again Yannick entered the improvised press room, instantly setting off a clamor of questions. With quiet authority he silenced the journalists, asking them to be patient, assuring them he was aware of their deadlines and would report the outcome of the meeting within seconds of learning it himself.

To his surprise, he was enjoying his role, and it occurred to him that perhaps, under stress, he had finally gained the confidence he had always lacked. The possibility was so dizzying as to eclipse the terror that had been building in him since the start of the scheme. Perhaps it would work out wonderfully, and in only a few hours he would find himself rich and powerful and by some miracle in possession of Robert's respect at last.

He would never press his advantage, however; he would give Robert a position that would allow him to maintain at least a semblance of prestige, and he would try very hard not to point out that Robert had never done the same for him.

He slipped back into the boardroom and joined the group of "executive assistants" standing just inside the door, available to carry out orders from their superiors. These men, each of whom possessed almost godlike authority in the world of finance, were seated around an enormous mahogany table that filled the center of the room.

Robert de Laine occupied the seat of honor at the

head of the table and Paolo Gianelli the secondary place, at the foot.

Yannick wondered whether Gianelli was aware of his presence where he stood so modestly by the door. Would he invite him to join him at the table when he launched his bombshell? Yannick resolved not to mind if the man were understandably too excited to include him in his moment of glory.

Marc Mielmont was seated beside Robert, and now he rose, making a visible effort, and began reading from a file of papers he held in his hand. His voice was weak, however, and after a few words Robert reached for the microphone that stood on the table and handed it to Marc. If Yannick had been capable of feeling pity for Mielmont, he would have pitied him for the look of gratitude he turned on Robert and the quavering voice with which he resumed his now-audible remarks.

Robert sat watching him with a smile of encouragement, which grew broader as the halting speech went on until, to the bewilderment of all but three people in the room, he was shouting with laughter, his head thrown back, and joyously slapping one hand on the tabletop.

Had his brother lost his mind? Yannick had not taken in the sense of Marc Mielmont's few stumbling words. Now he realized a bombshell had indeed fallen on the meeting, but from an entirely unexpected quarter.

Some of the young men beside him were buzzing excitedly; others stood silent and white with shock. What in God's name had happened, and why did Paolo Gianelli sit there so quietly when he should be rising to announce the culmination of his life's ambition—his takeover of de Laine & Cie?

De Laine's public relations people were going around the room handing out press releases, and Yannick took one and began to read. He concentrated on the words, trying to make sense of what in the light of his expectations made no sense. De Laine & Cie. was not to be the victim of a takeover; Robert's empire would not become Paolo Gianelli's plaything, after all. On the contrary, it would now be up to Gianelli to salvage what he could of his own company, for if Yannick added the figures correctly, control of Empire Resources had now been placed in the unforgiving hands of Robert de Laine. Somehow, in the greatest secrecy, Robert had acquired control of the voting stock; it was a coup that would shake Wall Street to its foundations.

Yannick felt sick and dizzy. In his mind he pictured Carole de Laine sitting in her lawyer's office with Helene Rocher, waiting for the triumphal telephone call. He imagined her face becoming distorted with fury, like a witch's in a fairy tale, while she absorbed the shock; then he imagined that fury turned on him.

His knees were buckling. He had to get out of there; but now he realized that the men around him were congratulating him. They were opening up a path, but one leading not toward the door, but toward the vast table where, to his horror, he saw that his brother was standing and, still smiling broadly, was beckoning him to come and share his triumph.

As Yannick began to stumble forward, a strangled sound rose from Robert's right, and he turned in time to see Marc Mielmont pitch forward in his chair. Robert reached for him, but Mielmont slid to the floor, his head bumping the edge of the table before he sank out of sight.

Robert shouted, "Get a doctor!" and, shoving the chair out of his way, knelt on the rug beside his friend. Yannick looked on, frozen in his progress. Someone ran to the door, nearly knocking him down; others were giving suggestions: open his collar, stretch him out, take his pulse.

Paolo Gianelli had risen and was slowly pushing his chair back. He seemed deaf to the voices of his colleagues, who were stridently competing for his attention. He straightened and peered slowly about the room until his massive head pointed directly at the motionless figure of Yannick. He stared into his eyes, his own as black and opaque as ebony, and in spite of the distance between them, Yannick read in his gaze a message of implacable hatred.

Carrie looked up from the page and seized her pencil to jot Yannick's name on her list. A strange one, she thought; it did not sound at all French. On the other hand, the name Mielmont still pricked at her mind. She returned to the story, but after only a few more pages she stopped again, recalling how at breakfast that morning the bees had come to hover around the honey pot until she covered it with a napkin. *Miel* was the word on the jar! Marc Honey-mont? An obvious parallel for Margo Honeywell.

She noted the two names and underlined them heavily, feeling the excited flush of discovery. Marc Mielmont was the loyal colleague of Robert de Laine and the object of Carole's enmity.

Had Margo, as a loyal colleague of Charles Melton, incurred the enmity of Noel? It was certainly possible, for Carrie felt no doubt that Noel Wright could be devious. His apparent fondness for Margo could be pretended; the camaraderie they appeared to enjoy could be skilled playacting—on both their parts. They were two highly intelligent, sophisticated people, both accustomed to keeping a gimlet eye fixed on their own best interests.

This could mean Margo was in danger. Carrie shivered, instinctively glancing toward the muscular *gendarme,* who snored on in spite of his uncomfortable position.

She went back to her reading.

With a murmured excuse that did not affect the conversation, Claude Dépouille left the table to fetch another bottle of wine. The mood of happy intimacy was too precious to risk by summoning a servant. Claude would have liked the evening to go on forever, with just himself and Kay and Robert dining together in the

candlelight that softened the contours of Carole's Art
Deco dining room.

He could well imagine how much Carole was enjoying the evening. It was not surprising she had declined to join them, on the pretext of being worried to
distraction over Marc Mielmont's precarious condition.

Yannick had begged off as well, but Claude felt
reasonably certain they were not sharing a cozy meal
à deux. He sighed as a thrill of happiness coursed
through his veins. He did not know whether to wish
Robert could share his secret knowledge or to pray he
never learned that he had nearly lost his empire
through the machinations of his own wife and brother.

Oh, those two would stay in line from now on! But
Claude's face sobered at the thought. As he searched
for a corkscrew he felt a familiar bitterness. For the
rest of their lives Carole and Yannick would share his
lot; they too would exist on Robert's sufferance. They,
however, would be spared the agony that was his
companion until death: the certainty that his only child
would never know her parentage.

That had been the stipulation all those years ago,
when Claude Dépouille was in no position to refuse it.

No more than forty-eight hours after he had left
Dépouille trembling on the floor, Robert had returned to the house, bringing Mimi with him. After
rescuing the child and finding her unharmed, his black
rage had subsided; still it was many days before he
would allow Dépouille to see her.

De Laine had to be assured that the horrors of
withdrawal were over and that Dépouille had returned to reasonably normal condition before he
would allow the little girl near him. He had needed
time, as well, to recover from his own repugnance, to
again become able to accept Dépouille as his friend—
as Dépouille had accepted him in his own time of deg-
radation.

"That is what makes it possible, Claude," Robert had said during one of their long afternoons of talk. "When I detested myself to the point of suicide it was your friendship that saved me. Remember how it was?"

"Thank God, I remember," Dépouille had replied. "I've often wondered, though, what I did to make the difference. I stayed with you, I know, and I felt I was your true friend, but that was all."

De Laine smiled. "You knew the world, I didn't. You weren't shocked by what I had done; you convinced me it was an aberration. And because of who you were I believed you."

"Well, it wouldn't have been the end of the world, Robert, even if..."

"For me, it made a new beginning. If I hadn't hated and feared the idea so intensely, I wouldn't have subjected myself to that extraordinary expiation. I sound immodest, I know; but it was the endurance I learned then that turned me into the man I became."

"I sometimes wonder about your friend de Cendre. Did you ever hear what happened to him?"

De Laine replied, "Our 'experiment,' shall we say, was apparently an isolated incident for René as well. Or so I gather by the fact that he married soon after, and what's more, has stayed married and fathered five children." He got to his feet and started toward the door, adding, "I suppose I'll never see him again and wouldn't know him if I did."

Dépouille drew a deep breath, then asked the question that was constantly on his mind. He said, "Robert, I hardly have the right to ask you this, but..."

De Laine swung around to cut him off. "You want to know my plans for Mimi, of course." He stopped and stood frowning at the floor. Finally he said, "I believe my mind is made up. Yes, it is time to tell you."

While Dépouille watched in an agony of suspense, Robert paced slowly to the window, where he stood peering out while he carefully chose his words.

He said, "I want to raise Mimi in my household, Claude, but not as my child. Since there is a possibility that Carole and I will have children of our own, I will not adopt Mimi. Aside from that, she will have everything I would provide for my own daughter."

Claude Dépouille sank into a chair and buried his face in his hands. "Thank God," he sobbed. "Thank God, you're not turning her out because of me or Katerina."

"You are still weak, Claude, or you would not grovel." Robert spoke with utter contempt, and Claude looked up angrily.

"I couldn't expect you to understand a father's feelings," he said, brushing at his wet eyes. "But you usually stop short of cruelty."

"Get used to it because I'm going to offer you a cruel choice." Robert's face was white and set; his features might have been carved in stone as he studied his friend. "You may live with us, Claude. I'll give you dignified work of some sort; you can manage the household, perhaps. You'll be near Mimi; you will know her and watch her grow up. And she will know you—but never as her father. That is my stipulation. Can you accept it?"

Claude gazed up at him, trying to think sensibly, but his mind was reeling.

Robert's face softened as he watched his struggle. He said, "I'm not cruel enough to insist on an immediate answer. Give it some time, Claude, and tell me when you've thought it through. Time won't affect my decision, however; that is unalterable."

Again de Laine started for the door, and again he stopped with his hand on the knob. He turned and Claude saw that he was actually smiling.

He said, "This may make it easier, Claude. It is time for Mimi to have a real name, so I've decided she will be called Katerina after her mother—Katerina Tourette. Do you like that? We'll call her Kay.''

Dépouille could not speak. His eyes were once more brimming as he watched Robert leave the room and quietly close the door behind him.

TWENTY-TWO

CARRIE RAN UPSTAIRS the minute she finished the manuscript, but the suite was empty. There was no sign of Ben in the bedroom, bath, or sitting room, and he had left no message regarding his whereabouts.

She telephoned the pool and waited while the attendant called Ben's name over the speaker. Clutching the phone, she pictured the scene, the half-naked sunbathers interrupting their reading of *France Soir* or *Paris Match* to see if this Ben Porter would answer the call, smoothing lotion on their burnished skin while they watched for him to appear.

Perhaps he had dived into the pool just as his name rang out. If so, he was in trouble, for the attendant went on calling and calling, and finally Carrie stopped waiting to leave a message and hung up.

She dialed La Rêverie; there was no answer, which exasperated her. Someone must be there.

Ben might have gone to Margo's, she decided. If he too had made the connection between Mielmont and Honeywell—and she couldn't believe he would miss it—he might have hurried over to Margo's house to warn her.

Carrie dialed Margo's number and received a busy signal.

The frustrations were piling up, and she could feel her nervous tension building like a head of steam. She paced to the terrace and back, then tried Margo again only to hear a repetition of the maddening bleeps.

She couldn't stay in that room a moment longer, and she snatched up her handbag, checked to make sure she had her sunglasses and a room key, then hurried out to the elevator.

Ben would have taken their car, but she could get a ride to Margo's house in one of the taxis that invariably waited outside the hotel.

As the *ascenseur* slowly bumped its way down to the lobby, she peered through the glass sides for a glimpse of the hotel entrance and saw no taxis there—another frustration, but the concierge would call one for her. Reaching the lobby, she stepped out of the elevator in time to see a tall, uniformed figure approaching the front door. It was the *gendarme* who had overseen her reading of the manuscript; surely he would be driving to the village.

Five minutes later Carrie was seated in the police van while the concierge directed her driver to the villa of Madame Honeywell. Margo's house was situated roughly halfway between the hotel and the village, hardly out of the *gendarme*'s way.

As they rolled along the hotel drive Carrie asked him, "Do you know the name Yannick?"

He peered at her brightly. *"Yannick? No, Madame, je m'appelle Victor."*

"I didn't mean..." She stopped, wondering how to ask the question properly. She tried, *"Comprendez-vous le nom Yannick?"* and the young man nodded.

"Oui, Madame," he said, agreeable but puzzled.

"Ah, qu'est-ce que c'est le sens de le nom Yannick?"

"Pardon?"

"I mean, *le significance!"* Hopefully, Carrie gave it her best French pronunciation; perhaps she could bend the language to her will.

But the young policeman was still baffled, and now he had turned onto Avenue Bellevue and was watching for Margo's road, which ran off it.

After they had made the turn he remembered something. He said, *"Ma cousin s'appelle Yannick."*

Carrie said, *"Oui?"*

They drew up before Margo's gate, and the *gendarme* turned to her and said, *"Oui, le père de ma cousin s'appelle* Jean. *Voilà, ma cousin s'appelle* Yannick!"

He smiled triumphantly; he seemed to have made a point, and although she had no idea what it was, Carrie felt grateful for his kindness.

"Merci," she said as she climbed down from the van. *"Merci beaucoup!"* and the young man drove off looking well pleased with himself.

Carrie walked up the drive toward the house, peering hopefully around for the sight of their rental car. The driveway was empty, however, and her spirits were further dashed by discovering the front door firmly closed, as it never was when Margo was at home. But Margo's line had been busy; she couldn't have left the house more than five minutes before.

Carrie knocked with the heavy ball-and-hand knocker and heard the sound reverberate loudly; if Margo were there she couldn't miss it. She knocked once more, then walked around to the patio at the side of the house. Although the flagstone deck was empty, as she had expected, the door leading to it from the kitchen stood slightly ajar.

She could get in if she wanted to. Margo wouldn't mind; she would be delighted to come home and find Carrie sitting in her house, preferably with a drink in her hand. But supposing she didn't come home? Presumably Margo would spend another night at La Rêverie—was probably on her way there right now.

Remembering that, and the reason for it, Carrie glanced around Margo's garden, suddenly uneasy. Where were the policemen who were supposed to be guarding the house?

She stepped onto the flagstone patio and approached the kitchen door calling, "Inspector Foch? Sergeant Clement? Is anyone there?"

There was no reply, and she hesitated outside the door, peering through to the dim, silent kitchen, feeling reluctant to enter the house. She should close the door, however; she felt certain of that, so after exploring with her fingers, she pressed the button that would lock it, then pulled the door firmly shut.

She walked uncertainly to the edge of the patio, wishing she had checked the house before allowing the *gendarme* to proceed to the village. His words came back to her: *"Le père de ma cousin s'appelle Jean; voilà, ma cousin s'appelle Yannick."*

A possible meaning of that apparent non sequitur suddenly occurred to her. He could have been saying that Yannick was a nickname, or a diminutive for Jean—something like Jack in English.

A small version of Jean. Jeanette.

Carrie stood frozen, gazing from the sloping lawn while her mind teemed with new possibilities. If Yannick represented Jeanette in Melton's novel, it might mean that Jeanette had attempted to deceive Melton in some way and that he had outsmarted her. Then, not satisfied with that, he had created a fictional situation to prove he knew what she had been up to.

How disappointed he would be if she never got the message. But perhaps she did. Perhaps it was her sudden comprehension of Melton's hidden meaning that took her to Margo's house on the night of her murder.

Jeanette, like Carrie, might have intended to warn Margo, and instead been most effectively silenced.

Carrie shivered; the air had turned cool, and looking at her watch she was appalled to see that it was six o'clock. The only thing for her to do was walk to the village, or to La Rêverie, whichever turned out to be closer. Neither could be more than fifteen minutes away.

She was about to set out when something moved at the edge of her vision. Fixing her eyes on the spot, she saw a dark shape emerge from the dense border of trees and bushes that sheltered Margo's lawn from the road. Carrie stood perfectly still, watching as the figure appeared to weave in and out of the wall of foliage. It was a man working his way toward the house, she realized, and her heart gave a leap of excitement. It could be Ben.

But something about the way the figure moved, in the brief intervals when it was clearly outlined, told her it was not Ben. Whoever it was would be sure to see her if she stepped out in the open, so she shrank back against the sheltering wall of the house, which was now deep in shadow. In her navy pants and beige blouse she would be well camouflaged.

Staying close to the wall, she slowly edged her way to the opposite side of the patio, where a hedge had been planted to provide privacy and hide a view of the kitchen garden at the side of the house.

Disturbing the branches as little as possible, she pushed behind the hedge and emerged on the other side, facing the vegetable garden. Now she could hurry around to the front of the house without being seen, then make a dash out to the road.

Carrie was not afraid, at this point; she was too preoccupied with escaping before being caught snooping around Margo's premises. She felt secure enough, with the hedge between them, to risk checking the progress of the unknown visitor. It *could* be Ben, after all, and how amusing that would be.

But it wasn't Ben, nor from the back did the man now standing on Margo's patio look like Inspector Foch or Sergeant Clement or any of the *gendarmes* she had met. He was slender, dark-haired, of medium height, and was not dressed in uniform, but in a dark blue shirt and pants that might well have been chosen for concealment.

The man stepped softly to the door, his face still turned away into the shadows. He bent, obviously listening for sounds from inside the house, then carefully tried the knob and pushed against the door. It did not give, and Carrie congratulated herself for that. At the same time, his furtive manner made her suddenly aware that she might be in real danger, and she hastily ducked down and began creeping as fast as she could along the vine-covered wall, past the neat rows of beans, lettuces, and onions.

Beyond the garden the ground sloped downward, falling away from the foundation that supported the west wing of the house. Cautiously peering down, Carrie saw that a low wooden door was set into the exposed stones, a curved, double door, its gray, weathered panels carved with the attention the French seemed to lavish on even the humblest of their doors.

Carrie made her way down the slope, stepping on the rocks that held the soil in place. At the base she stumbled and, tossing out her arm, struck a panel of the wooden door, which, instead of supporting her, fell slightly open to throw her further off balance.

Straightening, she peered in at a brick-lined cavern with a low, curved ceiling and, along the walls, shelves piled with bottles resting on their sides. She had stumbled on Margo's wine cellar.

Carrie pulled the door shut and was setting the iron latch when she was seized from behind and a hand clasped firmly over her mouth. In the same instant her arms were pinned against her sides and she was roughly hustled into the dark cavern.

The door was pulled shut and she was in darkness, struggling to get free of the man who pushed her farther back into the blackness, his fingers still clamped on her mouth in a bruising grip.

They bumped against a shelf and she heard the thump of rolling bottles, then the hoarsely panted words, "Will you be quiet if I let go?"

Incredulous, Carrie recognized the voice of Noel Wright.

She nodded her head as best she could, and his hand left her mouth. Still she was held immovable as he whispered, "Don't make a single sound, whatever happens."

Though he still kept a tight grasp of her arms, she managed to twist around and stare, unbelieving, into his white face. Through the darkness his bony features glimmered like a skeleton's while his gray-blue eyes bored into hers, cold and opaque and unreadable.

She opened her lips to speak, but the wintry eyes flashed an unmistakable warning.

"You have probably ruined everything," he whispered. "But keep quiet and we'll soon see."

The dark space fell quiet except for the rasp of his breathing and, for Carrie, the jarring thud of her own heartbeat.

BEN PORTER stepped into the funicular that carried swim-
mers to and from the level of the hotel pool and, as the car
began its steep climb, glanced anxiously at his watch.

It was six o'clock; his plan was already set in motion. He
could spend no more time searching for Carrie.

The little car stopped and Ben stepped out. He strode up
the brick path that bisected the hotel's lawn, entered the
building from the terrace, and went directly to the front
desk to leave a note for Carrie. His message was brief; he
asked her to wait at the hotel for his call and under no cir-
cumstances to look for him at Margo's house or at La
Rêverie. He closed with, *Don't worry,* then crossed that off
as alarmist and handed the note to the concierge.

He suddenly thought to ask, "Did you see Madame
Porter leave the hotel?" and the man nodded.

Looking up at the clock, he said, "Madame Porter went
out at about four-thirty," then, as Ben's face filled with
concern, added, "She accepted a ride to the village with
Pierre Dufour, the *gendarme* who was here this morning. I
think she is safe with him."

His smile was reassuring, but Ben said, "Will you telephone the *gendarmerie* for me? I would like to ask Pierre
Dufour where I might find my wife."

In a moment the call had gone through, and after a quick
exchange, the concierge reported that Pierre Dufour had
left for the day and that Madame Porter had not been with
him when he returned the car to headquarters.

Ben glanced anxiously at his watch, thanked the concierge, and started for his car. Carrie was probably shopping in the village, where the boutiques stayed open until
seven. She had been holding off, he knew, waiting for the
end of their stay to buy presents for the children; still, she
might have left him a note.

He climbed into the car, debating whether he had time to
stop at La Rêverie. Starting down the hotel drive he
dropped the idea. If that was where Carrie had gone he'd
soon know it.

Ben's face was grim as he paused at the gate, then turned
left onto Boulevard du Général-de-Gaulle.

TWENTY-THREE

THEY STOOD facing the door, locked together in what might have appeared a lovers' embrace. Noel's cheek was pressed tightly against Carrie's; if she opened her mouth to cry out, he would know it instantly. With one hand he held her arms pinned behind her back in a surprisingly strong grip, his long, bony fingers digging painfully into her wrists.

In Noel's other hand, he held a flashlight pointed at the entrance, but in the instant Carrie recognized what it was, he altered his tactics. Pulling her with him, he moved close to the nearest shelf, switched on the flashlight, and propped it between two wine bottles so that it continued to illuminate the door to the cellar. Then he drew a small pistol from the pocket of his trousers.

Carrie's heart lurched; she was suddenly dizzy with terror. But Noel pointed the gun, not at her, but at the door in place of the flashlight. Clearly, he now felt more concerned with protecting himself than with identifying whoever might suddenly appear in the doorway. His arm was trembling uncontrollably, however, so he shuffled still closer to the shelf and propped his elbow on the edge. Still his hand shook violently, and with a murmured curse he dropped his arm to his side.

"I don't need you at this point," he breathed in Carrie's ear, and hearing the quaver in his voice she was swept with a sensation verging on pity.

She whispered, "Noel," but instantly the hand that held the gun was slammed against her mouth—hitting her harder than he had expected—for with a muttered, "Jesus!" he pulled away and dropped the pistol into his pocket.

Holding her with one arm about her shoulders, he studied her face to assess the damage, obviously appalled by what he had done. Through a haze of pain Carrie heard him mutter, "You're all right, I think, but don't talk, Carrie. Don't talk at all."

She leaned against him, blinking the tears from her eyes, testing her swollen mouth with her tongue. She could feel his hot, panting breath on her face and the trembling of his tense body as he resumed watching the door. Obviously he expected it to swing open at any instant, and although Carrie could see that the vigil was absorbing all his energies, she had no thought of trying to escape; she felt too weak, too shocked. She stared at the door also, mesmerized by Noel's concentration.

He must be waiting for Ben, she decided; but with what purpose in mind? Was Noel afraid of being discovered there by Ben—or was this a trap he had set, a plot to get Ben out of the way?

Carrie straightened slightly, and Noel tore his gaze from the door to peer down at her. She tried to smile reassuringly—he seemed so frighteningly near the breaking point—but the pain in her bruised lips was too intense. His eyes softened as he recognized her attempt; she was about to risk a question when a slight sound drew his attention back to the door of the cellar.

They watched in horrified fascination as the thin crack of light slowly and silently widened. Carrie drew a deep breath, preparing to cry out a warning, but Noel suddenly pulled her down to the dirt floor, roughly pushing her into the black space behind a small barrel and cramming himself in behind her.

She felt him grope for the gun in his pocket as the door swung open. For an instant a dark figure stood silhouetted in a wedge of light. Carrie screamed, "Ben!" and felt Noel's hand clamp across her mouth. Then the door banged shut and the slice of light was gone as quickly as a snuffed candle. Noel's flashlight fell off the shelf and rolled into a corner, where it shone crazily against the stone wall.

There was silence. From where she lay curled in the dark, dirty corner, pressed against Noel's bony frame, Carrie strained her ears for the sound of breathing. Did the cellar now hold three occupants? And if the third was Ben, why didn't he come to her rescue?

Suddenly the cavern was filled with light, this time pouring surprisingly from the rear. A door had been thrown open back there, an entrance to the house, but Carrie, struggling against Noel's suffocating grip, could not see who was coming through, only hear rapid orders shouted in French and the thud of running feet.

A shot rang out, the door at the front of the cellar crashed open, Noel abruptly relaxed his hold, and Carrie raised her head in time to see a man—was it Ben?—leap through the door, then throw himself to the ground to dodge an exchange of shots between the police and someone who had been standing just inside the door.

There was a strangled cry of pain, and a figure lurched through the open door, clutching at the frame for support, then staggering determinedly forward in spite of shouted orders to stop.

Another shot, and the figure dropped to the ground, then slowly rose to a kneeling position as if daring them to finish the job, and, holding the pistol with both trembling hands, fired toward the cellar. Instantly the shot was returned, and the wounded man or woman—Carrie could not make out which it was—collapsed to the ground and lay still.

As Foch's men ran out of the cellar, Carrie saw Ben push between them and stumble toward her, his face white with concern.

At the sight of him Carrie began to cry with great gulping sobs. Tears poured down her cheeks while she pushed at Noel, struggling to get free, then as he remained silently slumped against her, Carrie sank back in horror.

"What's wrong with him? Oh, Ben, he's hurt, he's dead, you shot him, you shot him!"

Carrie's voice soared hysterically. Terrified and repelled, she burrowed deeper into her dark corner until Ben reached across Noel's motionless form and dragged her up and into his arms.

"You're not hurt, are you? Oh, Carrie, your face! What happened?" He held her tight against him, cradling her poor, swollen face against his shoulder, stroking her hair, her back, until the shuddering sobs abated.

Pulling her down with him, he knelt beside Noel and cautiously turned him onto his back.

Noel immediately moaned, and Ben said, "He's alive, thank God." He searched for a pulse. "He's ticking along, but he's been hurt. Inspector Foch, will you give us a hand here?"

The inspector came toward them, saying, "Madame Porter, I fear you have had a terrible experience."

"But I'm all right. Or I will be." Carrie tried to stand, but her legs would not cooperate, so she sank back and watched the two men work to revive Noel:

He moaned again and his eyes fluttered open; then as they carefully raised him to a sitting position he cried out in pain and the inspector's eyes brightened.

"I think..." he began, gently lowering Noel to the ground, "I think he has been shot in the...ah yes!...forgive me, Madame Porter, but M. Wright has been shot in the *derrière!*"

"Oh, no!" Carrie began to laugh weakly. Her voice trembled as she added, "He'll be all right, won't he? Poor man, he was so frightened."

"*He* was frightened?" Ben gazed at her in wonderment. "You're worried about Noel after what you've been through—after what he did to you?"

"He was just trying to keep me quiet. Because of course I didn't know..."

With Ben's help Carrie pulled herself to her feet and slowly, almost reluctantly, began walking toward the door of the wine cellar. Together they stepped through and approached the knot of men surrounding the still figure on the ground. Without speaking, the men stepped back to allow Carrie and Ben to look down at the peaceful face of Lila Baines.

CELIA ROWAN climbed the steps leading to the entrance of the Negresco Hotel for the second time that day. She was smiling—she had spent a delightful afternoon—but her step was slow, and seeing her reach for the brass handrail, Raoul Bernet stepped down to help her in the unobtrusive way he had perfected over the years.

Anxiously, as if he had come down because he could not wait to know, he asked, "Are you enjoying yourself, Madame?"

At the same time he placed a supporting hand beneath her elbow, and Celia Rowan turned her smiling face to him.

"I feel as if I have come home, Raoul, to the happiest home I ever had." Her beautiful dark eyes shone into his, and Raoul felt a catch in his throat; for a moment he could not speak.

She laughed softly, still gazing at him with that look of pure joy. She said, "Even the cats make me feel welcome. One has been following me all afternoon—could it have something to do with the tiny box of chocolates I bought?"

"No, no, Madame, it is your charm, I am certain." Raoul had recovered his composure, and he ushered her into the lobby with his usual style, then returned to his post.

From behind his tall mahogany counter Henri, the concierge, watched Madame Rowan pause and look around her with a pleased, slightly dazed, expression, as if she could hardly believe her good fortune, and he felt an immediate desire to add to her pleasure.

"Madame Rowan," he said, holding up a small white envelope, and she turned and came toward the desk with a questioning smile forming on her lips.

"M. and Mme Vivier invite you to be their guest at dinner tonight—if you are not too tired?" He bent forward over the counter to study her face. Yes, she was tired but obviously delighted by the invitation; would she accept?

She began slowly shaking her head, though smiling still, and he added, "M. Vivier suggests a rather early dinner, here in the hotel, in the restaurant Chantecler. It is very good."

"Oh yes, I have heard excellent reports from my friends. And of course I would adore to spend the evening with M. and Mme Vivier, but I have had a very long day." She gazed at Henri helplessly, and he came around the counter to escort her to the elevator.

"Perhaps tomorrow night would be better, Madame. M. Vivier asked me to give you your choice. But perhaps, after you have rested . . . ?"

"I will see, Henri." She stepped into the lift. "I will rest and then I will send a note to M. Vivier. Meanwhile, please tell him I am overwhelmed by his thoughtfulness."

The glass doors of the elevator slid shut, and as the brass cage began its ascent, Henri heard the ring of his telephone. His assistant answered, and stepping into their enclosure, Henri heard him say, "Hospitalier de Ste. Jeanne? *Oui,* how may I be of service to you?"

TWENTY-FOUR

THEY TOOK Noel Wright to the hospital in Nice, where it was discovered that Lila's bullet had nicked his hip bone, then traveled through his body without damaging the spine. The wound would heal quickly, but for Noel the episode had been extremely stressful, he was weak with shock, and the doctors were not prepared to say when he might be allowed to leave the hospital.

"I may stay here for good," Noel said to Margo, who sat beside the bed, holding his hand when he would let her. "When I think of what I did to Carrie, that lovely girl . . . I who detest violence with every fiber of my being . . ."

"Darling, you were in frightful danger, both of you, and I think you acted extremely bravely. You should be proud, not ashamed. After all, you didn't have time to explain things; you protected her, you probably saved her life. Your method was a bit basic, that's all."

"I do hope she looks at it that way, but I don't suppose I'll ever find out." Noel closed his eyes wearily and with all animation gone his pale face appeared to have caved in. He lay so still that Margo felt her pulse flutter in alarm.

She took his hand again. "Noel," she whispered, "do you want to sleep? Shall I leave now?"

His eyes flew open. "Leave? Well, yes, this is dull for you. And of course you're expected somewhere . . . probably with Sonny. Don't let me keep you, for heaven's sake." He pulled his hand away from her, then ostentatiously tucked both hands beneath the blanket. His cheeks had turned quite pink and his eyes held a defiant spark as he watched for her reaction.

"Ah, that's better." Margo grinned at him happily, then saw his expression change as he looked toward the open door to his room.

She swung around to see that Carrie and Ben Porter had arrived and were standing in the doorway wearing the awed, hesitant air common to sickroom visitors. Carrie had carefully arranged her hair and had applied more makeup than she usually wore, but the swelling of her lips and jaw could not be concealed, nor could the dark streaks caused by the pressure of Noel's fingers.

She peered anxiously toward the bed, and Noel uttered a whimper of dismay and closed his eyes again. A trickle of tears emerged from his lids, and Carrie hurried to the bedside and embraced him as best she could, curling one arm around his head as she kissed his cheek.

With her head pressed to his, she murmured, "Don't feel so awful, Noel; you were taking care of me, I know that. You risked your life to protect me, and I'll always be grateful to you."

Noel opened his eyes, trying to smile. "Do you know, Carrie, I have never struck anyone before in my life?"

"You probably never held a gun before, either. Let's face it, Noel, you were out of your depth." Carrie attempted a smile, but winced and thought better of it. "The scary part was when I thought you were the killer; but that didn't last long because I could tell you were just as terrified as I was."

Noel sighed. With a shamefaced smile he said, "I'm afraid physical courage has never been my strong point. I'm only glad I didn't faint and leave you completely on your own."

"You turned out to be braver than you thought." Joining Carrie at the bedside, Ben reached out and shook Noel's hand. "Thanks," he said. "Carrie was a complication we didn't allow for. I'd say you coped with it admirably."

Carrie was staring wide-eyed at her husband. "Are you saying that you and Noel actually planned that confrontation, or whatever it was? My God, Ben, you could have warned me!"

"I didn't have a chance. I'd been pretty close to the truth, but I wasn't certain of anything until I read those last pages of manuscript. Then, when it hit me, I knew I had to act fast—Margo was in great danger—and I had no chance to explain it all to you." Ben paused and shook his head. "If I'd had any idea you were going to Margo's . . . well, naturally I would have done things differently."

"I'd certainly like to think so." Carrie moved from her perch on the edge of Noel's bed to a chair. "Now, how about explaining what you meant to accomplish by stationing Noel in Margo's wine cellar."

"Well, it seemed obvious to me that Lila would go after Margo, since Margo had the bulk of the manuscript in her possession at that point."

"She did?"

"Sure: her own chapters, Noel's, Jeanette's, and Celia Rowan's. The only ones missing were Millie's and Paul's, and presumably Lila already had those." Ben paused to peer anxiously at Noel. "This could wait, Noel, if you're tired."

"No, no, my head is teeming with questions." Using the electric control, Noel elevated the head of his bed until he was sitting up. "Firstly, I can't understand why Lila, who was so strong and capable—indomitable, I would have called her—should suddenly be compelled to commit such terrible crimes. It doesn't fit the woman, Ben, as I knew her. And yet there's no denying that she shot me—*me*! After all those years when I championed her, however much she exasperated Charles." Reaching for Margo's hand, he added piteously, "I may never recover from the shock."

"I can imagine, darling," she replied. "Lila has kept everything going at La Rêverie for—how many years?"

"Twenty-three." Ben spoke so decisively that they all looked at him in surprise. "I checked it out when I began to catch on to what was going on."

"Which was when?" Carrie's expression was grim.

"Only yesterday, Carrie, and my idea was too nebulous to talk about. It struck me all of a sudden that we'd been concentrating on straight, literal translations of the French names of Melton's characters, and it might be illuminating to get hold of an English dictionary and look for less obvious parallels, ones that might not spring to mind."

"Give me an example."

Ben smiled. "How about de Cendre, remember him? The fictional René de Cendre, with whom Robert de Laine had a brief homosexual affair?"

"Yes. Weren't we trying to match him up with Melton's love, Celia Rowan?"

"We were, and I did. Or rather Melton did, bless his devious heart. *Cendre* means 'ash,' right?"

"That's what I thought."

"Well, trying to connect the two love affairs, I looked up *rowan* in an English dictionary, and here's the definition: 'the European mountain ash.'"

"Ben..." Carrie breathed.

"I knew that!" Noel was glaring at Ben; his cheeks had turned bright pink. "Damn, why didn't I think of it! All those early English poets went on about the rowan."

Margo's eyes were shining with excitement. "Give us another one, Ben!" she said, but Carrie spoke up.

"I have one for you, Margo, one you should have caught before I did. Maybe you did?"

She grinned questioningly at Margo, who shook her head in bafflement. "Come on, Margo, what's *miel*?" Carrie asked her.

"'Honey,' of course. What about it?"

"What about the character, Marc Mielmont? Any relative of yours, do you suppose?"

While Margo stared openmouthed, Ben nodded his approval. "Good girl, Carrie," he said. "Did you get the Yannick-Jeanette connection too?"

"Indeed I did," Carrie replied, "with help, I must admit."

Ben said, "Me too. The hotel manager explained the name to me." He raised a pacifying hand. "But not till this morning, Carrie, I swear it, and I didn't have a chance to tell you."

Margo was muttering, "Honeywell—Mielmont, I don't believe it. Marc Mielmont stands for me?" She looked suddenly alarmed. "What about this Mielmont? He's a good guy, isn't he? In the story?"

"You are immortalized in Melton's pages, Margo, whether the general reader ever knows it or not." Ben paused, amused by the conflicting emotions Margo was making no attempt to conceal. "Yes," he went on, "Marc Mielmont is a good guy—he's Robert de Laine's most trustworthy friend. How does that make you feel?"

"I'm going to read every blessed word Charles wrote about the fellow; then I'll tell you how I feel." A ferocious glint had appeared in Margo's tawny eyes.

"I have no doubt you'll find a way to punish him if you're not pleased," said Noel. "Retroactively, of course."

Margo was not amused. "What were you saying about Jeanette?" she asked Ben. "Did you find her in the book too?"

"It looks like Melton intended Yannick de Laine to represent Jeanette," Ben replied. "As you must know, Margo, Yannick is a diminutive for Jean, so it's a good fit—especially since they're both relatives. In the story Yannick is de Laine's brother; Jeanette was Melton's niece. The question that emerges is, did Jeanette ever try to trick Melton, betray him somehow, as Yannick tries to betray Robert de Laine?"

Margo and Noel stared at each other, their faces solemn. After a moment, as if they had reached an agreement, they faced Ben, and Noel said slowly, "Jeanette is gone now, and unable to defend herself, so I prefer to keep my suspicions to myself."

"Shall we just say there was an incident involving a publishing deal—the rights to one of Melton's short stories—that could have been very profitable for Jeanette?" Margo looked questioningly at Noel and he nodded slowly.

"But Melton was too clever for her. A man of his complexity could never be fooled by Jeanette's transparent sort of scheming." Noel smiled as he reflected on the genius of his departed friend. "And he never revealed that he knew what she was up to, never. We admired him for that, didn't we, Margo?"

"We did indeed." Her face crinkled in a broad grin. "We also took it as a warning, at least I did. The wily old bastard was a jump ahead of everybody."

Noel looked shocked. "Really, Margo..." he began, but at that moment a nurse appeared in the doorway and glanced around the room in disapproval.

"Visiting hours are over," she said firmly. She glanced pointedly at the clock on the wall. "It is nine-fifteen. I must ask you to leave."

Noel said, "But Mademoiselle, my friends have some very important information to give me. May we have just a few more minutes, please?"

The nurse shook her head. "We must consider the other patients, Monsieur, as well as your own condition."

"I will be very agitated, I won't be able to sleep..."

"We can fix that, Monsieur. You will have no problem. Now, please bid farewell to your friends. They may return tomorrow morning at eleven."

"Yes, I am up to a nightcap. What I'm definitely not up to is being sent to bed like a child while you two go over all the juicy details. So let's go in, Ben, just for half an hour."

Carrie spoke from the front seat of the car Ben had pulled up to the door of La Rêverie, and Margo instantly seconded the idea.

"I can't possibly face Millie and Marie by myself," she said, as she began climbing out of the back seat. "God knows what state they're in, but anything's better than going home alone tonight." Margo looked toward the dimly lighted facade of the house and squared her shoulders.

"Maybe we should all go to the hotel," said Ben.

Carrie disagreed. "They need us tonight," she said, stepping out onto the gravel. "Especially Millie. I can't imagine the shock..."

"Oh, I don't know that Millie was all that devoted to Lila," said Margo.

Carrie looked at Ben. "I gather you haven't told her."

"Told me what?"

But Marie was opening the door to them. She wore a knitted pink bathrobe tied with a fraying cord over her usual shapeless black cotton dress. Her gray hair, usually arranged in a tidy, braided knot, hung down her back in a shaggy approximation of a pony tail. She might have emerged from an air-raid shelter.

The sight of them undid her. Her doughy face crumpled, and she began to wring her hands, wailing, "Oh, Madame Honeywell, I am so sad, so sad."

Margo put an arm around Marie's quivering shoulders and led her toward the kitchen, saying, "We all feel terrible about poor Lila. You know she must have been very sick to do such things."

"Very sick and very frightened," said Ben. "Now at least she is at peace, while Millie... Tell me, Marie, is Millie here now?"

"She is in her room." Marie drew a large handkerchief out of her bathrobe pocket and mopped her tear-stained face. "M. Stovall has been with her, but he has gone to send a cable in the village."

Carrie had followed, and she said gently, "Marie, I know you are very upset, but could you possibly make us a pot of tea?"

"Tea?" exclaimed Margo. "Not for me; I'm having a good stiff drink."

"Oh, Madame Porter, what happened to you? Your face..." Fat tears were once again coursing down Marie's cheeks as she went to Carrie and touched her chin with a tentative finger.

"It isn't as bad as it looks, Marie, but if you had an ice bag..." Struck by a new thought, Carrie swung around to Ben and said, "What are the children going to say when I walk in? They'll probably run out of the room screaming."

"You'll look good to them, don't worry." Ben studied her face admiringly. "Frankly, I think the swelling's an improvement; makes you look like Grace Kelly."

"I can see you're desperate to be forgiven, but I'm taking my time."

Marie produced tea and cinnamon toast on a tray, then when Carrie was snugly settled on the drawing room sofa, she brought another tray containing a plastic bag and a bowl of chipped ice.

"It is the best I can devise, Madame," she apologized, carefully spooning ice into the bag. "In the morning I will go to the pharmacy..."

"This will do nicely, Marie; thank you." Carrie looked past Marie's broad shoulder to see that Millie was watching from the doorway, looking pale and rather disheveled and puzzled by the scene before her.

"What happened to you, Carrie?" Millie's voice was a frail, invalid quiver, and Carrie pushed aside her tea tray and got up to embrace her.

"I'm fine—just a few bruises—but you, poor girl...I'm so sorry, so terribly sorry..."

"Will somebody tell me what is going on?" Margo had entered the room, carrying her drink, to find Millie weeping in Carrie's arms.

Ben had followed, and he said, "Millie has had quite a shock, Margo. Sit down and we'll tell you about it."

Marie, once again in tears, had hurried off to get another teacup, and Carrie drew Millie to the sofa to sit beside her.

"Do you mind, Millie, if we talk about what's happened? It seems important to get it straight."

"Mind? No, I need to get it straight more than anybody." Millie pushed her hair back from her tear-stained face. "But first, is Noel all right? He wasn't badly wounded, was he?"

Ben grinned. "He's fine, and since the scar will be well hidden, even his vanity can remain intact."

Millie managed an uncertain smile. "Does he know?"

Carrie said slowly, "Well, of course he knows it was Lila who shot him. That's what has shaken him the most. It's shaken all of us, I might add."

Margo said, "What no one has bothered to tell me is why; why did Lila kill Paul and Jeanette? Did she simply go mad?"

"There's nothing simple about any of it, Margo, but Lila's motive might be more comprehensible to you if I explain how the final two characters in Melton's novel match up."

"You mean you actually found the answer in that manuscript?"

Ben nodded. "You'll recall the tragic misadventures of Claude Dépouille—his drug addiction and its consequences?"

"Of course; a real tear-jerker. He gives his little girl away to get money for dope, but Robert de Laine saves her and takes them both into his home."

"The word *dépouille* has several meanings, among them 'shed,' 'skin,' and 'spoil.' I combed the English dictionary looking for a useful synonym and getting nowhere until I tried a different tack." Ben sipped his drink. "I concentrated on the two close associates of Melton's who so far had no counterparts in the novel: Millicent Girard and Lila Baines."

Margo said, "Girard is a proper name, Ben, in French or English, I should think."

"Right, and Millie—well, we'll get to that in a minute. *Lila* would be 'lily,' of course, or *fleur;* no help there, so I turned to Baines and looked up the English word *bane.*" Ben paused and looked around at them expectantly.

Carrie said, "Bane: baneful, bane of somebody's existence. I guess it means a curse or a blot."

"It also means spoil. 'A person or thing that ruins or spoils.' You can imagine my feelings when I stumbled onto that."

"I'd say Charles was reaching for it with that one." Margo wore the chagrined expression of one who has been tricked.

"He didn't want it to be easy, you know."

"I don't know why he wanted to do it at all!" Millie's dark eyes were tormented; her teacup was rattling in the saucer, and Carrie took it from her and covered her hand with her own.

"I can't believe he meant to hurt you, Millie. From all I can gather, Melton was very fond of you. I think he wanted to tell you something he felt you needed to know, even if you weren't aware of needing it."

Margo was staring at Millie and mumbling, "Baines—Dépouille. Are you telling me that Lila was a drug addict? Are you saying she had a daughter?"

Ben said, "The daughter in the manuscript has the most problematical name of all: Kay Tourette. For one thing, Kay is an English nickname; I couldn't find any way to relate it to a French name. In fact, there are very few French words beginning with K—no proper names that I could find—so I looked up Tourette and, again with help from the hotel manager, decided the word meant 'to turn a trick,' or 'trickery.'" Ben paused, but since no one applauded his cleverness, he went on. "I decided that was a hint from Melton that this name association was particularly devious and should not be expected to equate with the others."

"The sex!" Carrie exclaimed. "In all the others he switched the sexes. This was his way of saying that Kay Tourette's real-life counterpart is a woman."

"That's what I chose to think—partly because the only remaining member of Melton's close group of associates was a woman."

"But how about the first name, Ben?" Millie's voice was almost a whisper.

"Carrie, do you recall a business novel we read and rejected last year? The one with all the endless deal-making?"

"I wish I could forget it."

"We learned some business terms, remember? One was sprinkled through the story especially freely: the use of K as shorthand for 'a thousand.'"

Millie breathed. "The French word for 'thousand' is *mille*."

Ben said, "So here's our theorem: if Kay equals Millie and Kay is the daughter of Dépouille, whose daughter is Millie?"

Margo gasped. She stared at Millie, clutching the arms of her chair while she absorbed the shock.

Finally she said slowly, "Millie is Lila's daughter? I don't believe it."

"I wish I didn't believe it," said Millie. She looked at her watch, then rose to her feet, moving as feebly as an old woman. "I'm going to put in a call to my mother—my adoptive mother, I mean—and tell her what's happened."

TWENTY-FIVE

IT WAS CLOSE TO noon the following day when Ben and Carrie returned to La Rêverie. As usual at that hour, Finesse lay sprawled on the lawn near the driveway, where he could bask in the sun and at the same time keep an eye out for arriving visitors.

Watching him bound toward them on his long, stiff legs, Carrie said, "There's one character Melton forgot to match up in his manuscript."

She climbed out of the car and knelt to give Finesse the hug he expected. "I'm going to miss him, Ben. Don't you think it's time we got a dog? For the children?"

"Certainly, if you want to take it with you to the office every day. You're so much better at training animals than Terry and Brooke and me."

"You have a heart of stone, Ben Porter." Carrie stood up, brushing the dust from her linen trousers. "How do I look in this light?" she asked him. "Has the swelling gone down at all?"

Ben tilted her chin to one side, then bent to kiss her lips. "You always look beautiful to me," he murmured.

"Thanks, darling, but that's not an answer." Carrie smiled up at him, her blue eyes crinkling, the shining blond hair falling back from her face. "Never mind; I feel a lot better than yesterday. I'm not worrying about facing the children any more; I just can't wait!"

With arms about each other, they approached the house, where the front door stood open to let the morning air warm the dim hallway. Carrie tugged at the bell, then they stepped inside just as Millie ran down the stairs saying, "Come in, come in. I have a lot to tell you."

"How are you doing?" Carrie said as she kissed Millie's cheek. "I hope you got some sleep, poor girl."

Millie nodded, but her dark eyes were misted with tears as she looked at Carrie. "I'm having a hard time taking it in," she said, "but I talked to my mother last night. That helped."

She led the way to the drawing room, saying, "Margo is bringing Noel home—in the Marchands' car, need I say— and Hank has gone to the village to get you an ice bag, Carrie." She turned to examine Carrie's face. "But you don't need it, I see. What a relief for Noel!"

As they all sat down, Ben said, "What was your mother's reaction to your news?"

"She was absolutely horrified, though she said she's been feeling uneasy ever since she heard about Melton's legacy. She knew him pretty well, you see. Of course she feels terrible about Lila, and inclined to blame herself, though I hope I talked her out of that."

"Why would she blame herself?"

"Because she was the one who got Lila her job with Melton, and then years later suggested me for mine. She thought she was doing Lila a favor, placing her in a spot where she would see me occasionally without my ever finding out the truth. It's typical of my mother's kindness."

"I should say she was taking quite a risk," said Carrie. "Tell me, how did Melton get involved in the first place?"

"He and my parents were friends. He was older, of course, but my father met him when he was starting out in publishing. They lived in the same apartment building in the Village, and I gather they saw a lot of each other when my parents were first married. When Melton first came to live over here they visited him fairly frequently. They both had jobs, and no children, so they were quite free, and he always put them up. Mother has often told me what riotous times they had in those days."

"And then they adopted you. Have you always known?"

Millie said, "Yes, they were completely open about it." She paused, smiling to herself. "In fact, after my brother was born they made such a thing of it: how special I was because I was carefully chosen, not just born haphazardly,

that I had to ask them to stop. I was always perfectly comfortable with the idea—probably because they were great
parents and we were very close.''

"You were lucky and so were they," said Carrie, "but
Millie, why were they in touch with Lila? That's very unusual.''

"My parents decided to adopt a child at a time when
white, Caucasian babies were in short supply. It was the
effect of the birth control pill, I suppose. Anyway, they
were passionately determined, so they resorted to slightly
questionable channels.''

"Ah, that's where money comes into it.''

"I'm afraid so." Millie sighed and sank back in her chair.
"And of course that's what made Lila so desperate to hide
the truth. She didn't exactly sell me, though." She laughed
abruptly and said, "Do you know how funny it feels to say
that?''

"I can imagine," said Carrie. "Was Lila a drug addict,
though, like Claude Dépouille? Is that why she couldn't
keep you?''

Millie nodded. "She was, yes, and when I was born I was
addicted. I went through withdrawal, can you imagine that?
A newborn baby? I gather I almost died, and Mother says
I was a pathetic, scrawny creature when she took me
home.''

"That would account for the shady method of place-
ment, I suppose.''

"The strange thing was that as soon as Lila accepted
whatever amount of money she got—probably a fraction
of the so-called social worker's profit—she became determined to cure herself. She was that appalled by what her
habit had made her do.''

"Like alcoholics who have to hit bottom before they can
start up again.''

"When she got well she began to long for her baby, so
she tried to get me back, but by then my parents were devoted to me and refused to give me up." Millie smiled. "I
was in great demand, wasn't I?''

"Isn't there a time limit for a mother to change her mind?"

"Yes, I believe it's six months, and by the time Lila was healthy, I was eight months old. My mother couldn't have been expected to give me back to Lila—it would have been a terrible loss to her by then—but she felt such sympathy for her that she tried to make it easier." Millie's face filled with sorrow. "And that sympathy is what caused all this agony."

Carrie said, "Don't blame your mother, Millie. She was young and tenderhearted; she thought she was doing a good thing."

Ben said, "Probably the 'social worker' encouraged Lila to try to get you back, thinking he could collect another fee."

"It must have been something like that. Anyway, my parents consented to meet Lila, and discovering what an exceptional woman she was, arranged for her to work for Melton. That got her out of the country, you see, so it appeared to be a good solution. She accepted the job partly because it gave her a chance of seeing me now and then."

"Obviously Melton was filled in on the situation," said Ben.

"Yes, but Lila never knew that—until she began reading his manuscript, his legacy, and realized what it could mean to her."

"She was pretty smart to catch on so quickly," said Ben. "What happened? You showed her your chapters first, I suppose?"

Millie nodded. "Yes, and then she must have found Paul's, wherever they were hidden. She must have become alarmed by the direction the story was heading—you know how your antennae go up when you sense a personal threat. Then she probably began dreading that I would catch on as easily as she had. She must have brooded about it for a while, because she read my part right after I got it—weeks before she stole it."

Carrie said, "She probably thought she could get away with it because she wasn't one of Melton's heirs. They were the only ones who might be expected to steal or kill for possession of the entire manuscript.''

"And she didn't know about Jeanette's copier. She thought she could prevent anyone ever reading the complete story.'' Alerted by the sound of tires on the gravel, Ben stood up and went to one of the tall drawing room windows. "Here's the convalescent,'' he said, "with Hank right behind him,'' and they all jumped up and hurried to the door.

"THANK YOU, Marie. The custard was delicious.''

But the crystal dish was half full, and Noel's voice sounded petulant. Lying on the sofa against a mountain of pillows, he looked to Marie like a frail old man.

She bent over him anxiously. "Have just another spoonful, M. Wright,'' she coaxed. "You must make yourself strong again.''

"Your good cooking will do it, Marie,'' he said, forcing a smile to his lips. "Nothing could cure me as quickly as your bouillabaisse or one of your lovely ragouts.''

Marie frowned in disapproval as she reluctantly took the dish and set it on the tray. She studied him for a moment, then turned to leave the room, muttering, "A good beef broth, that is it. A beef broth today and tomorrow perhaps an omelette.''

When she had gone Noel said plaintively, "What have you told Marie about my injury? She seems to have the impression I was shot in the stomach.''

Ben laughed, helping himself to *terrine de canard* from the coffee table. To be near Noel they were having a buffet lunch, but with a marked difference in menus.

"Here, darling,'' said Margo, "now that she's gone you can have some of this nice pâté.''

"No, thank you, my appetite is ruined.'' Noel sank back against the cushions and closed his eyes.

Ben said, "I suppose Margo has filled you in on Lila.''

Noel's eyes flew open. "Oh dear God, I've been so wrapped up in myself I haven't said a word to you, Millie. What a frightful shock you've had. I'm so sorry.'' He reached out his hand, and Millie put down her plate and went to him.

"You've had a shock too, Noel dear. It's going to take us both a while to feel normal again." She kissed his forehead, and added, "Are you exhausted? Do you want to go to your room and be quiet?"

"No, no, I want to go over everything with you. It is so difficult to take it all in, especially to realize that Charles knew all those years and never revealed it to anyone—even to me, his closest confidant." Noel's expression turned sullen. "It makes me wonder what else he kept from me," he added.

Margo chuckled at his disgruntlement, her amber eyes narrowing to slits. "You needn't feel singled out," she said. "He kept it from all of us: Paul, Jeanette, me. He couldn't take a chance on Millie finding out."

Millie cried, "Then why did he want me to know now—or ever?" There was such anguish in her voice that Hank stood up and tried to draw her to her feet.

He said, "Come on, darling, you've had enough. Let's go for a walk," but Millie shook him off.

"This is important, Hank," she said. "I really need an answer."

"Melton didn't exactly tell you, Millie, you have to admit that. He disguised the information so that you wouldn't just stumble on it, you'd have to go to a lot of trouble." Carrie bent forward earnestly to make her point. "He might have thought it was his duty to make the truth available to you somehow."

Ben said, "I'm betting it was the challenge: Melton would implant a secret in what he must have suspected would be his last novel. Would it ever be discovered by the only people to whom it mattered?"

"A secret is a form of power, isn't it?" said Carrie. "You can manipulate events, either by keeping quiet or telling."

"And Charles loved power," said Margo. "He told me it was one reason he became a novelist—he could control his characters as he could never control the people in his life."

"I never thought of that," said Hank. "Then this was a way to continue controlling people after his death."

"How absolutely demonic!" Millie's dark eyes were bright with anger. "I *hate* thinking Charles Melton would be capable of such meanness."

Carrie said, "But Millie, he couldn't possibly have predicted that his conundrum would result in murder. He must have seen it as a game, a sort of treasure hunt."

Millie was not appeased. "I can't believe he would be so cruel as to deliberately expose poor Lila," she said. "She was so completely helpless."

Noel shifted his position, punching at the pillows they had packed around him. "I maintain that Lila overreacted. She didn't commit a crime by putting her baby out for adoption; quite the contrary, since she was an unfit mother."

Carrie spoke up at once. "Mothers don't reason like that, Noel. All Lila saw was that Melton's novel could destroy her relationship with the daughter who had been miraculously restored to her—as a friend, at least. It wouldn't be the adoption per se that would alienate Millie, but the money, the idea that Lila had sold a helpless baby—a baby who might not even live because of her addiction." Carrie's face was somber. "No mother could stand to have her child learn that."

They all fell silent until Ben got to his feet and said, looking around at the others, "Tonight is our last evening in France, and Carrie and I are hoping you can put your troubles aside for a few hours and help us enjoy it. We invite you all to join us for dinner at La Reserve." Ignoring Carrie's stunned expression, he added, "You too, Noel. I've already booked a table and told them we require one extra-comfy chair with a nice soft cushion. Now come along, Carrie, we've got to pack."

TWENTY-SIX

WHEN CELIA ROWAN opened her eyes her bedroom was deep in shadow, and she could not think where she was. She felt her heart speed up; panic was approaching, and to fight it off she made herself lie very still and let her eyes range slowly around the room until she found her bearings.

In a moment she had identified the bulky shape of the armoire that held her clothes, then a panel of light that was the dressing-table mirror, then the subdued shimmer of the brocade that draped the two tall windows. Those draperies were a pale rose color, she reminded herself, matching the fabric on the walls, and in the bathroom the towels and even the soap picked up the same rosy tone.

She was in the Negresco, of course, where she had already spent two days and where she would be pleased to spend the rest of her life. She felt very good there, free and cared for at the same time. Going around Nice, doing what she liked, she seemed to function like an adult again, smoothly and reasonably, instead of like some unpredictable—she backed away from the word *unstable*—adolescent.

She smiled to herself, sitting up and reaching for her robe. Would she become terribly spoiled if she stayed forever in the luxurious world of the Negresco? Next question: at her time of life, what would it matter if she did?

Celia Rowan wondered, as she tied the satin robe around her waist, why being spoiled had always seemed a fate to be avoided at all costs. Her mother must have implanted the fear of it, yet there had been no spoiling in Celia's childhood, either of her or her sister; as daughters of two college professors they were taught to value scholarship above riches, above beauty, above all worldly pleasures, and she was glad of it.

She turned on a light and went to the dressing table to brush her hair. Had her sister also been glad they were brought up as they were? she wondered. It was too late to ask, but she remembered Charles pointing out to them once how their beauty might have distracted them if not for the values instilled by their parents. As it was, they might have been unconscious of their wonderful looks, and their lack of vanity made them irresistible.

Charles saw everything, understood everything. How deep he went, probing for the secrets that gave meaning to life. Celia sighed with happiness, thinking of him. Dreamily, she wandered into her sitting room, now filled with the warm, golden light of late afternoon. She must go out to her balcony and enjoy the sight of the western sky reflected in the ocean. But on the desk that stood between the two pairs of French doors lay the small white envelope containing M. Vivier's dinner invitation, and Celia Rowan felt a twinge of conscience as she realized she had not answered it. Too late now to write; she would telephone and hope the concierge had prepared M. Vivier for her refusal.

She picked up the telephone and chatted briefly with Madame Vivier, her husband being occupied, and although Madame Vivier sounded somewhat vague, almost as if she were surprised to hear of the invitation, they agreed to dine together the following evening. After she hung up Celia poured herself a glass of Perrier and stepped onto the narrow balcony.

Her room faced south, across the Promenade des Anglais to the pebble-strewn beach and the sea beyond—not the quietest location in the hotel, but for Celia the most prized because of the life that swirled by outside the windows. At this hour the warm tints of the approaching sunset were pushing the blue from the sky, and the vast expanse of barely moving ocean had taken on a matching tawny glint.

The golden color flashed in the windows of the cars that moved along the boulevard and turned the faces of the strolling people bright orange, like faces in a child's drawing. Celia touched her own face, wondering if it looked orange to anyone who might glimpse her standing there.

Amused at the thought, she peered down toward the walk three stories below, but none of the passersby took time to look up at her; they pressed on with a purposeful air after their day of work or shopping or sight-seeing, as if headed for some highly desirable destination.

That was the only thing missing, Celia thought—the reward at the end of the day; and of course for her that meant Charles.

Looking up at the sky, she saw that in only seconds the colors had changed, becoming an almost garish mix of tangerine, rose-red, and yellow. She drank it in with her eyes, letting herself sink into it, until she sensed something of Charles there in the sky. Sometimes she thought she could really lose herself in that sensation of Charles's presence, could merge with the sea and the sky where his spirit lingered. All she needed was the courage to drop the thread that bound her to reality.

Pushing the thought away, Celia glanced down to see a car pull up at the entrance and Raoul step out from beneath the fan-shaped glass awning to open the door. He bent to hand a lady out, but when she started up the stone steps he did not go with her, but turned and looked up, almost as if he knew Celia was watching.

She smiled down at Raoul and waved her hand. He waved to her, then made a low bow, sweeping the plumed hat from his head in a theatrical flourish.

As he straightened, grinning up at her, Celia heard her telephone ring, and she waved to Raoul once more, then hurried inside to answer it. Henri, the concierge, was calling to announce a visitor—a friend, he said, who had asked permission to surprise her.

Laughing, she begged him in vain for some small clue, then hung up and went to put on some makeup. Looking into the mirror, she paused with the lipstick poised in her fingers.

Henri had not sounded playful; when he refused to help identify her visitor his voice had been somber. Of course it was his busiest time of day and perhaps he considered the "surprise" a nuisance.

But Celia was a favorite of Henri's; he loved attending to her modest needs, that was obvious. In fact, he often seemed to wish she would be more demanding.

She peered into the mirror and carefully applied the lipstick. She leaned forward, close to the mirror, studying her own face as if searching for some elusive answer. Clinging to her image as if afraid to let it go, she listened for the bell. She felt suspended, loosened somehow from her surroundings, and again she pictured herself linked to reality by a fragile thread loosely held in her hand.

A silvery chime sounded, and Celia straightened, still gazing intently into the mirror. After a moment she began to walk into the drawing room, not hurrying, moving as if she had something very absorbing on her mind.

The bell chimed again, and Celia seized the brass knob and pulled the door open. She was not surprised to see Anne Rouffet standing in the hallway, looking kind and anxious, as the dear girl always did. Next to her stood M. Vivier, his face sad and embarrassed, and behind him the director of La Hospitaliere de Ste. Jeanne.

Celia stepped back to admit them, smiling absently, distracted by the feeling of elation she associated with Charles, but stronger than ever before, overwhelming her until, with a joyous sense of freedom, she allowed the slender thread to slip from her fingers.

TWENTY-SEVEN

THE PLANE CLIMBED steeply after taking off from the Nice airport, and Carrie pressed her face to the window, memorizing the steep hills covered with scrubby green, the roads looping across the rocky ledges, the terraced vineyards and flower gardens, the bright blue lozenges that were swimming pools.

They pierced through a bank of plump, white clouds and leveled off, staying above them. The view was gone, nothing to see now but clear blue above, and below, the fluffy layer of white, like a soft feather bed waiting to catch them. Carrie sighed and leaned back, dropping Ben's hand, to which she always clung during takeoffs and landings.

But Ben took her hand again, asking, "Sad to be leaving?"

Carrie shook her head. "Not exactly. It's time. But it'll be an adjustment."

"Let's not make it too abruptly." The stewardess was coming up the aisle with the drinks cart, and Ben loosened his seat belt in order to reach his wallet.

"Champagne," he ordered with authority, and Carrie turned to him, surprised.

"I don't know, Ben," she began, but he ignored her.

"Some good champagne, please, if you have it," he said to the stewardess, and while she took inventory he added to Carrie, "It's the only thing; trust me."

When the Dom Perignon was opened and poured, Ben touched his glass to Carrie's. "To a bright new future for Porter Publishing," he toasted, "with more business trips like this one."

"I'll second that," Carrie replied. Smiling, she sipped her wine. "But you can't call this a business trip."

"Why not?"

"You know perfectly well why not. You haven't done a lick of work for two weeks and neither have I. Unless..." She turned to him suspiciously. "You're not thinking of setting up as a detective, I hope. Just because you figured out one crime, Ben..."

"Two. Three, counting Greg Dillon."

"Ben, you're making me very nervous."

"Well, you needn't be; you're probably set for life."

"What are you talking about?"

Wearing an enigmatic grin, Ben reached into his jacket pocket and slowly withdrew a folded sheaf of paper. He took his time carefully opening and smoothing the document, then handed it to Carrie and sat back to watch her reaction.

"Ben, it's a contract," she said. She glanced swiftly over the typewritten paragraphs, then turned awe-filled blue eyes to her husband. *"Mirror Image,"* she whispered. "We're going to publish *Mirror Image.* Charles Melton's last novel."

"Charles Melton's greatest novel."

"But Ben, what about Sudmann's? They publish all Melton's works."

"Not any more." Ben drew the champagne bottle from the ice bucket the stewardess had left with them and refilled their glasses. "Noel and Margo and Millie each came to me to ask if they couldn't somehow reward us for our efforts, and the idea came to me quite effortlessly. Surprising, isn't it, when I never know what I want for my birthday?"

"Your birthday, indeed. Ben, this is an enormous plum for us; but can Noel and the others really do it? Do they have the rights?"

"Sure. Whoever puts the whole manuscript together has the rights. Anyway Noel controls all of Melton's copyrights, so it's no problem."

"Except for Paul Clifford's pages, and Jeanette's, and poor Celia Rowan's."

"I would never refer to her as 'poor Celia,' Carrie; not that incredible woman." Ben lifted his glass as if toasting the memory of Celia Rowan. "There will be a few legalities, but Noel assures me we have a binding contract."

"We'll have to hire some people." Carrie was frowning as the complications mounted in her mind. "Ben," she said, "let's not get too big, okay?"

"Just big enough for one business trip to France every year, how's that?" He kissed her cheek, then leaned back and closed his eyes.

"Or Italy. I do want to see Italy." Carrie finished her champagne and tilted her own seat back.

"Florence," she murmured, "and Venice. Find an author who lives in Venice, Ben." Her voice trailed off as she fell asleep.

A DEB RALSTON MYSTERY

THE MENSA MURDERS

 ## LEE MARTIN

DEAD BODIES LEAVE NO TRAILS....

Three women are murdered—in identical and very unusual ways.
The killer is solicitous—first breaking their necks, then tucking
them neatly into bed before cleaning the house and tending to the
pets.

With no trail to follow—since the killer insists on straightening up
the mess—Fort Worth detective Deb Ralston looks beyond the
scrubbed floors to discover the victims were all members of Mensa,
an organization for the superintelligent. Deb quickly discovers that
the group's members are not all as sane as they are smart.

"A believable sleuth in a superior series."   *—Booklist*

AN INSPECTOR NICK TREVELLYAN MYSTERY

HOPE
AGAINST
HOPE
SUSAN B. KELLY

First Time In Paperback

DEATH IN THE FAMILY

Aidan Hope is bludgeoned to death in his hotel room in the hamlet of Little Hopford. The prime suspect is Alison Hope, the victim's cousin, a brash, beautiful, wealthy businesswoman who inherits sole ownership of a lucrative software business. Alison maintains she bought Aidan out years ago. So why had Aidan suddenly appeared to claim his rights and his money?

Fighting his growing desire for the red-haired Alison, Detective Inspector Nick Trevellyan undertakes the investigation. Alison has no alibi . . . and every reason to have killed her cousin. But as Aidan's unscrupulous past comes to light, and a second body turns up, Trevellyan begins to hope that Alison is innocent . . . although that may mean she'll be the next to die.

"A pleasant diversion and a promise of good things to come."

—*Library Journal*

W⊕RLDWIDE LIBRARY®

A PORT SILVA MYSTERY

GRANDMOTHER'S
HOUSE

JANET LAPIERRE

First Time In Paperback

PORT SILVA—LAND TO KILL FOR?

Situated on California's beautiful northern coast, Port Silva had escaped the rash of land developers eating up the state's prime real estate. But when a posh San Diego firm finally offers small fortunes to persuade the people on historic Finn Lane to sell out, everyone jumps at the chance. Except thirteen-year-old Petey Birdsong. The house belonged to his grandmother. He's not selling. Charlotte, his mother, stands adamantly beside him.

But how far will Petey go to defend his home?

"LaPierre is something else . . . real talent."
— ***Mystery Readers of America Journal***

The Hour of the Knife

SHARON ZUKOWSKI

First Time In Paperback

A BLAINE STEWART MYSTERY

REST, RELAXATION...AND MURDER

Blaine Stewart found work and self-pity moderately effective ways to cope with her husband's death. Tough, tenacious, burned-out, she was getting on everybody's nerves—including her own. A trip to the Carolina coast was going to give her the chance to tie up a case and then the time to catch some R and R.

But when her client—and friend—was found dead in the marsh, Blaine started asking questions.... Vacations had never agreed with Blaine, anyway, and this one wasn't about to change her mind...especially when it was highly likely it would be her last!

"The fast paced action, assortment of characters and the unsolved death will keep you reading far into the night."
                                                        —*Polish-American Journal*

Available at your favorite retail outlet in July, or reserve your copy for June shipping by sending your name, address, zip or postal code, along with a check or money order for $3.99 (please do not send cash), plus 75¢ postage and handling ($1.00 in Canada) for each book ordered, payable to Worldwide Mystery, to:

In the U.S.

Worldwide Mystery
3010 Walden Avenue
P.O. Box 1325
Buffalo, NY 14269-1325

In Canada

Worldwide Mystery
P.O. Box 609
Fort Erie, Ontario
L2A 5X3

Please specify book title with your order.
Canadian residents add applicable federal and provincial taxes.

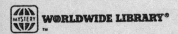

MYSTERY **WORLDWIDE LIBRARY®**
TM

HOUR

ZERO at the BONE

A KATHERINE DRISCOLL MYSTERY

First Time In Paperback

Mary Willis Walker

UNSUSPECTING PREY

It had been thirty-one years since Katherine Driscoll had seen her father. Then he sent a cryptic letter. He knew she was in trouble—about to lose her home, her dog kennel and her beloved championship show dog, Ra, to creditors. He was offering his help.

Katherine went to meet him at the Austin Zoo where he was senior keeper of the large cats. But she just missed him—he'd been mauled to death by a tiger.

With nothing to go on but a key and receipt from a storage warehouse, Katherine took a job at the zoo and started probing into her father's bizarre death.

> **"Walker is terrific at goosebumps."**
> *—The Philadelphia Inquirer*

WORLDWIDE LIBRARY®
™

ZERO